To everyone else, he looked like just another marine in the company.

But he wasn't. He was a true hero. And her hero. Love smothered her other ragged emotions for a moment. Infused and overwhelmed, Megan stood there feeling her heart open wide to this man with broad shoulders who walked with confidence born from experience. His face was ruggedly handsome. She recalled the unexpected kiss they'd shared earlier. Lips tingling in memory of that moment that had changed her life, Megan looked away. No one could know how she felt toward Luke. He couldn't know she was falling in love with him. Not now. She had a job to do.

Dear Reader,

I'm thrilled to announce that *Beyond Valor* opens a new series encompassing many military romances to come in Harlequin Romantic Suspense and Harlequin HQN. This story features continuing characters from Black Jaguar Squadron and earlier romances. Stay tuned for more details on this news!

In *Beyond Valor,* you'll meet U.S. Navy hospital corpsman 2 Megan Trayhern, a combat medic and the daughter of Noah and Kit Trayhern. Those who love the Morgan's Mercenaries series will recognize Noah as the younger brother of Morgan. As Megan's story opens, she's been deployed to Afghanistan, to a marine corps company near the Pakistan border, a real hot spot. All Megan wants to do is prove women can handle the stress of combat. Her commanding officer orders Luke Collier, also a combat medic, to keep her out of combat situations. Both Megan and Luke are unprepared for the powerful attraction they have for one another. I hope you enjoy their story!

You can always get ahold of me at www.lindsaymckenna.com. For more updates on this series and the books to come, drop over and check it out. I love to hear from my readers!

Lindsay McKenna

LINDSAY MCKENNA

Beyond Valor

HARLEQUIN® ROMANTIC SUSPENSE

Recycling programs
for this product may
not exist in your area.

ISBN-13: 978-0-373-27809-1

BEYOND VALOR

Printed in U.S.A.

LINDSAY MCKENNA

served her country in the U.S. Navy. She was an "air dale," aerographer's mate third class, also known as a weather forecaster. And it is from this background that she helped create the military romance subgenre in 1983 with *Captive of Fate* (Silhouette Special Edition). She writes what she knows. As a romantic suspense author, she likes to combine action with romance. Creator of Morgan's Mercenaries, a long-running family saga, she stays true to her military roots. She does a lot of hands-on research: she has flown in a P3B subhunter, flown a day and night mission in a B-52 bomber, and in a "chase" plane on a test flight at Edwards Air Force Base, and she has interviewed military people up and down the chain of command. She has worked with officials in the Pentagon and was the first romance writer to sign her books in the Pentagon bookstore. Since she was in the navy, she felt it was only right to tell stories about the the U.S. Navy SEALs. Visit her online at www.lindsaymckenna.com.

Dedicated to all the women who have been or are in combat presently, whether the military wants to acknowledge your courage and service or not. To all the women who have been killed in combat, to their families and loved ones, prayers and grateful thanks to all of you for your ultimate sacrifice. Gender should never determine who volunteers out of patriotic duty to defend our country. Only physical strength should be the final determination of whether a woman is fit for combat, duty or not.

Chapter 1

"**Y**our number's up, Luke," Sergeant Bucephalus warned.

Navy field medic Luke Collier looked up from what he was doing. Their Marine Corps company had just been choppered into Lar Sholtan in the Nuristan Province of Afghanistan. He stopped adding medical items to a cabinet he'd just hung on the wall. As he studied the grizzled thirty-year-old Marine Corps sergeant, his mouth curved. "I'm going to set up a Scrabble tournament as soon as I can, Buck. I know you like to play. And win."

The sergeant ambled over to the dusty desk where Luke was working. "I know you like your Scrabble tournaments because you win a pot of money, but this has nothing to do with it."

Outside the room was a small mud-and-rock structure where he and several other men from Lima Company had been assigned to sleep. It also doubled as his medical facility. Luke looked toward the open door. The early June sunlight was strong, shafts entering and making it easier to see around the Afghan hovel.

"What, then?" Luke asked. Tension mingled with urgency because Lima had just replaced another Marine company for the next year. The Afghan village of Lar Sholtan was a dangerous place. The villagers were equally scared of the Taliban and the Marines.

"Sit down," Buck said, and gestured to a nearby wooden keg. He pushed his fingers through his short brown hair. "I just got done talkin' with Captain Hall, and he's one unhappy dude. He's only happy that this assignment is gonna land in your lap and not his." He added a toothy grin, revealing that one of his front teeth was missing.

Frowning, Luke stared at the hillbilly-born Marine sergeant. Buck ran the company and had nearly as much power as the captain and the executive officer, Lieutenant Speed. The Kentucky sergeant was the glue between the officers and the one hundred thirty enlisted Marines in Lima.

"Uh-oh," Luke teased. "I guess this is a sit-down moment?" What on earth could Buck be talking about? Luke was on his third deployment in Afghanistan, and nothing surprised him much anymore. He set the bandages aside, pulled up the wooden keg and sat down.

Buck took the other keg, wiping the sweat off his darkly sunburned face. "The captain just got a call from Black Jaguar Squadron at Camp Bravo. You know about 'em, right?"

Searching his memory, Luke shrugged. "Not a whole lot. I've been stationed down south in Helmand Province for the last two tours. I know Camp Bravo is a big

CIA forward operating base. They have a lot of stealth stuff going on. Their mission is to stop the Taliban from crossing into this country."

Buck settled his large, spare hands across the thighs of his desert camouflage utilities. "You've got good scoop. I've been over here for—" and he held up his fingers and counted "—three tours. Comin' here to Lar Sholtan is number four."

"You win that round," Luke said, enjoying the humor dancing in Buck's green eyes. He liked the hillbilly sergeant, but so did everyone else. His Kentucky drawl and his easy way of managing the Marines had earned him trust among the men. "For once, you look serious. This *must* be bad news."

Buck rubbed his hands slowly up and down his thighs. The heat was stifling, nearly a hundred degrees in the early afternoon. "Well, the cap'n sure thinks it is. But—" and he shrugged a little "—I don't necessarily think so." His grin widened considerably. "But I'll let you tell me how you react to the news."

"Okay, you got me curious."

"You're a scrounger by nature, so you always like knowin' the little details." Buck chortled.

"Every company has a scrounger," Luke said proudly. That was a person who could get items that no one else could. Luke had spent enough time in-country and knew the ins and outs at the U.S. military headquarters in Kabul. Anyone who needed anything came to him. Luke got results. As a field medic, he was trusted by the men with their lives. As a scrounger, he was a demigod who could perform miracles.

"Well, the cap'n just spent a half hour explaining what's gonna happen tomorrow mornin'."

"What *is* going to happen?" Luke asked, meeting

the sergeant's foxlike smile. "Is this a person, place or thing?"

Chuckling, Buck pulled out his canteen and unscrewed the lid. "Naw, this ain't some Scrabble game, Luke. It's a person we're talkin' about. And I've gotta say, it's a sweet deal in my eyes. The cap'n thinks he's just been handed his biggest career killer to date." Buck guzzled some of the water. His Adam's apple bobbed up and down as he drank half of the contents. He then wiped his mouth with the back of his sleeve, screwed the lid on and placed it back in his belt. "How'd you like to be assigned another field medic?"

Luke's brows rose. "Well…sure. I'm busy 24/7. I could use another pair of hands around here. There should be four medics assigned to every company, but there's only me at Lima."

It was no secret that Navy corpsmen were some of the highest casualties of the war. They were the ones who braved hostile fire to get to their injured Marines.

"Is this what it's all about? Another field medic is being rotated in here to help me?" Luke asked. What could be bad about that? Nothing, in Luke's opinion.

Holding up his hand, Buck said in a warning tone, "Now, son, don't get your hopes set too high. There's more to my story. Did you know there's a supersecret group of women Apache drivers at Camp Bravo? They're called the Black Jaguar Squadron. When you see Apaches in this area, they're being flown by all-woman crews."

"Hey, that's cool," Luke said, admiring the whole idea. "I didn't know."

"Not many do. The woman who started the BJS is General Maya Stevenson," Buck said. "She formed a plan to have U.S. Army women flying the Apaches in

Peru to stop cocaine from leaving that country to the United States. She went to the Pentagon and argued it could be successful. The boys, of course, said she'd fail. But the opposite happened. That was fifteen years ago. Since then, Maya Stevenson has proved having women in combat works and works well. She's a general in the Army, stationed at the Pentagon, and came up with another idea involving women."

"She sounds like an effective leader," Luke said. "I knew nothing about this."

"I know," Buck said. "Remember, this is a top secret black ops."

"What does all of this have to do with me?"

"General Stevenson is at Camp Bravo right now. She's spearheaded a new strategy plan through the Pentagon. JSOC, Joint Special Operations Command, has given its full approval."

Curiosity burning bright, Luke could barely sit still as the sergeant, who was well-known for his long-winded stories, took his own sweet Kentucky time. "Okay, okay, so how does it involve us?"

"You always want to ruin a good story, Luke. Ya can't sit still longer than two seconds. You're always flittin' around like a hummingbird."

"Guilty," Luke admitted, holding up his hands. "My mother blames it on the fact that I'm a Gemini, and they're the tumbleweeds of the world."

Buck laughed. "That sounds about right. Okay, so here's the scoop. General Stevenson asked women volunteers to train with the Marine Corps. This group of women came from all branches of our services. They went through one year of combat training and learned Pashto. Some are specially trained to go into the villages and befriend the women. Of equal importance, these gals could get information from the women that none of the men leaders could give the military. In other words, they're a brilliant intel weapon."

Luke sat thinking about the concept. "It's not a bad idea. Given that in the Muslim tradition here in Afghanistan, women are totally subjugated, they must hear a lot."

"Exactly," Buck agreed. "Women hear everything. They're married to the chief of the village. They talk to the other wives in the village. And you know from being over here, the chiefs of a village often play both sides of the deck with us. They do that because they're afraid of reprisals by the Taliban."

Luke became sad. "We've lost a lot of men to injury and death because a village chief would know where the IEDs were being planted by Taliban sympathizers, but they wouldn't warn us."

"Right on," Buck said. "But what if one of these women soldiers befriends the women of the village? What if she's able to get dental and medical help for a woman and her children? These gals are trained to make connections and then be there if an Afghan woman wants to speak with them. Muslim women aren't allowed to talk to male strangers. It's taboo. Why not use the women instead?"

"That's a helluva plan," Luke agreed, finding the concept fascinating. "Are we getting one of those women here? In our company?"

"Your mama didn't raise a dummy, did she? Yep, we sure are." Buck pulled out a notebook from his pocket and flipped it open. "This gal's name is Megan Trayhern. She's a U.S. Navy Hospital Corpsman second class." He looked over at Luke. "Not all the women volunteers are in the field of medicine. They're all trained in first aid and the like, but Megan is a qualified field medic, so I figure that's gonna make you a happy man. She can actually help out the women and children in this village like you do the boys and men."

Brightening, Luke smiled. "Hey, this sounds great. She's the same rating I am." Finally, he'd have help taking care of the daily health issues of the men of Lima Company.

"Yep, she's your equal. The captain was happy to hear Megan was a field medic, but he sure as hell was unhappy about having a woman in an all-male combat company."

"I can see why," Luke said, thinking about his good fortune. "We've never had women in combat companies since it's against U.S. law."

"Yeah, yeah, I know all that, but General Stevenson argued women are *already* in combat whether they want to be or not. There are no more front lines. Congress just has to get over it, is all."

"Captain Hall doesn't think women can handle combat?"

"You got that right. Me?" Buck snorted. "This officer is a Northerner. He don't know hillbilly women at all. Hell, they can shoot just as good as any man, or better. They're tough, smart and hardy. Cap'n Hall is a rich city boy who has a very narrow view of women."

"I don't see her as a problem, Buck. Afghan women here won't talk to us. Megan might be a real resource."

"I think so, too, but the cap'n is sour on it. He's worried this woman will get kidnapped or killed on his watch."

Luke could appreciate Hall's dilemma. "If these women have had a year of training in combat and weapons, that should minimize the risk."

"You'd think," Buck said. He tore off the paper with the notes scribbled across it. "Here, you're gonna need this. The woman doc is flyin' in by CH-47 tomorrow at 0800. You're to meet her. The cap'n wants her to stay with you. You're in charge and responsible for her."

Luke laughed. "Oh, great! So if she gets injured or killed, it's *my* fault?"

"That's about it in a nutshell, Luke. Hall wants nothing to do with her. Out of sight, out of mind."

"Okay, so I meet this woman. What then?"

"Well, she's assigned to this house. She's now one of the boys. No special treatment, okay?"

"Okay." Luke was suddenly excited by the promise of a woman, a field medic, living among them. "I'll take care of her."

"Yep, you will. I'm sure her needs as a woman will be different from ours. I'm havin' some Marines build an outhouse and a private shower stall for her."

"That's special treatment. The Marines probably aren't happy about it, but it would give her some privacy."

"I like women. I don't see that as treating her special," Buck said with a wily grin. He rose and picked up the rifle he'd leaned against the dusty table. "And I know how strong they are. My only worry is you won't respect or admire them like I do. I don't want you pullin' a Hall on me."

"No worries on that score, okay?"

"Okay," Buck said, settling the helmet on his head. "But if you got problems, come to me first."

The shaking and shuddering of the CH-47 helo deepened as it began its descent into the valley toward Lar Sholtan. Megan sat tensely in the nylon-webbed seat squeezed between the aluminum hull and a large shipment of pallets beneath netting in the center of the bird. The loadmaster, a young blond Army spec, sat opposite her. He seemed bored. Looking to her right, Megan felt relief. Her cousin, Captain Rachel Trayhern-Hamilton, was flying. Next to her, in the copilot's seat, was her husband, Captain Ty Hamilton. They were recently married and were now assigned to the Black Jaguar Squadron. Megan's red-haired cousin was guiding the huge, unwieldy workhorse helicopter into a circle to land.

Megan saw glimpses of a wide valley notched between two huge mountain ranges. With her helmet on, she could follow chatter between the Marines on the ground and the pilots in the cockpit. Everyone was looking for a flash from the slopes of the mountains. This could indicate that a Taliban soldier had fired a grenade launcher or rocket against the incoming helo. There was tension in everyone's voices.

Megan held her medic pack across her lap. The shuddering of the helo and the roar of the two mighty engines above them made her anxious. Would she get on the ground in one piece or not? Craning her neck, Megan could see the blue of the sky dotted with fluffy white clouds. Below, she spied the sharp, rocky brown mountains. Everything looked dry and dead, like a desert.

The helo jostled as it hit an early updraft of heat from the valley below. As she gripped her pack, Megan's heart sped up. Her cousin dropped the helo swiftly toward the ground. If it hadn't been Rachel at the controls, Megan would probably have screamed. She held her breath as the aircraft dropped out of the sky. At the last minute, Rachel flared the helo, the nose coming up. In seconds, all Megan could see was yellow dust rising in thick clouds around them. Rachel had warned her this would happen. It blinded both pilots and they had no instrumentation to tell them how close they were to the ground except for an altimeter.

Breath exploded from Megan as the wheels touched the earth. She felt relief. The helo sagged and suddenly the engines were cut. The shaking stopped, the blades whirling more slowly.

The loadmaster was up and hurrying toward the descending ramp. Megan saw Rachel unstrap and squeeze out of the cockpit. She grinned at Megan and gestured for her to get up and move out of the helo. Haste was part of their life here.

Megan quickly jumped up, held on to her pack and hauled her duffel bag behind her. Rachel picked up the other strap and they carried the heavy bag down the ramp.

The dust still swirled and moved around them. Megan coughed and choked. Bits of dust got into her eyes as Rachel guided her off the ramp and toward some unknown point she couldn't see. Eyes watering, Megan felt the tears running down her cheeks. Hurrying, the duffel bag weighing more than ninety pounds, Megan followed Rachel. She was amazed her cousin seemed to know where she was going.

Finally, they emerged from the dust. Megan could hardly see, her eyes tearing up, dust and grit blinding her.

"We're here," Rachel called above the noise of the helo engines, dropping the duffel to the ground.

Megan was happy to let the bag drop to the yellow earth. She wiped her eyes, trying to remove the dust. When she looked up, she noticed two Marines standing in front of her. One was a lanky sergeant with a big welcoming smile on his face. The other was a tall, broad-shouldered Marine in desert fatigues, helmet on, his eyes narrowed speculatively upon her.

"We got her, Captain," the sergeant told Rachel as he came forward. "Take off!"

Rachel nodded, turned and hugged Megan. "Gotta go, Megan. We're sitting ducks here on the ground. Let Ty or me know if you need help. I love you. Stay safe!"

Megan hugged her and nodded. In seconds, Rachel disappeared back inside the cloud of dust, heading back to her helicopter. The tall, broad-shouldered Marine with hazel eyes stepped forward, hand extended. Relieved he was offering his large, calloused hand, she took it.

"Hi, I'm Megan Trayhern. Thanks for meeting me."

"Field medic Luke Collier. Welcome to Lar Sholtan, Doc."

His smile was warm and sincere. Her tension instantly melted beneath his firm handshake. Luke's hand was strong, his eyes conveyed intelligence and his smile made her feel more hopeful. "Thanks, Doc." She saw the medic insignia on his fatigues. One of her kind. There was kindness in Luke's face and his low, monitored voice convinced her that she was genuinely welcome.

"Come on, let's get back inside our fort," Luke said. "This is Sergeant Buck Payne. He's our go-to guy in the company."

The rotors on the helo's engines spooled up. She quickly shook Buck's hand and turned. The bird was already taking off, the sound earsplitting. More dust rose in the wake of its ascent into the blue sky.

"Let's move inside," Buck told her. He easily picked up the heavy duffel bag and led the way. The entire

Marine company lived within a large area that resembled a fort.

Megan nodded and hurried to catch up with the long-striding sergeant. Luke walked at her shoulder. She felt his protective energy, and it was exactly what she needed going into this unknown situation.

Eyes wide, Megan took in her new home. There were huge, round nylon bags filled with thousands of pounds of sand. They formed a tight circle around the company facilities. On top was a razor-sharp concertina. But now wasn't the time to linger. She hurried to keep up with Buck and go into the opening.

A number of curious Marines stood near the opened gate, gawking openly at her. She must have looked like a mess. Tears were still running down her dusty cheeks.

Once inside the metal gate, Buck ordered it closed. The sergeant headed toward one of mud-and-stone huts that sat in the middle of the enclosure.

Luke could see the anxiety on Megan's face. Despite her helmet and Marine fatigues, a rifle over her shoulder and the medical pack, she was obviously a woman. And a beautiful one at that. Strands of red hair had escaped from beneath her helmet. He smiled to himself, that he wanted to protect her. He cautioned himself against unwanted personal feelings. This wasn't the time or place.

"You can relax," Luke told her. "These grunts are curious about you, is all." He met her gaze head-on. "They don't bite." He couldn't help noticing the gold flecks set in the dark blue of her eyes. Megan was very attractive. Surely, she had a significant other. She was about five foot seven and maybe weighed around a hundred and thirty pounds. Even the baggy camouflage utilities couldn't hide her swaying hips or long legs. Someone loved this woman.

Anxious over the stares from the Marines, she flashed Luke an uneven smile. "Are you sure?" Something about this medic calmed her. It had to be his personality and that he was a healer.

"Absolutely," he said. Her anxiety seemed to ebb, and he was glad that she trusted him. His heart opened wide as her smile deepened. Megan had a quiet kind of charisma that couldn't be quantified or explained. More than curious about her, Luke decided his luck had changed for the better.

Buck led them into the large mud-and-rock house. He dropped the duffel bag in the corner near an empty cot. "This is your home away from home, Doc," he told her. Luke here is assigned to you. You're both medics and you'll be working exclusively with him. You come to me if you can't resolve a problem. And if I can't, then I'll be the one goin' to see Cap'n Hall, our C.O. He's expecting you, so as soon as you get squared away here in your new digs, Luke will take you over to HQ to see him."

"Got it," Megan assured him.

"Good. Later." He lifted his hand goodbye, turned on his heel and exited through the opened door.

Turning, Megan noticed Luke pulling her duffel bag aside. "That's my bed?"

"Yeah, you're bunking in with six guys, including me. We thought you'd like the corner? If not, we can move you to wherever you want."

"I really appreciate your help. I was honestly scared of coming here. My cousin Rachel, who flew me in, filled me with all kinds of horror stories about these outpost villages close to the Pakistan border."

"Amazing you have family over here. We're in Dodge City here and there's a lot you need to know so you can be safe while you're with Lima. It's my job to get you acclimatized."

Luke had scrounged up a bedroll for her. Even a pillow, which no one else had. The cots were Marine issue, olive-green canvas and on aluminum legs. The bedroll would make sleeping a lot more comfortable. He tried to shrug off the tender look that came to her face. Megan was open, Luke realized, unafraid to show her feelings. He responded to her whether he wanted to or not.

Luke was simply too handsome. He was powerfully built, but then, he was a field medic who routinely went out on squad and platoon missions in these rugged surroundings. The deep tan only made his hazel eyes more prominent. His nose was straight, his jaw clean and set in a square face. A small, thin scar ran alongside his left brow. Combat injury? Without thinking, Megan glanced at his left hand. Surely, he was married, though most men did not wear their wedding rings in a combat area. Why did she care about this?

Alarmed at herself, Megan looked around the dimly lit hovel. It had no electricity or running water. There was a square, dusty wooden table with a kerosene lamp. Only light pouring in through the opened door allowed enough light to see within the home. "When I was in training at Camp Pendleton in California, they tried to impress upon us the terrible conditions we'd be living in." Lips compressed, Megan added, "This is a really dirty place...."

Luke got the cot squared away for her and moved her duffel to the end so she could easily reach it. Laughing softly, he said, "Trust me, medics know cleanliness is next to godliness." He straightened and looked over at her. "This is the dustiest place on earth, except for where I was born."

"You were born in a desert?"

"Yep, Phoenix, Arizona. That place is a dust bowl, too." He grinned and gestured around the hovel. "Made me feel right at home here in Afghanistan."

Megan stood uncertainly. The medic was tall and terribly handsome in a rugged kind of way. His smile went through her like sunlight and helped her relax. Maybe it was his warm hazel eyes that made her feel safe. "I like your attitude."

"You've got to develop one out here," he told her. "Here, have a seat. I scrounged up a beat-up teakettle and I got real coffee on hand." He went over to a hot plate lodged in the corner, turned it on and set the copper teakettle down. "We'll sit down, chat and share a cup of the good stuff."

"But…this place has no electricity. How does that hot plate work?"

"Oh," Luke murmured, "I'm the company scrounger. On a flight into Kabul HQ last week, I found this little discarded generator and brought it back. I've got the wires running under the adobe and stones here. One of the grunts is an electrician, so he wired it up." Giving her a humored look, Luke added, "This company is a full of coffee hounds. You'll get used to the foot traffic in and out of here."

Megan smiled. "So you're a real scrounger? That's great. The Navy ship I was on before I volunteered for this assignment had a chief petty officer who got us anything we needed it. Scroungers were absolutely essential to an outfit. They make our day, to say the least." She noticed Luke preening. For a moment the man disappeared and she caught a glimpse of the little boy beneath. Megan had to stop herself from simply staring at Luke. He was eye candy of the finest sort.

"Whatever you need, all you have to do is ask. I'm starting my third tour over here and I have connections." Luke heard the water begin to boil in the kettle. He was drawn to Megan. She had a solid, quiet demeanor that bred confidence. He imagined she was an outstanding medic. Patients would instantly trust her. "You'll feel better after a good cup of hot coffee. I get my beans from Brazil. They're the best."

Setting her medic pack down on her cot, Megan laughed. "It's a good thing I ran into you, then." Looking down, she appreciated the Persian rugs of various colors and designs that covered the dirt floor. Suddenly, all her trepidation about this assignment melted away. Luke Collier was intelligent, sinfully good-looking and he made her feel safe in a world she knew could kill in a heartbeat.

Chapter 2

"Shouldn't I get over to Headquarters and let Captain Hall know I've arrived?" Megan asked.

"After coffee. Right now the day's getting into high gear. The captain will have his hands full with the squads going out looking for IEDs along the road to the village." Luke glanced over his shoulder as he made coffee and took note of the worry in her eyes. "Things are done different out in the field. I know he's not expecting you to show up right now."

Megan watched the activity outside the door. It was early June and the valley sat at five thousand feet. The weather was cool, but not cold. She was glad to be wearing the flak jacket because it kept her warmer. "I'm used to being on a carrier out in the middle of the Pacific," she said somewhat as a joke.

"How long you been in the Navy?"

"I've been in since age eighteen and I'm twenty-six."

Luke brought the two chipped ceramic mugs filled with steaming coffee to the table. "Cream? Sugar?"

"Neither. Thanks."

He sat down opposite her on another wooden barrel. "Buck said you're an HM2?" he asked, lifting the cup to his lips.

"That's right. What's your rating?"

"Same." He grinned. "Makes us equals." Luke tried to ignore her hair. Even though it was drawn up into a ponytail, he could tell it was shoulder-length. Mentally, he tried to picture it framing her oval face. Her complexion was pale, her cheeks stained pink. What would it be like to loosen that thick, coppery hair and allow it to fall through his hands?

"I didn't know who I'd be paired up with once I got here. We were taught in training that we'd have to work directly with the C.O." It was so easy to stare into Luke's warm green-and-gold gaze. She liked the gentle energy she felt around him. Most field medics were humble and passionate about helping others. Luke was no exception.

"Captain Hall may or may not do that," Luke warned. "He's a manager, not a control-freak kind of officer. For example, I man the dispensary at Lima. I pretty much have the run of the company to do what I want. My main contact is Sergeant Buck Payne. I know you have to report for duty over at the C.O.'s office, but I'm guessing he's going to tell me to be your main contact."

"Is Captain Hall on board for this experiment?" Megan wondered aloud.

Luke shrugged. "I don't know." It was important Megan feel a part of Lima, not abandoned by it.

"How about the rest of the Marines? Have you heard anything?"

"I think most of them are curious. So am I. I like the idea of a woman being with us to deal with the villagers. As a corpsman, I can't examine a woman or a little girl who is seven years or older, by Muslim law. That means the females in a village are never taken care of medically like the men are."

"It's a stupid law."

"It has its drawbacks," Luke agreed, hearing the growl of frustration in her husky voice. He smiled. "So, tell me about yourself. For some reason, the name Trayhern rings a bell."

"You're thinking of my uncle Morgan Trayhern," Megan said.

"That's it!" Luke snapped his fingers. "Your uncle Morgan is part of Marine Corps history. He had his company wiped out in the Vietnam War and then suffered a head injury. If I recall right, he spent time in the French Foreign Legion afterward because he couldn't remember who he was."

"Right," Megan said. "Eventually, his memory did come back and he came home. The newspapers made him out to be a traitor and he wasn't. He cleared his name with Laura's help, who was a military archivist in Washington, D.C." Megan's voice softened. "They fell in love during the time of proving him innocent. She's a wonderful person and I'm proud of our military family history."

"You should be. Your family is a military dynasty. Every child, if I recall, does at least six years of military service?"

"Yes."

"And you chose to become a field medic. I thought most of your family were officers in the different branches of the military."

Shrugging, Megan said a bit defensively, "I did get an invitation to train at the academy of my choice, but I didn't see myself as a leader. I had other priorities I felt were important to follow."

Luke studied the frown gathering on her brow. Her eyes, once light, were now shadowed. He sensed sadness around her. "Like what?"

"I've never been a proponent of carrying a weapon and killing another human being," Megan said, setting the mug on the table. "I just can't see myself doing that. At the academies, you're taught to shoot to kill. I wasn't cut out for it. So—" and she drew in a deep breath "—I decided to become a registered nurse."

"Then you went into the military after graduating?"

"Yes, but not as an officer. They let me have my pick of career positions. I wanted to use my medical knowledge as a nurse and I chose to become a hospital corpsman. Field medicine really appealed to me, so I made it my speciality."

Luke rubbed his chin and gave her a respectful look. "You've been in the Navy for four years and you're already an HM2? That means you're pretty spectacular at what you do."

Hearing his admiration, Megan felt heat move from her neck up into her face. "I love what I do," she admitted in a soft voice. "I believe love heals all. And our actions as medics are based on compassion."

Her depth resonated within him. There was grit in her eyes, a stubbornness that showed her strength despite her feminine softness. There was something unique to Megan that intrigued him. Tearing away from his thoughts, he asked, "So, why volunteer for this outback duty? Why not go with an NGO in some other foreign country where it's a lot safer?"

"I'd read articles about Afghanistan. It angered me that women and little girls are overlooked in this culture and they suffer terribly without proper medical care. They aren't animals." Glancing toward the door, Megan saw a number of Humvees lining up with Marines getting ready to leave the massive compound. "I wanted to make a difference, Luke. I'm driven to help them...."

"Are those your Trayhern genes talking?" Luke asked.

She thought for a moment and moved the cup between her hands. "I guess, maybe a little. My family, even my uncle Morgan, was disappointed with my choice." She saw curiosity in Luke's face. The light and dark shadows gave his square face a sense of strength. She liked Luke's insightful nature and figured he had a family waiting at home for him. Maybe that was for the best since she was still smarting from her poor relationship choices. "I just didn't want to pick up a rifle and kill. At heart, I'm a pacifist." She studied his expression carefully; *pacifist* was a dirty word in the military world. Luke's brows dipped, but there was no censure in his eyes.

"I think that people like us who are corpsmen are basically pacifists," Luke said, treading carefully. "We do carry weapons when we go out into the field. We have a duty to save lives, not take them, if possible." He frowned. "But as I understand it, the women who volunteered for this one-year experiment were trained to shoot a weapon and defend themselves?"

Megan nodded. "That's correct. It was easy for me to shoot at a lifeless target." She smiled a little. "Out here, I'm hoping Captain Hall will acknowledge my medical status and allow me to forgo carrying a weapon."

"That's a tough one," Luke replied. "I don't know

what Hall will decide." He stood up. "Ready to go over to HQ and meet your new C.O.?"

Standing, Megan left the emptied cup on the table. "Yes, let's get this over with. I've got a feeling he's not going to be very happy to see a woman in his company...."

Luke walked with Megan across the dusty, busy yard within the compound. Two lines of Humvees had just left the fort. He pointed to another small mud house. "That's our headquarters."

"Couldn't tell it," Megan said. Since she was dressed in full combat gear, few Marines realized she was a woman until they saw her up close. And then their eyes would widen with momentary surprise. It made her feel alien. Would these Marines accept her or not? Megan had been warned in training to expect push-back by some who wouldn't want a female in their midst.

As they walked across the powdery red earth, Megan noticed how the Hindu Kush Mountains literally surrounded the wide, long valley. They rose like lords over the desert. There was little green on the rock-strewn slopes and it looked dead to her. This was an inhospitable place of brutal harshness. Afghanistan's economy was one of the weakest in the world, comparable to Somalia's. Only the toughest survived in this mountainous country.

As they entered the busy command post, or C.P., Luke guided her toward the rear. She recognized Buck at a messy desk. There were a number of radios hanging on the wall and on the strategy board in the center of the area. The talk was nonstop.

"Sergeant Payne? Megan is coming here to meet Captain Hall. Is he available?"

The sergeant nodded. "Yep, go right in, Trayhern. He's expectin' you."

Nodding, Megan moved around Luke, her orders in hand. "Thank you, Sergeant."

"Luke, you're to go in with her."

"What?"

"Yeah, the cap'n wants to see both of you."

"Okay," Luke murmured, surprised by the odd request. "You sure?"

"Do I look like a bump on a log? Get your butt in there."

Shrugging, Luke followed Megan to the rough wooden door.

Megan knocked firmly.

"Enter," a voice called from behind it.

Megan stepped into the cramped, tiny office. A number of radios and a GPS phone sat on the C.O.'s cluttered desk. Megan set the order on top of the mess and came to attention in front of the desk. "HM2 Megan Trayhern reporting as ordered, sir."

Hall, who had his back to them and was sticking colored pins into a map behind his desk, muttered, "At ease, Trayhern."

Megan relaxed into an at-ease position, as did Luke, who stood at her side. She was unsure why the sergeant had ordered him to join her. When Hall turned around, she saw the deep scowl on the Marine officer's face, his stare intense. The man was around thirty, at least six feet tall, lean as a whippet and darkly tanned. It was his hard jaw and the line of his mouth that made her tense. He was not happy to see her.

Hall snapped a look at Luke. "Collier, you're in charge of this medic. You take her with you when you go to the village."

"Yes, sir."

Hall glared at Megan. "And off the record, Trayhern, I'm not a fan of this little experiment. I know you're trained, but unless they carry me out of here boots-first, you aren't going on any missions with my men. You either stay here at the fort or you work at the village."

"Yes, sir."

Hall picked up her orders and perused them, the silence thickening in the stuffy office. "You're an expert marksman," he said.

Megan heard the astonishment in his voice. Expert meant she had shot accurately enough to be the best. Only sniper-quality shooting was above her ability. Few men or women qualified as expert. She saw his face moving into a surprised expression. "Yes, sir, I am."

"You're not carrying arms," he said, dropping the papers on the desk. "You're the Pentagon's latest experiment, so when you are outside our compound, you *will* carry a weapon and you *will* use it. Got it?"

The intensity of his expression made her tense. "Yes, sir." Megan wasn't about to tell him she'd never kill another human being. Hall wouldn't want to hear it.

Grabbing the papers again, he read down the list of her duty stations. "You were in Iraq for a year? Tell me about that."

"I was stationed there after completing field medic school. I was assigned to Baghdad and I worked with the Lionesses group. The Lionesses were women in the military, usually military police, who had to pat down women in burkas who might be hiding weapons or explosives. Eventually, the Lionesses formed liaisons and positive connections with women in the areas where they were assigned."

"Hmph. I see you also took a one-year immersion course in Pashto?"

"Yes, sir."

"Well," he said, rubbing his jaw, "I just might steal you from Collier from time to time to do a little translating for me. The translators I got are Afghani and they don't speak the dialect this village does. Maybe you can."

"Yes, sir."

"You've seen combat, Trayhern?"

"Not directly, sir. We got mortared from time to time in the Green Zone, but that's all."

Hall snorted. "Collier, get her out of here. She'll assist you. Trayhern, Collier is your boss. Got it?"

"Yes, sir."

"Give these papers to Sergeant Payne. Dismissed."

Turning on her boot heel, Megan was more than ready to run out of the hot, stuffy room. She clenched the orders in her hand. Buck Payne gave her a slight smile as she handed them to him.

"Cap's in a foul mood this morning, but I guess you saw that," he said, stamping the orders and placing them in a file folder. "Don't worry, Trayhern, he'll get over the fact that you're a woman." Grinning and showing the gap between his front teeth, Buck added, "I'm sure once he finds out you're a translator, he'll forgive you for being a female. We've been havin' a hellacious time with getting someone who can accurately translate between us and the elders of the village. Here you go, here's info you need to read." He handed her a manual.

"Thanks, Sergeant."

Buck looked at Luke.

"Okay, I'm headin' into the village at 0900. Meet me and my convoy at the gate."

"We'll be there," Luke promised.

"Go saddle up."

Luke knew they had about fifteen minutes to get their medical gear together. He looked at Megan. Her face was unreadable, but he could tell she was disappointed in Hall. "Let's go," he told her.

Once outside and crossing the grinder, as they referred to the wide-open dirt area between the buildings, Megan said in a low voice, "Hall is absolutely pissed I'm here."

"Yeah, I heard from Buck a week ago that he called General Stevenson personally to complain."

Megan sucked in a breath. "He did?"

"Yeah. Why?"

"I got to meet General Maya Stevenson at Camp Pendleton a year ago. She's a force, let me tell you. A one-woman army at the Pentagon. Her track record on proving women do just as well as men in combat is unquestioned."

"Which is probably why the Pentagon approved this experiment," Luke concluded, stepping into their sleeping quarters. He gathered his medic bag and other needed supplies.

"I hope I can prove myself to be an asset and not a pain in the ass," she said with a chuckle, sliding the strap of her medic bag over her shoulder. Whether she liked it or not, she picked up her rifle, as well.

"Hall's not a bad sort. He just wants to bring his men home on two feet and not in body bags." He stood at the door and watched her place items into her large medical pack. Her fingers were long, her movements graceful. Her curvy hips gave away her gender. The Kevlar that would protect her upper body from a bullet fully hid her breasts. Overall, he liked what he saw. Luke tempered his pleasure, reminding himself a romance had no place in a combat situation.

"Ready," Megan said, meeting him at the door. "Let's go."

Nodding, Luke led her to the left of their sleeping quarters. There were four Humvees mounting up with Marines. Other missions were already out and clearing the dirt road of IEDs going into the village of Lar Sholtan. A truck at the front held instruments and a television camera to keep an eye for suspicious dirt. Those areas could house recently buried IEDs. The last truck in the convoy contained a machine gun. The slopes of the mountains always hid Taliban insurgents who watched the company through binoculars. Often enough, they fired into the compound. There was no safe place.

Luke led Megan to the Humvee behind the IED truck. He opened the rear door for her. "Climb in."

Megan was familiar with Humvees from her Iraq duty. She placed her medic bag in back and squeezed in.

"Hey," the driver called, raising his hand. "I'm Shorty. You the gal assigned to us?"

Settling in, Megan said, "Yes. HM2 Trayhern. Nice to meet you, Shorty."

Luke climbed in and shut the door. There wasn't a lot of room between him and Megan in the tight quarters. "Hey, Shorty, Megan is a field medic."

Shorty grinned. "Good news. Now if we hit an IED we have two medics to save our sorry asses, instead of just you, Doc."

Chortling, Luke could see Hall approaching the Humvee. "Two for one," he agreed with the private. With a tilt of his head, he warned Megan that the C.O. was striding up to the vehicle.

Once Hall settled into the front seat of the Humvee, he radioed the column to move out. Megan sat behind him, glad that the officer couldn't see her. He hadn't acknowledged them, either. That was fine with her.

The vehicle growled and jerked forward. The five miles to the village were done at a crawl. The IED truck determined the speed along the dirt road, which was deeply rutted. It gave Megan a chance to look around and study the desert terrain. From time to time, Luke pointed out certain areas. Massive black and gray boulders piled up together usually meant a hiding place for a Taliban spotter. It was from these points that grenade launchers were lobbed into the Marine enclosure.

"How often do you get attacked?" Megan asked.

"Maybe once or twice a month. Most of the Taliban in this area are another tribe from the other side of this mountain." He pointed to a fourteen-thousand-foot peak to the east of them. "Lar Sholtan is a major choke point for the U.S. to stop al-Qaeda insurgents from coming through this area."

Megan nodded, knowing how Taliban soldiers often fought other tribes in the area. The U.S. military tried to help one tribe, and if the other took offense, it attacked. Al-Qaeda soldiers were different. They came out of Pakistan and other Middle Eastern countries to fight in Afghanistan for a strict Muslim way of life for all Afghans. Sometimes, the Taliban and al-Qaeda joined forces, as they did in this border area.

"What does the chief of the village feel about us being here?" she asked. Did the elders respect the Marines, and vice versa? Did Captain Hall play fair with the villagers?

The heat in the Humvee rose. She was glad Shorty turned on the air-conditioning. They couldn't open the windows because if they hit an IED, the shrapnel could fly in and kill them.

Rolling his eyes, Luke said, "Timor Khan, the leader, is about fifty, with a gray beard and blue eyes. He was a Mujahadeen fighting the Russian soldiers early in his life. He's got tribal Taliban friction, but nothing like the al-Qaeda soldiers who threaten to kill his people if they work with us. He's cagey, from what I understand. The other C.O., who just left with his company, did not create strong, trusting ties with the Marines. It's up to Captain Hall to change things. Timor could tell us where certain villagers of his who are Taliban sympathizers are planting these IEDs, but he won't. He fears reprisal by al-Qaeda operatives."

"It was like that in Iraq," Megan said. "You had to read between the lines with the leaders over in Iraq, too."

"Same here," Luke said. "I don't blame the people. Khan's the leader and he's responsible for protecting his village. In my time in Helmand Province, we did people-building and got the trust of a number of villages. They'd tell us where the IEDs had been planted the night before." He frowned. "It's not like that here, and Captain Hall is working hard to get Timor's trust. I come into the village twice a week to hold medical clinics. The people really appreciate it and Timor seems to be softening his attitude toward us. But we have a long way to go."

"I don't care what country you come from, or who you are," Megan said, "you want to be treated with fairness and respect."

"No disagreement. At least our C.O. is on top of the situation." He smiled. "That's where you can really help us make a difference, Megan. You can talk to Khan's wife, Mina, and find out how you can help the women and children."

"How long has Lima been here?"

"Just a month."

Nodding, Megan gazed out the dusty window. The landscape reminded her of the moon: barren and un-livable. Yet, as the road rose over a small hill, she noticed a verdant area down below them. Lar Sholtan was beautiful with its fields of corn and wheat growing in large, rectangular patches. Three-foot-high rock fences cordoned off each rectangular field. "Do they grow poppy crop here?"

"No. Only in south and central Afghanistan where it's warmer. Here in this area, it's colder and the growing season is barely ninety days. These poor people have one shot at growing grains, fruit and vegetables or they die of starvation."

"It's so dry and dead-looking," Megan remarked.

Despite this difficult new assignment, she started to relax. Was it because of Luke? She liked the alert look in his hazel eyes. He didn't seem to miss much. Megan felt safe sitting with him. It was silly, because no one was safe out in Dodge City, the slang term for this country.

"What can tip the balance in our favor is getting a well dug for the village," Luke said. "Like I said, I was born in Phoenix, Arizona. The pioneer coming into this state built concrete dikes to bring water from the Colorado River." He gestured out the window. "The last Marine company C.O. stationed here ignored Timor Khan's request for a well. Captain Hall is trying to get the Pentagon to let go of enough money to sink a well for this village. If he can get approval, it would go a long way in building trust. Water is always a problem in Afghanistan."

"Can't you scrounge up a drilling rig to sink a well?"

A crooked grin worked its way across his mouth. "I'm a fine scrounger, but that's way beyond my pay grade. I was thinking that nongovernment organizations would be the route to take, if Captain Hall can't get Pentagon money."

"Let me think on this, Luke. I might have some connections to a charity."

Brightening, Luke leaned over and whispered, "If you could do that, the captain would worship the ground you walk on. He's not getting positive signals from the Pentagon, and he's frustrated."

Megan thrilled at his unexpected closeness. The moisture of his breath grazed her neck. A ribbon of pleasure wound through her. "Oh, I don't think he's going to see me as a positive force in this company. I need time to talk with Mina Khan and see what she feels her people need first," she said, keeping her voice low.

The Humvee lurched forward. They were speeding along at ten miles per hour. Megan became excited as they finally pulled into the walled village. "How many people here?"

"Two hundred," Luke said, craning his neck to look at the men standing at the gate of the village. All were farmers. Some owned donkeys and others had primitive farm implements to plow the stubborn soil. The grain fields surrounded the village. He saw a few little boys and a few scruffy dogs playing nearby.

"Do things look quiet?"

"Yeah, from what I can see. The men and their sons are going out to tend the fields."

She saw them in baggy cotton pants, their long vests over long-sleeved shirts. Most wore turbans or caps, and they all had beards. It was a Muslim law that no

man could be clean-shaven. This was an easy way to
identify non-Muslim in this country, which was why
the SEAL teams always wore beards. "They're hard-
looking," she said. Their faces were darkened by con-
tinuous work under the sun, many lines and creases
deeply etched into their leathery skin.

"The stats say people in Afghanistan die in their
early forties," Luke said. "This land is a challenge, and
only the hardy survive."

"It's tough enough trying to survive in this environment," Megan said, feeling for the people. "Add to that
al-Qaeda threatening to kill them if they talk to us."

"Yeah." Luke sighed. "It's not a good situation.
Timor Khan has a truce with the tribe on the other
side of the mountain—for now. You can bet some of
these men are al-Qaeda sympathizers. Some may be
burying the IEDs in the road at night, hoping we'll
drive over one the next morning. There's no way to tell
who's good or bad."

"I'm sure Khan knows who they are," Megan said.
The Humvee came to a halt and Hall climbed out.

"He does." Luke watched the captain go up and give
the Muslim greeting to the elders standing at the entrance. "The captain knows just enough Pashto to get
some rudimentary greetings out of the way."

Megan had a dark green cotton scarf stuffed in her
pocket. She pulled it out and took off her helmet. Placing it across her head, she said, "We were taught to wear
a scarf because it honors Muslim law."

"My advice is tie it around your neck and always
wear your helmet when outdoors," Luke said. "I don't
think Hall will let you traipse around the village with
a scarf on your head. He'll want you fully protected.
Don't forget, there could be al-Qaeda sympathizers

among these people. We don't know what they might do if they see you." His voice turned soft. "Megan, you're a target whether you want to be or not…."

"Good advice." Megan took off the scarf and instead allowed it to hang around her neck and shoulders.

Megan saw the captain walk away from the elders. "Greetings are completed. I guess we go into the village now?"

"Yep. The C.O. will drive to Khan's home to talk with him. Protocols are very important to follow here."

"Do we get out at Khan's home, then?"

"I would think so. Hall will probably want to introduce you to the leader. Timor Khan will then decide whether or not to allow you to talk with his wife. Women never attend meetings of men. They're not allowed."

"Do you know anything about Mina?" Excitement thrummed through Megan. At last, she could put a year's worth of hard work into play.

"No, all I ever see her in is a burka. I don't even know what she looks like." Luke grinned as Hall climbed into the Humvee and shut the door. "Maybe Mina will invite you in for tea. They don't wear those burkas inside. You can tell me later today what she looks like."

Megan found the Muslim laws unwieldy and unfair to women, but she said nothing as the Humvee lurched through the opened gate and passed the men standing nearby. These young men in their twenties had a flat and expressionless look in their eyes. Who among them hated the Marines? Which were friendly? Swallowing hard, Megan tried to still her excitement. At least she hoped to help the women and children of this village.

Women, their babies and young girls would no longer have to go without medical intervention. This was her silent promise to these villagers and to herself.

Chapter 3

Megan's heart beat a little harder as the Humvee rolled slowly down the main dirt road. It was one thing to be shown slides and photos of the area and another to see it. Most of the homes were single-story and made from mud. Others were made of stone, or a combination of the two. Afghans used whatever raw materials were available.

Children, barefoot and in ragged clothes, ran down the street. Their faces were filled with smiles, and they held their hands out toward the Humvee.

"They're asking for candy," Luke told her.

"My trainers told me to always carry a bag of candy in my pocket." She patted her left thigh pocket.

"Some kids, the older ones, can be a problem," Luke warned. "The Pashtuns are a tribe and they live all along this border region between Afghanistan and Pakistan. The Taliban threatens them, and some of the villages work with them. Others do not. Most Afghans hate al-Qaeda rule, but they can't snub them or they'll come into a village and murder everyone. It's sad."

"Maybe I can help turn this around if there are al-Qaeda sympathizers in this village," Megan said. She memorized what the homes looked like. Older men stood near the street, staring at them. A few women in burkas, which covered them from head to toe, moved quickly, heads down.

They passed a donkey cart with sticks and branches piled high. When she'd flown in earlier, she'd seen how denuded the landscape was for several miles around the village. Those in the business of collecting and selling firewood had to travel many miles farther to find fuel.

"This is going to get interesting," Luke said. "The kids have never seen a female soldier before. It's going to fascinate them. Afghan women stay at home and cook, clean, weave and take care of their children. You're going to be very popular."

Megan grimaced. "I don't like being popular. You get less done that way."

"It comes with the territory," Luke said. What he didn't say was the teenage boys might do more than stare. Captain Hall hadn't said anything yet, but Luke knew he was going to have to protect Megan the best he could. He worried someone in the village might try to kill her. She was like a lamb going to live in the lair of a wolf pack.

"I love children," Megan said. She glanced at Luke and saw worry in his eyes. Worry about her or the situation? Unsure, Megan inhaled deeply. Captain Hall had ordered Shorty to drive them to Khan's three-story rock home. Holding Luke's gaze, she asked, "Is Timor Khan anti-American?"

"No," Luke said with some hesitation. "He's in a precarious position between al-Qaeda, the Taliban and the Marines. His duty is to keep his people safe. Outwardly, he pretends to help us. The departing company commander warned Captain Hall that Khan was a sly old fox and never to trust him." Shrugging, Luke added, "I heard the past C.O. didn't do any relationship-building with Khan. Now Hall is trying to change things around. The captain knows the only way to get support is to treat the people fairly and with respect. Because of the other C.O., Hall has to mend fences, bridges and get Khan to trust him."

"Sounds like a tough order," Megan said, seeing Hall in a new and more positive light.

"It is." Luke looked out the windows. Children were racing alongside the Humvee, laughing and waving. He waved back. "There are so many rules and laws to the Pashtun tribe, too. Hall has to thread the needle on this, and so do we. We're basically emissaries for America."

Wrinkling her nose, Megan said, "I have a *real* problem with how women are treated here."

"Yeah, the old 'barefoot and pregnant' idea is alive and well in Afghanistan." Luke's mouth curved with irony.

"Maybe I can be a role model in more than one way."

"Just be careful," he cautioned. "You need to be with a group of women at all times. Never walk down one of these streets alone. Always have a village woman as an escort."

Frowning, Megan asked, "Why?"

"It could be dangerous. There are al-Qaeda sympathizers here in this village. We don't know who they are, and Khan isn't telling us. These men will hate you. You're a woman doing a man's job in their eyes. And you're not conducting yourself like a Muslim woman should. You're flying in the face of their laws regarding women. Your ally will be Mina, the wife of Timor Khan, and she is queen of her village, so to speak. She's thirty-five years old and they have two boys and two girls. Mina is Khan's fourth wife."

Brows raising, Megan asked, "What happened to the other three?"

"They all died in childbirth," he said sadly. "It happens a lot out here, Megan. Right now in this village there are five women who are pregnant. I can't examine them, much less see them to prescribe prenatal vitamins to them, because I'm a man. With you here, I'm hoping all five will deliver healthy babies."

"That's so depressing," Megan whispered.

"Well, let's get this meeting with Khan over with first. There's an empty house next to Khan's home. I'm hoping Mina will set it up as a medical clinic where you can work. The women and children could come there for treatment. I just hope Khan blesses the idea."

The Humvee pulled to a halt in front of the home. Megan climbed out when Hall ordered them to follow him. A two-foot rock wall surrounded the home. A dirt path was lined on either side with large gray and black rocks. As Megan followed the captain up the thick wooden stairs, children gathered at the bottom, outside the wall. The men's faces were sharp and alert. This sent a frisson of danger through her.

Mina Khan answered the door. She wore a long gray vest over her pale pink dress that fell to her slippered feet. She smiled and swung the door open.

"Welcome, Captain Hall. My husband is expecting you. Please, come in." She stepped aside.

Megan and Luke followed Hall into the home. The

wooden floors were swept clean of dust. A huge dark blue Persian rug filled the center of the room. Megan smelled bread baking. Taking off her helmet, she pulled the green scarf over her head. Mina wore a bright pink scarf, her blue eyes intelligent-looking and clear.

Mina shut the door. "My husband is in the library, Captain Hall." She pointed toward an entrance that led to another room.

Hall nodded. "Thank you, ma'am." He gave Luke a glance and they walked toward the library.

Mina turned. "And you must be Megan Trayhern."

Megan gave the Muslim greeting in Pashto and touched her fingers to her heart as she spoke.

Mina reached out to guide Megan toward a set of stairs. "You speak our language quite well. What a delight! Please, follow me. My two daughters will serve the men tea, and then they will serve us."

The scent of baking bread became stronger as they approached the wooden stairs.

"Thank you," Megan said.

"The kitchen is always the warmest place in our house. We'll have tea at the table and chat."

Megan liked the woman's warm, sincere smile. Mina was tall, confident and pleasant. Tucking her helmet beneath her left arm, the rifle slung from her left shoulder, Megan thunked across the floor in her desert combat boots. She glanced around, thinking the house was tastefully furnished. Dark brown chairs and a sofa sat on beautiful Persian rugs. Gold curtains hung at each of the small windows. Mina walked like the queen she was.

In the kitchen, two young women hurried around gathering up cups, a teapot and silver trays. They stopped and anchored for a moment, staring at Megan. Mina chided them and they quickly returned to their duties. In moments, they had left the kitchen for the library, where their father was holding audience with the Americans.

"Alone at last," Mina said with a smile. She gestured to a small wooden table at one end of the large kitchen. "Have a seat, Megan."

"Thank you," Megan murmured. She pulled out the highly carved chair, her back to the stucco wall. After setting down her helmet and rifle, Megan returned her attention to Mina.

"Do you like chai?" Mina asked, pouring two cups. "I do."

"Good." Mina brought over the dark red ceramic cups and placed them on the table. She sat down opposite Megan. "Captain Hall promised an American woman doctor would come to help us. I can't tell you how much I have counted the days."

Megan picked up the steaming cup of chai and cautiously sipped it. Sweet honey combined with hot milk and nutmeg. It was delicious. "I'm not a doctor, my lady. I'm a Navy field medic, but I'm also trained as a registered nurse. I was hoping to get your help and advice on how best to serve the women and children of your village."

"First, please call me Mina. And we're delighted you're here."

"Is your husband all right with me being here?"

"Yes, of course. Like me, Timor knows that Luke cannot see, talk or examine a woman or little girl because of Muslim law. The last Navy medic assigned here was also a man." She wrinkled her long, fine nose. "We lost three wonderful mothers in childbirth last year. We lost their babies, too." She pressed her hand over her heart. "I have not stopped crying over those losses. Sometimes it is too much to bear." Tears shone in Mina's eyes. She had luxurious black hair beneath the cotton scarf.

Without thinking, Megan reached across the table and touched her work-worn hand. "I'm so sorry to hear this. I'm going to do everything in my power to help the women and children, Mina. That's why I'm here. You just tell me where I can set up my medical clinic, and I'll get to work."

Mina wiped her eyes. "I was hoping you would have a great heart, and you do. I was born in Kabul, the daughter of very rich parents, and was sent to Europe to study. I received an economics degree from the Sorbonne in France. I was used to the refinement and luxuries of life until I met and fell in love with Timor. I know the people suffer greatly here compared to those who live in a city." She raised her hand and pointed out the dust-covered window. "Out here, there is nothing but survival. My husband is a good man, but we have little means to bring in medical help."

Megan saw the frustration in her face. Her cultured voice was husky with tears. "I will help as best I can. So, you also speak French?" Clearly, Mina was not an ordinary Afghan woman out on this frontier.

Smiling shyly, Mina said, "I speak fluent Pashto, French, English and Italian."

"That's remarkable," Megan said, admiration in her tone.

"If you'd like, we can speak English. I have no one to practice my English with."

"Of course, that would be great," Megan said. She sipped the delicious chai. "Do you have a plan for a clinic?"

"Yes." Mina pulled a paper from the pocket of her

gown, opened it and flattened it across the table. "There is an empty home next to ours. I have had our four widows cleaning it up for your arrival. Their husbands have been killed and they have no support for themselves or their children. Our village is so poor even their relatives cannot take them into their homes to feed them. I have been trying to give the widows work and pay them with daily food. Right now the four of them are preparing your clinic. After chai, would you like to see your facility?"

Megan nodded. "Absolutely."

"Can you come daily?"

"I don't know, but I'll ask Captain Hall and let you know."

"Of course," Mina said. "I like this captain. He's far nicer than the other one who was here last year."

"I believe Captain Hall is trying to heal the damage done," Megan said.

"He is already succeeding," Mina said with a slight smile. "My husband likes this young man very much. He is sincere, he listens a lot and asks questions. Those are signs of respect."

"Yes, they are," Megan agreed.

"And your job is to be here to help our women and children for a year, I hope?"

"Yes, it is. You are my priority." She saw Mina's eyes grow moist. There was hope burning in her large blue eyes. It made Megan happy that she would make a difference here.

"Good, because you can come over here to our home and eat your meals and share a cup of chai with me." Mina smiled fully. "I'm so glad you are here!" She reached out and gripped Megan's hand for a moment.

Megan gently squeezed Mina's hand and released it. "Let's go see my new clinic."

Rising, Mina nodded. "More than ready!"

Megan picked up her weapon and helmet and followed the joyous Mina.

The home next door was pockmarked with bullets and shrapnel on the outer walls. The windows were all broken. Some were patched with cardboard, while others had duct tape across the cracks. Megan noticed the cardboard had *U.S. Marines* written across them. The Afghan people wasted nothing and found uses for discarded American garbage.

Stepping inside the door, Megan spotted four women in black robes and black scarves over their heads. All were busy scrubbing a white tile floor until it sparkled. Mina closed the door and called the women over to meet Megan. The widows, some young, some middle-aged, dropped what they were doing and rushed over to the wife of the village leader. Megan saw hope burning in the women's faces.

"Now," Mina told her, "I want you to meet your helpers. I am employing them to help you, Megan, because it is a way to serve the village." She switched to Pashto and introduced the four excited women.

Megan performed the Muslim salutatory greeting with each of them. A look of surprise and then happiness filled their faces as they shyly returned the greeting. The eagerness in their eyes touched her deeply.

Mina showed her the two examination rooms and several cabinets to hold medical supplies. Megan was pleased with the small kitchen. It had an iron stove with which to heat water, a large concrete sink and a large wooden table. There was no running water. It had to be transported from five miles away in huge clay jugs carried by donkeys. The nearest stream was snowmelt from the mountains above.

Mentally, Megan ticked off items that had to be done or things she needed. Luke came to mind because he was the company scrounger. She'd have a list for him tonight.

"What do you think?" Mina asked. They halted in the waiting room, which had Persian rugs spread across the floor, along with chairs and pillows.

"You've done a great job, Mina," she said, gratitude in her voice. "I need to go back to the compound and get my medical supplies and start getting set up here."

The widows were already hard at work finishing the cleaning of the floor.

"And tomorrow morning, you can receive patients?"

"Yes."

"Good. What else do you need that is not here, Megan?"

Not wanting to insult Mina, Megan lied and said, "Everything I need is here."

A look of relief crossed the woman's face. She touched Megan's shoulder. "I know this is a developing country, but once I was informed you were coming, every family in our village donated something they could not spare in order to create this clinic. For you, a wooden chair may be commonplace. Out here, it is a luxury because there are no longer forests to cut down wood in order to make one. The rugs you see on the floor are a hundred years old and were given by families who know each one's long history. Every cup, plate and hand-embroidered tablecloth is meaningful to its owners."

Touched, Megan whispered in a choked tone, "I understand. And their gifts won't go in vain. We're going to improve lives here, Mina. You have my promise...."

Toward dusk, Luke found Megan busy at their house. He'd just come back with a group from the village after holding the weekly clinic for the men and boys. Dropping his large medical pack next to his cot, he saw her smile a hello in his direction. It touched his heart and he felt dizzy for a moment. Her lips were soft and the corners of her mouth curved. What would it be like to kiss that mouth of hers? The thought burned through him.

"How did your day go?" he asked.

"Great." Megan sat at the table, writing in her notebook. "I just made a pot of coffee." She gestured toward the corner.

"Good, I need some." Luke walked over and poured himself a mug. "When did you get back from the village?"

Megan closed the notebook and watched him approach the table. He had a boneless grace that spoke of just how athletic he really was. "Shorty has been driving me back and forth all day. Mina had the house next to her home set up as a clinic for me. I've gotten all the medical supplies hauled over to it so I can open it up tomorrow morning." She watched him sit down, feeling an invisible energy between them. When his large hands wrapped around the mug, a tiny shiver went up her spine. Megan was stymied by her instant attraction to him. She wasn't looking for a relationship, but she couldn't resist the merriment in his hazel eyes.

"You look exhausted."

"I just finished my fifth run a half hour ago. I'm whipped."

He sipped the coffee, grateful for this time alone. "What were you writing?"

She touched the notebook beneath her hand. "I'm creating a list of things I need for the clinic. Do you think you'd have time to look at them later?"

Luke glanced at his watch. "Sure. We'll be expected over at the chow hall in twenty minutes."

Megan nodded. He looked tired, too. "How did it go today for you?"

"Busy. But it always is. I hold a clinic twice a week. Today, there seemed to be twice the number of patients than usual."

"Mina told me when I open up the clinic at 0800 to expect half the women of the village to be standing in line waiting for help."

"You're going to be slammed," Luke agreed. "I wish I could help you. You're going to need a second pair of hands."

Megan smiled. "I'm used to the rush. In Iraq, it was the same."

"Is anyone able to assist you?"

"Mina has four widows who will be helping me out. I'll teach them as I go." She told Luke about Mina's impressive background.

"They're lucky to have Mina," he said. "I'm sure she's a joy to work with."

"She is," Megan agreed, tearing a piece of paper out of her notebook and handing it to Luke. "My wish list," she said, her grin growing even wider.

As Luke reached out for the paper, their fingers briefly touched. He felt like a sneaky coyote stealing a touch from her. While they worked together, Megan could never know he was drawn to her. Focusing, he studied the list. "This is a helluva list, Megan."

"I know it is. I'm asking for the moon."

Grinning, Luke looked up and held her softened gaze. "Sort of…"

"They need so much out here, Luke…."

"I'll see what I can do. I know a sergeant in medical at Bagram Air Base. She's really good at getting things that women need. I think she can fill some of this for you."

"Wonderful!" In that moment, Megan wanted to walk around the table and throw her arms around his broad shoulders. The need was visceral, especially with the air so charged between them. She saw his eyes narrow slightly, as if he were reading her mind. Her heart pounded for a second and warmth swept up from her neck into her face. Oh, God, she was blushing! Megan looked away and fumbled with the notebook. She scrambled to break the sudden sexual tension between them.

"Sorry," she muttered, "I get all giddy when I'm excited."

Luke managed a weak smile. She made him feel desired and powerful. The attraction took him by surprise. "It's okay. I like it."

Megan could see the warmth dancing in his eyes and the way his mouth curved wickedly. "I'm going to call my cousin Emma Cantrell-Shaheen. She was an Apache pilot in the Army before she got injured and couldn't fly anymore. Now she's a civilian working out of Camp Bravo with her husband, Captain Khalid Shaheen. He's very rich and they run a foundation to help people just like Mina and her village. Emma knows I was assigned out here, and she told me their foundation would foot the bills to get the things this village needed if the military couldn't."

Raising his brows, Luke murmured, "Hey, that's good news. They're an NGO?"

"Yes. Khalid and his sister set up the foundation a couple of years ago to bring books, desks and teachers to the border villages. It's working really well and they've enlarged their scope to include medical supplies, as well."

"That'll be good news for Lar Sholtan." Luke watched her as she released her red hair and it curved sensually about her shoulders, a perfect frame for her soft face. She was gentle. The toughness of being in the military had not eroded her unique personality in the least. His heart and body responded simultaneously as the low light gleamed in the strands of her hair. Megan was off-limits. She *had* to be.

He was going to spend a year here with her, and fraternization would not be tolerated. Even though they were both enlisted personnel and the same rating, a relationship would never fly. Every man in this company had loved ones back in the States. An attraction would be the worst kind of distraction and could put them in danger. No, he had to keep his distance.

Luke had a faraway look in his eyes, and Megan wondered what he was thinking. "I know this list is extensive," she offered with apology.

"No, no, it's okay. I'll look at it after chow tonight." Luke glanced at his watch. "Let's go eat. Charlie, the Navy cook, hates it when we show up late."

"Sounds good." She walked over to retrieve her desert camouflage utility cap and settle it on her head. "Do I take my rifle?"

"No, leave it here. Always wear your pistol, though. The last company here said they were shelled at least once a month. One time, al-Qaeda tried to take over the compound. Always keep a weapon on you, whether you're inside or outside the fort." Even in her bulky desert utilities, he could see her shapely body.

"Roger, read you loud and clear." She placed her cap on her head after pulling her hair into a ponytail once more.

Luke felt sad as she gathered up her thick red hair and tamed it behind her back. She was incredibly beautiful with that crimson frame showing off her oval face. Those huge blue eyes were compassionate and alert. "Okay, let's saddle up." He pulled his keg away from the table and stood up.

Megan prepared herself for the stares when they walked into the cramped, busy chow hall. The largest adobe building served as a central place to feed the company. There were many wooden picnic tables squeezed in close together filled with hungry Marines. The noise level was high, and the constant chatter and laughter liftied her spirits. She spotted Captain Hall eating with Lieutenant Speed near the rear of the large room. The odors of spicy chicken, mashed potatoes and gravy made her mouth water. Real food was a luxury not to be wasted.

She and Luke were invited over to the Motor Pool group of Marines. Shorty, their driver, grinned a welcome as Megan sat opposite him. Luke sat at her elbow. Proudly, Shorty introduced her to the other four Marines. None of them seemed to consider her an outsider. Instead, the meal conversation surrounded the new women's clinic.

"Hey," Shorty said, "you know we got ten other picnic tables that are broke? I can get some of the grunts to scrounge up enough wood to repair them. That way, you'd have some tables where the women could sit down and wait instead of standing in line in the hot sun."

Megan was touched by the Marine's sensitivity. "That's a wonderful idea, Shorty. I'll take you up on it."

Shorty gave Luke an evil grin as he spooned the potatoes and gravy into his mouth. "Maybe, if we do a little nation building with these folks, there will be fewer IEDs for us to find every morning along the road."

Megan chuckled. "When you treat people well, Shorty, they usually aren't out gunning for you."

The Marine grinned widely. "Amen to that, sister."

Heartened by the camaraderie, Megan felt a part of the group. She'd worried about her arrival in an all-male combat company. So far, so good. Still, she was glad Luke was sitting next to her, their elbows brushing each other's occasionally.

Luke had a lot of depth, she decided. He always seemed in a good mood, easygoing, cracking a joke or making the Marines feel better, but she saw more in his eyes. Megan swore she could tell what he was really feeling and thinking. This man didn't miss much. She ached to have more time just to talk with him, to explore him as a man, not just as a field medic. Would that ever happen? Megan doubted it, feeling sad about the loss without ever having experienced it.

As they walked in the dusk away from the chow hall, Megan looked around. She slowed and so did Luke. At four positions around the compound were twenty-foot towers manned by Marines with .50-caliber machine guns. They wore night goggles so they could spot anyone trying to sneak close to the outpost. The wind was cold and she was glad for her warm thick jacket over her Kevlar vest. Luke seemed pensive as they slowly made their way toward their house.

"You're well liked," he said.

"That's nice to hear. I was hoping I would fit in— and not out."

"I've never met a field medic who wasn't instantly embraced by the Marines."

"Comes with the job, maybe?"

Luke glanced over at Megan's profile. She was a few inches shorter than he was. A silent joy expanded his heart as he hungrily took in her darkened features. Her lips were full just above a stubborn chin. He pushed down his desire. "I'll bet you're like most of the grunts here. You have someone at home waiting for you?"

"Ugh, that's a sore topic," Megan muttered. She gave Luke an apologetic look. His face was unreadable except for the glint in his eyes. "My life is complicated."

Luke halted at the house and opened the door for her. "Whose isn't?" he teased.

They were alone, although Megan knew the other four Marines would be wandering in sooner or later. She wished much later. She pulled off her jacket and heavy Kevlar vest. "Just between us," she said in a low tone, "I stupidly fell in love with an officer over in Iraq a number of years ago. It just happened." She hung up her jacket and vest on two hooks on the mud wall. "Please don't tell anyone. I'm still embarrassed by it. An enlisted person like me is not allowed to fraternize with an officer. Period."

Luke sat down on his cot. "How old were you?"

"I was twenty-three and knew better," she said wryly. Sitting on her cot, she realized Luke's head would be near her own when they slept. Somehow, the idea of him being so close made her feel safer. "He was a doctor. A wonderful surgeon. He knew I was a registered nurse and had four years of college under my belt."

"In his eyes, you were an officer even though you chose the enlisted route?" Luke guessed.

"Yes." Unwrapping her hair, she ran her fingers through it until it settled like a cape around her shoulders. "He was a lot like you, Luke. Warm, funny and compassionate. About two months into our relationship, we tried to hide it from everyone. I got called on the carpet by the X.O. of the facility. He told me to break it off or face court-martial."

"Ouch."

"Yes." Megan winced. "I ended it. And it broke my heart and his. I have such high standards for a man in my life. My sisters always tease me that I'm too picky. But I know I'm right."

"I'm sorry it didn't work out. He sounds like a fine person." Luke had to stop himself from standing and going over to sit next to Megan. He saw suffering in her eyes, the way her mouth was pursed as if to stop feeling the grief she still carried.

"Norm died a week later," she whispered. "A sniper's bullet. He died instantly. I heard about it on the radio at the facility as the medevac was flying him in. It was such a shock...."

"That's tough to take," Luke agreed quietly, wanting to lighten her sadness. "Hey, at least we have one thing in common."

Lifting her head, Megan stared over at him. "What's that?"

"I had a high school sweetheart. Hope. We waited until we graduated before we got married. I had already joined the Navy and was leaving for boot camp right after our honeymoon. My dad is a cardiac surgeon and my mother is a registered nurse. They tried to talk me out of marrying Hope. My father, who had been a

U.S. Navy doctor, warned me the separation would be too hard on her." Luke gave her a wry look. "I should have listened. With boot camp, then medical schooling, I've been overseas for the last six years. I'd go home on leave for two or three months and turn around and come back to Iraq or Afghanistan. Hope divorced me because it just wasn't going to work out. I was gone for too long a time."

"A lot of marriages have broken up because of the constant duty rotation. I'm so sorry, Luke. She must have been a terrific person for you to fall in love with her," Megan said.

"She was, but two wars got in the way."

"Any children?"

He snorted. "I wasn't home long enough to get her pregnant."

"And now?"

"Single. You?"

"Oh," she said as she sighed, "single. I'm still not over Norm's death. Some days I think I'm ready for another relationship, and then I change my mind the next day."

"Grief has its way with us," Luke said gently. He smiled warmly at her and saw Megan respond. Her lips parted slightly. It was enough to make his heart speed up. If only… *Wrong place, wrong time,* he warned himself.

"I've decided to put relationships on hold until after I've finished my six-year enlistment. I can't handle another heartbreak. When I leave the Navy, I'll allow myself the luxury of trying to find the right man."

"Not a lifer?"

"No." Megan smiled a little. "I'm an R.N., and a good one. I want to go back into civilian life and pursue what

I love so much. I'm doing six years in the military because of the Trayhern family tradition."

"And what an incredible tradition," Luke said, secretly elated Megan was single. That powerful connection with her was growing. Above all, he'd have to be her friend. Not her lover. Somehow, he had to control himself....

Chapter 4

Megan was torn out of her sleep by a bomb blast. Disoriented, she automatically rolled off the cot and onto the floor of the darkened house. Outside the window, red and yellow colors flared into the night.

"Attack!" Sergeant Payne yelled. "Everyone to their stations!"

More grenades were lobbed into the compound.

Megan scrambled to her feet, bumping into two other Marines who had been sleeping. The door jerked open, and the sergeant hightailed it out into the night.

Another explosion detonated. The house shook, knocking her off her feet. Completely disoriented, Megan felt fear overriding her ability to think.

"Down," Luke yelled, grabbing her by the shoulder and pushing her to the floor. "Get your gear on!"

Breathless, fear racing through her, Megan heard yells and orders overriding the attack. This wasn't what she had expected. Fumbling in the dark, she found her helmet. Where was her Kevlar vest? Already, the house was empty, the Marines in full gear, running to their assigned positions. Megan hadn't been told where to go.

She had no idea what time it was, and the darkness only amped up her anxiety. Megan finally found her vest. She sat up and, with shaking hands, pulled it over her utilities. Gulping, she crawled to the corner where her weapon was propped up against the mud wall. While she grabbed it, Megan tried to think. She winced as return fire and the heavy boom of artillery began from within the compound. Glancing out the door, Megan saw muzzle fire flashes on the dark mountain. She shoved on her boots and rose unsteadily. Somehow, she made it to the door.

A snapping sound passed close to her right ear.

Gasping, she realized the enemy up on the slopes was firing down at them. She leaped outside the house and hit the deck, spread-eagled, bringing the rifle up to a firing position. Winking yellow spots could be seen up on the mountain slope. A terrible sense of vulnerability rushed through her. They were like fish in a barrel.

Men bellowed orders and she could hear the roar of a howitzer spitting out shell after shell toward their attackers. Her ears hurt from the artillery. In seconds, the shells hit, the sides of the mountain lighting up with red, yellow and orange arms of fire exploding into the night sky.

Within minutes, the attack was over. Megan slowly got to her feet and stood outside the door. The darkness was complete. How did the men see in this gloom? Night goggles would solve the problem, but none had been issued to her. Marines muttered and cursed around her. She wondered if any of the men had been wounded,

Megan scrambled to her feet, took her rifle inside, grabbed her medical bag and ran toward Headquarters.

She bumped into another Marine near the doorway. There was a small light to drive away the gloom. Captain Hall's face was grim, eyes angry.

"Sir, is anyone wounded?" she called.

"Not this time. Go back to your assigned house."

Nodding, Megan moved out of the way as Sergeant Payne strode into the small house. Heart thundering in her chest, Megan left the noise of the radios and the chatter behind. What time was it? She lifted her watch, the radium dials showing 3:00 a.m. Groaning, Megan stepped carefully, her eyes unable to adjust to the darkness. Without a moon to guide her, she felt her way forward with her boots. In one area, she suddenly pitched forward. Landing with a thud, Megan realized she'd fallen into a crater created by an enemy grenade. She got to her knees and searched blindly for her medical pack. After grabbing it, she climbed out of the crater. Oh, for a flashlight! Megan knew that would be impossible. A light would simply draw the fire and attention of their enemy. Moving slowly and deliberately, Megan finally got to her assigned house.

Inside, she found Luke and another soldier, Lance Davis.

"You guys all right?" she called to them.

"Fine," Lance answered. "Pissed off the bastards woke us up in the middle of the night, but that's what they do best."

Luke was relieved to hear Megan's voice. He moved toward the door where she stood. "You were supposed to stay here. What happened?"

She could barely see the outline of his face and helmet even though he was a few feet away. "I couldn't hide, Luke. It's my job to see if anyone is wounded."

"You haven't been given egress training or an assigned position if we're attacked," he told her in a censuring tone. "You should have stayed here."

"I don't have time when the enemy is going to lob grenades into our compound," she said in a cool tone. Shouldering by him, she found her cot. She sat down and placed her weapon in the corner. She heard Payne's soft Kentucky voice even though she didn't see him enter the house.

"Ya'll okay?"

"Everyone's fine, Buck," Luke said.

Buck grunted. "We're puttin' out extra guards. Davis, get your rifle and get over to the south tower. Keep Johnson company. You'll be relieved in three hours."

Lance cursed softly. "Just when I thought I was going to get a decent night's sleep."

Buck chuckled. "Now, you know they ain't gonna let that happen. Get going."

"Yes, Sergeant."

"Is there anything I can do to help, Sergeant Payne?" Megan called out in the darkness after Lance left.

"No, Sweet Pea, you just lie down and get as much beauty sleep as you can before we get reveille at 0600."

Under ordinary circumstances, Megan would have called the sergeant on the way he'd responded to her. It wasn't military; it was personal. Her heart was still beating with fear and she felt shaky. Luke was pissed off at her for leaving the house. What did he expect? Lying down, hands behind her head, she closed her eyes. "Sergeant, I want that egress training as soon as possible," she called out. "And a pair of night goggles."

"Yep, I hear you. After chow tomorrow morning, I'll get you squared away."

"Good," Megan muttered. She sounded like a petulant child, but that's how she felt. "Do these attacks happen often?" she asked no one in particular.

"The last company said al-Qaeda was very active during the dark of the moon," Buck Payne drawled. "And this is the first night of the new moon, so I 'spect we can get more attacks in the next six days. Just means we sleep in our Kevlar vests."

Groaning, Megan laid her arm across her eyes. "Great."

"Welcome to our world," Payne said.

"Really," Megan muttered.

"Combat isn't pretty. We're sittin' ducks out here with mountains surrounding the compound. The enemy can use us as moving targets any time they want. Cap'n Hall is madder than a wet hen and he's already ordering up huntin' parties tomorrow morning."

"Hunting parties?" Megan asked. "What's that?"

"It means me and the other sergeants will be taking out squads of Marines to go up into the slopes of that mountain where the fire came from, find the bastards and put out their lights."

Megan said nothing. "Luke? Will you be going with them?"

"I'm sure I will."

"You'll be in my squad," Buck told him.

"Can I go?"

"Sorry, Sweet Pea, but you're confined to the village only."

"But," she protested, "I'm a medic! I was stationed at a forward medical facility in Iraq and we got shelled at and shot at all the time."

"Megan, give it up," Luke pleaded. "Hall's not going to change his mind and let you go out with a patrol. Let's try and get some sleep."

Megan was starved when she woke up two hours later. The Marines around her were stirring, too. Dull light shone through the only window in the house. It gave her enough light to find her boots. Sitting up, she noticed Luke was gone, along with Sergeant Payne. Despite the adrenaline rush and fear of the attack, Megan was surprised she'd dropped off to sleep so quickly. She felt wide awake.

"Good morning," she called to Lance Davis, who entered.

"It will be when I can get over to the chow hall and get a cup of coffee," he said.

Smiling a little, she asked, "How did it go out there last night?"

"Boring as usual. It was quiet. Sergeant Payne was telling us that the last company here had the Taliban try to sneak in and they slit the throat of one of the Marines on guard."

"That's terrible," Megan said, chilled.

Lance nodded. "Yeah, the dude lived. That's the good news. Let's go eat," he said.

Though she'd lost some of her appetite, she walked with the lanky Marine across the chewed-up compound. In the dawn light she spotted the crater she'd fallen into last night, along with several others. A bulldozer was already pushing dirt to fill them in. Shivering in the cold, she kept up with Davis.

Luke was just leaving the chow line to find a place to eat when he spotted Megan with Davis. He waved to them and found a table with two other empty seats. His heart swelled with joy as he saw Megan. At the same time, Luke felt dread for her. She'd seen some combat in Iraq. Did she realize that one of those grenade launchers could have flattened one of the mud houses within the compound? Every time the enemy attacked, the possibility of people dying was very real. He couldn't protect her completely, as much as he wanted to.

He could see the tension on her face.

Within a few minutes, Davis and Megan arrived at the table. They sat down opposite him. Luke tried to ignore Megan's soft red hair framing her face. She was like a bright flower among the sea of camouflage desert colors. Her tray had little food in comparison to theirs.

"First combat?" Luke asked her.

"No. We were shelled in Iraq about once a week." She shrugged. "It was scary as hell last night. I couldn't see a thing."

Davis laughed. "That's why bunkers beneath the ground are great. Harder to target us and we have light."

"Yeah," Luke said with distaste, pushing the scrambled eggs onto his fork, "you forgot to mention how dank and airless those pits are. You can't sleep."

Megan slathered jelly on her toast. Her stomach was tied in a hard knot. She still felt shaky but wasn't going to admit it. She forced herself to eat. Food was fuel. And today, she was going to open the women's clinic in the village at 0800.

"How are you doing?" Luke asked, meeting and holding her gaze. Her face was ashen. Yesterday, Megan's cheeks had been rosy. Now there was darkness banked in her blue eyes. Luke caught a slight tremble in her fingers as she scooped up some eggs.

"I'm okay," Megan lied. "A little tired."

"You look pretty pale," Luke said in a quiet tone.

Megan shrugged. "Lack of sleep." She glanced over at Davis, who was chowing down as if there were no tomorrow. "You guys don't exactly look like *GQ* candidates, either." She managed a sour grin.

"Maybe it's your Trayhern military genes kicking in to help you deal with combat?" Luke wondered.

Megan forced the food down, trying not to be swayed by the burning look in Luke's hazel gaze. He cared for her, she could tell. Did anyone else see it? "I hope so."

"At Camp Pendleton," Davis said, "did they put you gals in live-fire situations?"

"No."

"Pity," Davis said. "They did us. We had to crawl under barbed wire with real bullets flying above our heads and blasts going off on the sides of us. Sure got you acclimated to what you were going to see out in the field."

"Sounds like fun," Megan griped. She picked up a third piece of toast and finished off the grape jelly across it.

"No live fire?" Luke said, shaking his head.

"No."

"Last night had to shake you up, then."

"No more than you guys." Megan wasn't about to implicate herself.

"Hmm."

"How can you see in the dark?" she demanded of Luke. "I felt blind as a bat."

"You get so you place your stuff where you can reach it in case of an attack," he told her, wiping his plate clean. "Tonight you'll put your boots near the head of your cot with the Kevlar hung across them and the helmet on top. That way, when we get bombed again, all you have to do is roll to your left, grab and go."

It made good sense. "I've got a lot to learn."

"Don't worry," Luke reassured her, "you did fine last night."

"I didn't panic."

"No, you didn't. But when we're under attack, I have to take my position at the clinic next to HQ. I didn't want to leave you there alone, but nothing else could be done."

Megan drowned in his worried gaze. "That's okay. I understand. I'm sure the sergeant will show me the ropes this morning so I know where to go next time we get attacked."

"He will," Davis answered. "There's only one place for medics, and that's at our clinic. You'll be there with Luke."

Megan felt good about that. She said nothing, however. "Where will you be today?" she asked Luke.

"Out with the patrol," he said.

"I'll be at the village, safe and sound." There was irony in her tone. She worried for Luke and the rest of the Marines who would be out as a hunter team trying to find the elusive enemy on the mountain slopes.

"It's not a secure village," Luke warned her. "Just because Mina is helping you doesn't guarantee that a Taliban or al-Qaeda soldier won't walk into that village, hunt you down and put a gun to your head, Megan. You *have* to remain on guard at all times. Do you understand?"

A chill of fear went through her. "Yes, I'll stay on guard."

Megan couldn't believe her eyes as Shorty drove the Humvee up to the women's clinic. At least fifty women and children were standing patiently in line waiting for the door to open. Mina came down the steps, smiling a welcome. After thanking Shorty, Megan climbed out and retrieved her rifle and medical pack. He got out and opened a side door where boxes of supplies had to be carried into the clinic. Since he was a man, he couldn't do it.

"Mina, can the widows come over here and take the supplies into the clinic?"

"Of course." Mina signaled to the four women in black burkas to help.

Megan had no time to think about last night's attack. She had set up two examination rooms. Twenty women and children crowded into the waiting room. The others waited outside in the chill of the morning. Mina was astute and got the four widows to become her helpers. Once the supplies were in the building, Megan had one widow, Aryana, put the dressings, bandages and other medical supplies in one room. In another, Mina had brought over a large wooden cabinet where all the drugs and antibiotics would be kept under lock and key. Megan assigned Rabia, a thirty-five-year-old widow, the responsibility for the cabinet.

The house had no central heat. Later, Megan discovered a small stove in the kitchen, but that heat didn't transfer to the rest of the building. With cold fingers, she put a stethoscope across her neck. She shed the Kevlar vest and put it with her helmet and rifle in the kitchen. Megan worked with Lona, the third widow, who would perform the secretarial duties. Lona sat at a dilapidated-looking front desk near the door. She would write down the name of each patient and her complaints, then give the patient a number. When the number was called, the patient would go to one of the exam rooms.

Mina's managerial abilities made the coordination

easy for Megan. Within thirty minutes, she was ready to see her first patient. A young mother of twenty brought in a two-month-old baby girl in her arms. Megan took the baby and gently laid her on the gurney covered with a thick, warm blanket. She talked to the mother while listening to the baby's heart and lungs, and it was clear the child had pneumonia. Megan wrote a prescription, telling the mother to keep her baby warm and out of cold drafts. The mother's green eyes teared up. This was her first child and she was so afraid of losing her. Megan patted the woman on the shoulder and asked her to return with the baby in three days.

Megan was surprised when the woman threw her arms around her, squeezed her and tearfully whispered a thank-you. Inwardly, Megan lived for these moments. She returned the young woman's embrace and picked up her baby and handed her to the mother.

Mina came into the second examination room. "It's time to eat," she called to Megan. "When you're done, let's go to my home."

"Right." Megan looked up. Where had time gone? To her surprise, she'd become so immersed in her duties that she'd completely forgotten her lack of sleep or the attack. She heard Lona announcing to those waiting that Megan must eat before helping the rest of them this afternoon.

"So, how is it going?" Mina asked her a few moments later in the warm kitchen of her home. She served Megan a plate filled with spicy lamb, couscous and some goat yogurt.

Megan sat at the kitchen table. "Good. Really better than I thought it would. Those four widows are a force to behold. Your ability to manage really makes the difference, Mina." Megan took the mouthwatering plate.

Laughing lightly, Mina filled her own plate and came to sit down opposite her. "Since I am the leader's wife, management comes easily to me."

"You're very good at it," Megan said between bites. The flavor of spices mixed with curry made the lamb delicious. The kitchen swam in the fragrance of many spices, and Megan inhaled the wonderful odors.

"You're very fast and very good with my people," Mina said. "I'm hearing from those who saw you that you are very gentle and kind with them. Thank you."

Meeting the woman's gaze, Megan nodded. "I think I've lived for this moment all my life, Mina. All I've ever wanted to do was help those in need."

"You are a healer, not a warrior."

Megan smiled and nodded. "I wish we could find a better way to settle our differences than with war. Three children I saw this morning all had a leg blown off by an IED. There's *got* to be a better way."

"Indeed."

Frustrated, Megan added, "I'm going to talk to Luke tonight. He's got connections. I want to try and get prostheses for these three little girls. They shouldn't be going around on a pair of crutches."

"That would be wonderful if you could help," Mina said, suddenly tearing up. She reached out and gripped Megan's hand. "The other Marine company wouldn't do anything like what you're suggesting."

"That's why the idea of embedding a woman into an all-male company is a good idea."

"It truly is," Mina said. "It's a blessing and a prayer coming true. You have no idea how many nights I've lain awake crying for these children, crying for those who have so little. I am just devastated by the constant suffering of these people."

"I'm beginning to understand," Megan said in a quiet voice. She picked up a cup of hot tea and sipped from it. "I'm in shock myself. I didn't understand how little they have." Her voice became firm. "I promise you, Mina, while I'm here, I'll do everything I can to help them."

"And yet they have the heart of a snow leopard. They subsist, they struggle, they battle the cold and the snow. And somehow, they survive things I never would. I have nothing but admiration for them."

"So do I." Megan looked around the small but warm kitchen. "I'm glad it's quiet here at the village. We got attacked last night."

"I'm so sorry," Mina whispered. "We heard the blasts and gunfire." Looking out the small window toward the mountains, she added, "I hope no one was hurt."

"No, just shaken up."

"This is a dangerous area," Mina whispered. Pressing her fingertips to her wrinkled brow, she released a sigh. "You must be careful, Megan."

"As careful as I can. We're in combat, Mina. We're trying to help all Afghans by stopping the al-Qaeda soldiers from coming into your country. We *want* you to be safe, happy and live a life in peace." She saw the woman's eyes cloud with worry. Did Mina know something she wasn't divulging to her?

"For the first time since I've been here, our women and children are finally getting medical help. I've tried to persuade a doctor to come out to our village, but we're so remote. The only roads are horse, donkey or goat paths in and out of this area. I wish…I wish things were different…."

Hearing the pain and wistfulness in Mina's voice, Megan reached over and touched her hand. "You're doing the best you can. And I can see the people love you. They truly love and respect you."

Mina lifted her head and choked back tears. "It's not enough. We're so poor we can't even afford a teacher for our children. The Taliban won't allow our girls to be educated."

Seeing Mina's frustration, Megan decided to broach another topic with her. "My cousin Emma is married to Captain Khalid Shaheen. He's the only Afghan Apache pilot in the U.S. Army. His family comes from Kabul. Perhaps you've heard of them?"

"Why, yes. Yes, I have. That's amazing."

Nodding, Megan said, "Yes, and not only that, but Khalid has an NGO, a charity he and his sister created. They fly in desks, books and a teacher to villages like your own. I'd like to call them on the radio and ask them to get in touch with you and Timor. They bring all classroom supplies and hire a teacher who will be here six months of the year to teach boys and girls. Do you think your husband would want a project like this?" Megan saw Mina's eyes widen with hope.

"I'm sure he would! Could you truly do this? Would Captain Shaheen consider us?"

"I see no reason why he wouldn't," Megan said, finishing off the lamb. She picked up the cup of cooling tea. "I can ask Khalid and Emma to fly in to talk with your husband about the program?"

"Yes, yes, I will tell him about this tonight."

"I thought the Taliban in this area don't want girls to be educated."

Grimacing, Mina said, "That is true, but I don't accept their dictates. They are from another tribe. They have no business trying to make our tribe believe or live as they do."

placed them in a small sink. "Are you ready to begin your afternoon clinic?"

"I am," Megan said, swallowing the last of the delicious tea. Elated, she could hardly wait to return to the compound and tell Captain Hall what she'd just found out. Even though Hall didn't think much of the program, she was going to prove him wrong.

Chapter 5

Captain Doug Hall sat at his planning table in the dusk light listening to Megan's information. Lieutenant Speed and sergeants were present, and he'd asked Doc Collier to be there, as well. He wrote some notes in a small notebook as she spoke.

Megan stood at ease at the end of the table where all the Marines sat. "And that's all I have for you, sir."

Raising his blond brows, Hall said, "You've given us a treasure trove, Doc."

"Really, sir?" Megan asked, flushed with his unexpected praise.

Hall held up his spare hand. "First, you've given us the name of the local Taliban leader, Jabbar Gholam. You've also found where he's living. And the name of his wife. Now I can feed the intel into our system. We may get a hit on him and we may not. What matters is identifying them because they're the ones the U.S. has to monitor. And if Gholam is one of the bomb makers, he goes on our hit list. We want the bomb makers dead."

A cold chill worked its way up Megan's spine. Killing was abhorrent to her. She wondered for the thousandth time why she had allowed Trayhern family tradition to push her into this life. In all fairness, Megan understood it was her choice, but other factors had shamed her into it. When would she learn to stand up for herself?

Megan's glance moved to Luke, who stood behind Buck. The dusk light shadowed everyone. At night, no lights were allowed because the Taliban could spot them.

"But, sir," she spoke up, her soft voice carrying across the cramped room, "you can't bomb Gholam."

"Why not?"

"Because Mina, the wife of the elder here at the village, is going to visit Tahira."

"Do you have *more* intel?" Hall asked.

Megan shrugged. "I don't know, sir."

"Give me *everything* you got today, Doc."

Seeing the censure in Hall's eyes, Megan said, "I thought, sir, you wouldn't want talk between two women. Tahira's eight months pregnant."

"Don't you decide what is or isn't important," the officer said. "Give me everything. I'll sort it out."

For the next ten minutes, Megan gave them information she felt they wouldn't want. Hall's eyes flared with surprise and then he hid his response. Finished, she waited for the C.O. to speak.

Hall looked over at his X.O., Speed. "What do you think?"

The lieutenant shrugged. "We have to think about the strategic value of the elder's wife having a connection with this Taliban leader. If she's going over the mountain to visit the pregnant wife to try and persuade her to let this village have school supplies, we might have a chance to turn Gholam from enemy into friend."

Hall nodded and flashed a look over at his sergeants. "Buck, any thoughts?"

"Sir, this is excellent intel. We're supposed to be over here the winning hearts and minds of the Afghan people, not bombing them back into the stone age if we don't have to. I'd say trying to turn an enemy into a friend is a better way to go here. Besides, Timor Khan is well respected in this province. I don't think it would look good if his wife was killed over there if the order's given to blow that village off the slope of the mountain, do you?"

Hall rubbed his jaw. "No. Our job is to protect these villages, make life better for the people living in them."

Buck gave Megan a nod. "You've gotten us more intel than anyone has since the Marines have been putting a company in this area, Doc. Great work!"

"Captain Hall, you aren't going to bomb that other village?" Megan's heart beat hard in her chest. She couldn't live knowing she'd caused the deaths of others.

"Not yet…"

"Sir, I am not here to be the cause of innocent people being killed!" Megan said hurriedly.

Hall nodded. "Stand down, Doc. We don't want to kill anyone, either. Relax." He smiled a little. "I do want you to continue to be Mina's friend and keep your eyes and ears open. I'm all for some friendly movement between these two different tribal villages." He chuckled and looked around the room at his men. "We all know that the wife rules the roost. Right, gentlemen? Gholam thinks he's in charge, but in reality, the woman runs the show."

Laughter erupted around Megan. She saw the men, many of them likely married, sagely nod in agreement. Hall's face relaxed with an easy grin. Luke gave her a wink. Managing a slight smile, Megan said, "Well, sir, I wouldn't know about that. I'm single."

Hall rose to his full six feet. "I believe it's genetic in all women to run the world. Men are just fooled into believing they do. Everyone's dismissed."

More chuckles followed as the meeting broke up.

"Doc, you did good work," Hall praised, looking at his watch. "It's chow time."

Megan left with Luke. The dusk was deepening but not so much she couldn't see where she was walking. The air chilled. The day was blisteringly hot, but as soon as the sun dropped behind the western mountains, the temperature fell hard and fast. As they walked, their hands accidentally brushed. Megan found the contact comforting.

"You did great," Luke said, opening the door to the chow hall. "The captain is really pleased."

Megan picked up two aluminum trays and handed one to Luke. "Thanks." She looked around. Half the tables were filled with Marines. The air was pungent with curry and the delicious smell of lamb. There were five men in line ahead of them.

"How did your day go? I haven't seen you since this morning," she said.

"Okay. Captain Hall said a couple of SEAL teams are operating up in the Hindu Kush Mountains to the north of us. He got orders from Islamabad HQ to work the slopes east of our compound."

"Navy SEAL teams?"

"Yeah, four-, six- or ten-man teams are dropped in by helo near major routes between Pakistan and here."

Luke shrugged. "Damned dangerous work. The Taliban and al-Qaeda bomb makers haul their materials over on camels. When a predator drone or satellite finds them, Apaches or jets are called in to destroy them. Major Taliban warlords are in cahoots with these bomb makers from Pakistan. And the SEALS are dropped to eliminate them."

Shivering, Megan saw she was next to get some of the delicious-smelling food made by the cooks behind the counter. "That's dangerous work."

"The most dangerous."

"Do you think Captain Hall will send the SEALS after Jabbar Gholam?"

"Only if it's proven he works with al-Qaeda. If he doesn't, then it's a question of if he's a Taliban-minded leader or not." Luke picked up his utensils. "We may find out more about Gholam in the coming days. If he's an ally to Timor Khan's tribe, then the Marines aren't going to bother him."

"I just don't want his village bombed, Luke. His wife has two kids and she's pregnant with a third one." The Navy chef put a huge leg of lamb on her tray along with scoops of white rice, carrots and a slice of white cake with pink frosting. It was enough for two men, but out here, Megan was discovering she would eat it all.

"I don't think that will happen," Luke said. At the table, they sat alone and opposite each other. The din of men chatting, some laughter and the clink of utensils provided background music of a sort. Megan dug into the curried lamb. She noticed Luke was quieter than usual. He'd been out on patrol for nearly twelve hours. In a way, Megan was glad she wasn't expected to go out on these dangerous missions. Luke looked tired. His cheeks were more hollow because his beard had grown back. She found herself wanting to lift her fingers and push several strands of dark brown hair off his brow. Stopping herself, she realized how powerfully drawn she was to the medic.

While she drank her coffee and enjoyed every bit of the sweet cake, she asked Luke, "What do you do tomorrow?"

"I'll be in the village holding a clinic again. I'm trying to be there two or three days a week."

"I'm going to call my cousin Emma after we eat. Captain Hall gave me permission to use the satellite phone. He's all for Emma and Khalid flying in books, desks and a teacher for Lar Sholtan. Does the C.O. think it will help stabilize the Marines' position with Timor Khan?"

Shrugging, Luke finished off his cake and pushed the tray aside. "Hard to say, really. You have to understand that all these villages are important to the Taliban and al-Qaeda. It's an uneasy alliance, at best. They can't operate within Afghanistan without village support. It's a double-edged sword the village elders have to walk with both parties. On one hand, if they appear to be pro-American, both will retaliate against the village. If they start killing off Pashtuns in a village, this can set the elders against them. And if that happens, they'll have gone too far and have lost that village's support."

"How do they entice these village elders, then?" Megan asked.

"Through food, clothing and medicine."

"But that's what we're doing."

"Precisely." Luke sipped his coffee. He saw the confusion in Megan's blue eyes. Several strands of her red hair peeked out from behind her delicate ear. Without a helmet on, she was attractive, and he found himself appreciating her as a woman. "Are you aware of *Lokhay Warkawal?*"

Nodding, Megan said, "Yes, I was introduced to the Pashtun code of life when I took the one-year immersion course in Pashto. The Pashtun are not ruled by any government. Their code, which has been in place for thousands of years, helps them live peacefully with one another. It's also called the *Pashtunwali.*"

"Right," Luke said. "I saw it in action once before. The Taliban were leaning on a village of Pashtuns who happen to live in Helmand Province. Most Pashtuns live in the mountain area along the border, but this group had migrated to the desert. Anyway, long story short, a local tribal Taliban leader was going to come into their village to capture a wounded British soldier who had asked for asylum among them. The elders met with the Taliban leader and told them that they had given the wounded soldier *Nanawatai* or asylum."

"Really?" Megan's brows shot up with surprise. "The elders protected a British soldier?"

"Yep, they did. If the Taliban had tried to come in and snatch the Brit, the whole village would have sworn vengeance and death on the offending tribe. The same goes for al-Qaeda soldiers. These different political factions *need* these villagers. It's where they hide when the Americans and Brits are seeking them out and killing them."

"Wow," Megan said, impressed. "I've never heard of *Lokhay* being invoked to save a life of a British soldier. That's taking a heck of a chance."

"Well," Luke counseled, "you need to understand this code because you're in the line of fire even in that village. I know Mina likes you and you're creating a bond of trust with her. The other part of this code is

Namus, which means the Pashtun must defend the honor of all Pashtun women. No one can come in and vocally curse at them or physically harm them in any way." His voice grew deep with warning. "You need to ask Mina to get Timor to bestow *Lokhay* upon you, Megan. If not, you are an outsider and if a Taliban or al-Qaeda soldier comes into their village, he can kill you. No one in the village will protect you. The Marines aren't in that village all the time. We're out on patrols hunting down the enemy in the mountains surrounding this valley."

"I—I never thought about this aspect of it." She saw how gravely concerned Luke had become. His hands were wrapped around the white ceramic coffee mug. His mouth thinned.

"Timor Khan may do it. You need to ask. You're a woman, not a man."

"Has he given *Lokhay* to the Marines in this compound?"

"No way."

Mouth quirking, Megan said, "But the Marines do so much for this village. You'd think he would."

"If Khan did, it would mean whoever is shelling us at night would have to stop. And then they would probably turn against the people of Lar Sholtan and murder all of them."

"I see...."

"You're a noncombatant, Megan. You need to get this idea across to Mina. You're there to help."

Nodding, Megan said, "I'll ask about this. Thanks for letting me know."

"There's a lot out here in the field you'll never be taught back in a schoolroom."

It was a somber conversation. "I'm just glad I have your friendship, Luke. You have no idea how safe it

makes me feel." She eyed him shyly. "Oh, I know we're
not safe anywhere out here, but you just have that sense
of protection around you."

Something in Megan's voice stirred his heart. Her
blue eyes danced with sincerity. And her husky voice affected him as would a lover trailing her fingertips across
his sensitized flesh. The light coverlet of freckles across
her nose and cheeks deepened. Was she blushing?

"Hey, you have no idea how much I look forward
to seeing you. It's nice to have a woman around. I feel
damned lucky you're a field medic," he said softly.

Megan chuckled. "It's a big adjustment for everyone."

"So far," Luke said in a confidential tone, "I think
the company likes having you here. A lot of these grunts
have wives back home, and just seeing a pretty young
woman like yourself helps them not feel so homesick."

Heat flared up into her face and Megan knew she
was blushing. "I just hope I can prove to Captain Hall
and the other Marines that a woman isn't trouble. We
can be of use."

"You proved that to Hall earlier tonight. I thought
his mouth would drop open when you gave him that
laundry list of intel."

"I'll feel really good about myself if I can persuade
Emma and Kahlid to help Lar Sholtan. Cross your fingers the phone call I make to them goes well."

Megan felt as if she were walking on air as she
moved through the darkness from HQ to her hut from
the chow hall. Elated, she opened the door and closed
it. Luke was the only one in the hut at the moment.

"Where's everyone else?" Megan asked, making her
way to her cot.

Luke sat on his cot refilling his medic pack. "There's a poker game tonight."

"Oh…"

"Did you get ahold of your cousin Emma?"

Sighing, Megan said, "I did. And it's wonderful news. Emma and Khalid are flying out in a couple of days in their CH-47. They're going to talk with Timor Khan. There will be a *jirga,* a meeting of all the elders, when Khalid comes in to sell them on the importance of education for their children. I'll tell Mina tomorrow morning. I know she'll be so excited. I'm excited!"

Although he could hear the joyfulness in her voice, Luke could barely see an outline of her face. "That is good news."

"I really think we can help them, Luke."

"Don't get ahead of yourself, Megan. Just quietly present the possibility to Mina and she'll carry the info back to her husband."

Trying to ratchet down her expectations, she unlaced and pulled off her boots. "You're right." She placed them near the head of her cot. "Do you think we'll get shelled tonight?"

"Never know," he said, zipping up his bag and setting it beneath his cot. What would it be like to have Megan in his arms? She was so full of hope, a beautiful flower thriving out in this dangerous desert at five thousand feet. He worried about her enthusiasm. And her life. The enemy could move through the village like a shadow. He lay down on the cot. "Do you know how to recognize someone who's from the Taliban if you saw one?"

Megan got rid of her Kevlar vest. "No."

"They have a hatred of us. Their eyes are black and filled with hate. You won't miss it. And there are other

signs. These villagers are small. Wrinkles in their face
and their hands show their hard work. A Taliban soldier
is going to have soft hands because he doesn't work out
in the fields all day. They're hired by a warlord to ride
and fight. Their beards are well trimmed, whereas a vil-
lager's is not. Their clothes are cleaner and not thread-
bare and patched."

"I'll keep an eye out."

"Do."

Megan lay down and brought the four thick wool
blankets up to her shoulder as she turned onto her left
side. Snuggling into the hard pillow, she sighed. "Thank
you, Luke. You're a lifesaver."

Luke wanted to be more than that, he was discovering. Unhappy that he was powerfully drawn to Megan,
he closed his eyes. "Get some sleep, Megan. Busy day
tomorrow…"

Mina listened with delight over the invitation from
Emma and Khalid to her husband, Timor. Megan sat
with her in the warmth of her kitchen, drinking hot tea
before the clinic opened.

"This is wonderful news," Mina said, sipping her tea.

"I thought it was. Do you think your husband will
hold a *jirga* and discuss the possibility? Perhaps invite
Jabbar over?" Megan held her breath because if Mina
knew something she didn't, the plan could be axed before it ever got off the ground.

"He must think about it."

Nodding, Megan tried to hide her feelings of panic.
"I understand."

"Jabbar is not Pashtun," Mina cautioned in a low
voice. "He was born in Pakistan and he's not of our
tribe."

Confused, Megan said, "I don't understand what he has to do with what we're discussing."

"Jabbar knows of *Lokhay,* but Timor is not sure he respects it."

Megan was silently thanking Luke for telling her about their code last evening. "Does that pose a problem between your village and Jabbar?"

"I don't know." Worried, Mina looked around the brightly lit kitchen. The sun's slats shined through the dirty windows and filled the area with a golden color. "Jabbar is a very angry and deadly man. He works with al-Qaeda in this area. And no one is sure he is respectful of *Lokhay,* which is problematic."

"You mean, for example, he could come into your village and kidnap your older boys for service?" Megan knew the Taliban did that.

"Yes. If there is *Lokhay* between two people or two villages or tribes, both abide by the laws of it. Timor has met Jabbar once at a *jirga* and the meeting didn't go well. Jabbar is arrogant and he abuses the privilege of the power he holds. He threatened to burn our crops if we didn't give his men the food they demanded from us."

"Oh, no…"

"Yes." Grimly, Mina whispered, "You know how precious our food is to our village. In the code, we have *Melmastia,* or hospitality. We respect all visitors, no matter who they are or what tribe they are from. We will offer them our homes, our food and our blankets. Without question. Last year, Jabbar came riding in here on his white stallion. He had an army of a hundred men on horseback. And he demanded bags of beans we had grown to feed all his men. He told Timor that he owed the food to all of them because of *Melmastia.*"

"But you had no *Lokhay* agreement?"

"Exactly. We fed his men, fed his horses and offered them hospitality while they were here, but Timor refused to allow them to take our harvest. My husband realized Jabbar was bringing a show of force in order to scare us into giving our winter food to him. He is known for stealing from others."

"What happened?" Megan saw the anxiety come to Mina's green eyes.

"Jabbar tried to threaten the elders at a *jirga*. Timor stood up and told him if he took our tribe's winter food, they would rise, hunt all of them down and slit their throats. If Jabbar did not abide by *Lokhay,* he could never return and demand anything from us again."

"Wow," Megan murmured. "What did Jabbar do?"

"He cursed the elders, the *Lokhay* and Pashtuns. Some of our younger men, even though they are farmers, were outraged over such insults toward our elders. They attacked two of Jabbar's soldiers, slit their throats and promised to hunt the rest of his men down to do the same."

Eyes widening, Megan asked, "Then what happened?"

"Jabbar left in fury. He and his hundred men rode out of here, but they didn't shoot anyone. Since then, he's not returned. The Marines came here shortly after Jabbar left. Jabbar bombs the Marine compound all the time. He sends his men to plant those awful IEDs out on our dirt roads to kill the Americans." Her voice lowered and she added sadly, "All we want is to live in peace."

"It must be very, very stressful," Megan whispered, reaching out and touching Mina's hand. "I'm so sorry."

"The Americans want to stop the Taliban and al-Qaeda. The problem is our villages are in the way.

Timor hates both groups because they have no code of life. They are disrespectful and he sees them trying to bribe other villages with threats, intimidation, food or antibiotics. There are many villages up in the mountains above us that barely survive, and the bribes Jabbar offers them are like life itself. You know as a medic how important an antibiotic is for someone who is sick or injured. I can't tell you how many of our people have died over the years because we had no medicine."

"It sounds like Jabbar knows the needs, supplies them and then gets the village to agree to what he wants."

Mina held up her hands. "Yes. The mountain villages have done that. But we, in this valley, have not. We live by *Lokhay.* No one, not even the Taliban, can tell us differently. And this causes great friction between us and the Taliban. Timor does not want the Taliban running our villages. Even an American, if given *Lokhay* by our people, would be protected against Jabbar. And he knows that."

"Sounds like a standoff between you and Jabbar," Megan said.

Sighing, Mina said, "It is. Timor hates that his men are always out there at night planting IEDs on our roads and paths. Our own people walk them. And many of our men and boys have lost their lives or a leg to them."

"And yet you're friends with Jabbar's wife, Tahira?"

"Yes, because she is from southern Afghanistan and she is a good person. Tahira is the soul of kindness and is much like you. I believe the only reason Jabbar has not attacked our village and murdered everyone is her influence."

"She has real power over Jabbar?"

Mina shrugged. "Yes. She's very tiny but very firm with Jabbar."

"How did you get to know her?"

"After Jabbar's missteps with us, she came over the mountain a week later by horseback. She asked to talk to me, because, as you know, women cannot talk to men they do not know. We became instant friends. She has two young boys and of course, we talked about our children, the pressures of being the wife of a leader."

"And Tahira came from a tribe that was not Pashtun?"

"Correct. Tahira's father is a chief of another tribe in the south of our country. She was very lucky and was taught how to read and write. She recognized my education made me a better leader's wife. That is why I want to send a messenger across the mountain and see if she will welcome me into their home. I want to speak to her about the educational opportunity your cousin and her husband can bring to us. All of us."

Considering the jaded past with Jabbar, Megan worried for Mina. "Would Jabbar stop his wife from allowing you to ride over the mountain to visit Tahira?"

Laughing, Mina said, "Oh, no! Men rule, but they never rule us in that way. This is a visit between women. Whatever I would share with Tahira, she in turn would let her husband know. And even though Jabbar is a fierce warrior, he is a lamb toward his beautiful wife."

"I hope this works," Megan said.

"And what of you?" Mina asked, pouring more tea into their cups. "You are a beautiful young woman. You have Tahira's spiritedness. Are you married? Do you have children?"

"No, I'm not married." She saw sadness come to Mina's eyes.

"Are you lonely?"

Megan picked up her cup of hot tea. "I'm just trying to concentrate on what I'm doing here to help your village."

"I've watched that handsome young medic, Luke Collier, from time to time." She raised her thin black brows. "He's very appealing. Don't you agree?"

Laughing a little, Megan nodded. "Yes, he's very handsome. So even though you ladies are out and about in your burkas, you *do* look at men?"

Grinning, Mina whispered, "You know, a burka works two ways, my friend. We have a slit to look out of and no one can see *what* you're looking at." Laughing, she added, "And men, at times, are like dumb donkeys. We can look and appreciate a very good-looking, strong man and never get caught doing it. There's no harm in appreciating beauty, no matter whether man or woman."

Megan grinned with her. "You ladies are amazing."

"I know I've read articles where Americans think burkas are bad, but they hide and reveal much!"

The laughter made the room feel warm and secure for Megan. She felt utterly safe with Mina around. The young wife of Timor Khan was a force to be reckoned with.

"I have seen Luke stare at you," Mina said, a playful smile on her lips. "Have you noticed it?"

Caught off guard, Megan stammered, "Why...no. I had no idea."

Megan wagged a finger in her face. "Megan, for being such a young, beautiful woman, you are a donkey with blinders on! The first day you arrived here, I saw the medic stare at you like a lovesick stallion pining for his favorite mare!"

Choking on the tea, Megan covered her mouth and set the cup aside. Heat soared into her face and she saw Mina's wide smile and knowing in her eyes. After coughing some more, she managed a weak smile. "I'm here on business only, Mina. We have rules in the military that say you can't have a relationship with another person. It's not allowed."

"Umm," Mina said with mirth as she sipped her tea. "Well, someone should tell your handsome medic about that rule."

Chapter 6

"Tell me about your parents," Luke said. It was the first time in the past two weeks he'd had a chance to talk with her privately. He sat on his cot after coming back from morning chow. They had a busy day ahead of them, and both would be holding clinics in the village. Everyone else had left for duty. A lucky break.

Megan hauled her medic bag from the bottom of her cot and set it up on the table. "My dad, Noah, was a Coast Guard officer for thirty years. He's retired now as a rear admiral. My mom, Kit, is still a detective with Dade County, Florida. Why do you ask?" She cherished the small moments with Luke. Most of the time, they were separated by demands. Megan couldn't stare at him because it would have been obvious to the other Marines. The military's warning of "no fraternization" always rang in her ears.

"I was just wondering who you took after." Luke flashed her a grin.

"My dad, for sure."

"Is he like you? Quiet and thoughtful?" Luke saw her expression grow contemplative.

"Yes, he's like that. My mom is more intense, like a laser. She misses nothing. My dad is very laid-back and easygoing." She picked up some drugs from another pouch and placed them in her pack. "I have a twin, Addison, and she's exactly like my mom."

"And where's Addison?"

"She's graduated from Annapolis and is now a helicopter pilot aboard the carrier *John C. Stennis*."

"A hard charger? Gung ho?" Luke guessed.

"Addy is definitely a hard charger."

"So, what happened to you? Why didn't you join the Coast Guard?"

"My dad wanted me to, but I guess I had to bumble around and find out who I was first. I knew I had to complete the Trayhern tradition of serving our country."

"You didn't want to become an officer even though you've got a four-year college degree. Why not become an officer in the Navy?" He could hear Humvees firing up and getting ready to leave for the day's first mission. Judging from her expression, he could tell he'd accidentally stepped into a wound she carried.

"I guess Addy would tell you I'm like a shadow in comparison to her. I was always the quiet one who watched but didn't say much. I'm an introvert. I need peace and quiet. I believe in peace, not war."

"I don't like war, either," he told her. Cherishing their intimacy, he added, "I guess that's in part why I became a field medic. I'd rather save lives."

She melted beneath his hazel gaze. "You're an introvert, too?"

"Probably," he groused, packing dressings into the larger pack. "My father is a medical doctor. My mother is a registered nurse."

"You have medical genes for sure," she said, impressed.

"My father was always pushing me to become a doctor, but I wasn't into it."

"And your mother? What did she want you to be?"

He stopped and rested his hands on the pack in his lap. "Happy."

"I like her already. She sounds like my dad. He's an idealist and believes that human compassion is better than going to war and killing."

"I like his philosophy. I think you'd like my mother. She cries if she sees a dead butterfly on the sidewalk."

"Oh, so do I," Megan said, amazed. "So, do you take after your mother?"

"I do. But," he said teasingly, "I don't cry over a dead butterfly."

"What makes you cry?" Megan sat and watched his expression. Outside, the voices of sergeants bawling at their charges filled the air along with the roar of Humvees.

"Watching an old woman die because she didn't get proper medical help in time," he answered quietly. "Or a baby burned by pulling boiling water off a hot plate because the mother was busy with four other children. Over in Iraq, I saw it all." Gazing around the mud house, he added, "And it's even worse here because in Iraq there's infrastructure and government. In this country, it's all tribal and most villages have no road system."

"It's bad here," Megan agreed. She pulled some bottles out of a pack and carefully put them into the larger bag. "It's one thing to take an immersion course on Afghanistan and another to be here."

"You're still in culture shock," he warned. "It'll take a couple of months to wear off."

"Do you ever get used to the suffering?"

Shaking his head, he zipped up the pack. "No."

"How do you deal with it?"

"I hold it in. Sometimes, when I'm frustrated, I'll go somewhere and cry it out. But not often."

Megan bit her lower lip. "Well, at least we have each other. Right? I do cry. I hope you don't mind."

"I'm okay with it," he said with a wink. Seeing the warmth come to her blue eyes made his heart beat faster. The softness of Megan's lips called to him on every level. "I'm here for you," Luke promised. "I always look forward to seeing you."

Megan was caught off guard by this comment. The Afghan sun had darkened his skin, and his rugged good looks did nothing but make her yearn for him even more. "I like our quiet moments together," she said. "I wish…I wish we had more of them, but I don't want the Marines to think…well, you know…"

"I understand." He gave her a teasing smile. "You're safe with me." Luke wanted to say much more, but it was dangerous. He ached to walk over to her cot, lean down and graze her lips with his. He stood up and shouldered his pack. "Well, I gotta get going. You catching the second group leaving for the village?" He looked at his watch.

"Yes. I'm going in with Buck." She watched as he

put his helmet on and walked toward the door. "Stay safe out there, Luke."

Opening the door, he grinned. "Hey, no worries. You stay alert, too."

"You have helped many children and mothers this morning," Mina told Megan as they sat in the house sipping tea at lunch.

Megan smiled. "Thanks, but I couldn't do it without your help or the widows. You are all amazing." She finished off a plate of couscous and lamb. Outside, the day was cloudy and Megan wondered if it would rain. The village's crops relied solely on such moisture. There was no well and no irrigation to water them when the rain failed to appear.

A sudden explosion went off somewhere in the village. Megan's head snapped up, her eyes going wide. The house shook for a moment. "What was that?" she asked.

"It's an IED!" Mina leaped to her feet and threw her scarf over her head. "Come!"

Megan's shoulder radio blared to life as she followed Mina out the door and into the dirt street.

"Red Robin, this is Red Robin Two. I need your assistance at the gate. Over."

It was Luke's tense voice.

"Red Robin Two, I'm coming with my pack. Where are you located? Over." Megan ducked into the clinic. She grabbed her medic pack, threw on her helmet and ran out the door.

"The gate. Over."

"Roger. I'll be there in a minute."

Megan shouldered the pack. A year of training on the hard, rocky hills of Camp Pendleton in California had kept her in prime condition. Mina was hindered by her long robes. Several other women, many children and older men were rushing toward the explosion at the gate. Megan easily passed all of them. Turning at the end of the main street, she dug the toes of her boots into the red dust and turned left. As she rounded the corner, she saw Luke and several Marines, plus a Humvee parked near the gate. Megan raced toward them. Two children, a boy and girl, lay on the ground. Luke was working frantically over one of them. The Marines from the Humvee stood by, looking toward the slope of the eastern mountains, rifles drawn and ready.

As she skidded to a halt, breathing hard, Luke jerked a look up at her.

"Two kids hit an IED," he yelled. He threw several dressings over the unconscious boy's missing right leg. "Get to the girl!"

Dropping to her knees, Megan felt the world focus in on the little five-year-old girl sprawled on her back, unconscious. There was blood everywhere. Her right leg was missing. Megan quickly went into medical mode. The bleeding had to be stopped. She grabbed a small elastic band and quickly put it on just above the girl's knee. The child was so beautiful, her tan skin leeching of color as she bled out. Megan heard Luke breathing hard, heard him ripping and tearing open more dressings. She heard nothing else. It was as if the world were holding its breath.

Quickly listening to the girl's heart with her stethoscope, Megan felt momentary relief. The heart wasn't cavitating—yet. When enough blood was lost, the heart would stop beating. The blood pool congealed into the dirt around the child. Megan gave her a shot of morphine. If she became conscious, the pain would be horrendous. The child's beautiful dark blue gown had turned purple as it became saturated with blood.

In the background, a woman screamed. Looking up, Megan noticed someone racing toward them, her face contorted, her shrieks wild. It had to be the mother of one or both of these children.

"Buck!" Luke yelled. "Call in a medevac! These two aren't gonna make it unless we can get them to Bagram pronto!"

"Will do," Buck called, getting on the radio in the Humvee.

Frantic, Megan continued to work with the child. She quickly put in an IV with saline solution into her tiny arm to try and stave off her massive blood loss. The mother came flying toward her, her robes like wings.

"Get her back!" Megan ordered Shorty, who had walked up to help her. "I need room to work with this girl!"

Shorty shot forward. Mina caught up with her and threw her arms around the young mother. Gripping her neighbor, she held her tightly, pleading with her to stop.

Shorty stood between the frantic medics and the screaming mother who fought to escape Mina's strong arms. He knew, as all Marines did, they could not touch a village woman. It was taboo. He held up his hand, a signal not to come any closer.

Megan yelled at another Marine standing nearby. "Lance, come and hold this IV!"

The young Marine was wide-eyed over the sudden carnage. He trotted over and took the IV from her hand and held it above the unconscious child.

Megan's hands shook as she applied sterile dressings to the bloody stump. The IED had blown off the girl's leg just below her knee. Jerking a look toward the Humvee, she yelled, "Buck, is that medevac in the air?"

"Yeah, we're getting one outta Camp Bravo. They'll be here in less than twenty minutes."

Groaning, Megan didn't know if it would arrive in time. She listened intently to the girl's chest. The mother's frantic screams, crying for her two children, filled the air. There was a faint beat of the girl's heart as she listened intently through the stethoscope. The heart weakened by the moment. The girl needed a blood transfusion, but none was available out here. None. Lifting the child's legs, she forced what blood was in her body back toward her core. Instantly, her heart beat a little stronger. Relief flooded through Megan.

Another Marine knelt down beside her. He had a blanket rolled up. "Can I put this under her legs?" he asked Megan.

Grateful to the corporal, she said, "Yes, great. Thank you."

"What else can we do?"

"Nothing. We're going to have to pray and wait." Tears jammed into Megan's eyes. She touched the girl's long black hair and gently pulled strands away from her wan face. Anger tinged her, but her focus was to keep the girl stable. Her heartbeat came back stronger and steady as her legs were lifted by the green wool blanket placed beneath her knees.

It seemed like forever before the medevac arrived. With it came two combat Apache helicopters, armed to the teeth. Megan wanted the helo to land, but she realized the Apaches were flying across the eastern slope, looking for hidden enemy fighters. The medevac helo wasn't armed. And when it landed, it was a sitting duck for missiles or grenade launchers. *Hurry! Hurry!*

Finally, the helo landed outside the gate in an area the Marines had already cleared of any possible IEDs. Luke picked up the unconscious boy, his face taut with tension, and carried him toward the helo. A Marine walked beside him, holding the IV for the boy.

Buck walked over to Megan. He knelt down next to her and yelled above the beating blades of the helos. Above them, the two Apaches swarmed and created a moment of safety while the medevac was on the ground. "I'll carry her. I just talked to Captain Hall. He said for both of you to take these kids to Bagram. You'll both fly them in. Pick up whatever supplies you can and bring them back with you tomorrow morning. Got it?" He gently slid his arms beneath the child.

"What about the mother?" she yelled, standing and taking the IV from Lance.

"No go," Buck shouted, quickly carrying the child toward the helo. "Not enough room."

Nodding, Megan looked back, lifted her hand to Mina, trying to signal to her that the mother's children were stable. "Can you tell Mina the kids have a chance? They're stable."

"Yeah," Buck yelled over the rotor wash. There was a crew chief on board the medevac. Ahead of them, Luke had traded the boy off to the woman. He quickly climbed in and moved aside, ready to take the girl from Buck's arms.

Within a minute, Megan was in the medevac. It was crowded and they worked side by side. The blades spun faster. The sound in the helo was loud. The door was pulled shut. Luke donned a helmet and then handed one across to her. The gravity of the helo lifting off made Megan feel some relief. They were targets, pure and simple. More than one medevac had been blown apart on the ground trying to pick up wounded Marines or villagers.

The pilot put the throttles to the firewall, climbing sharply in a zigzagging motion. Megan plugged her helmet into the cabin intercom system. She heard the talk between the pilots and the hospital in Bagram. Working with the woman medic, they continued to keep the children monitored. Adding several more blankets would keep the children from going into deeper shock. The helo shuddered around Megan and she briefly looked out the window. It was raining, the sky turning a dark, depressing gray color. Moving her gloved hand over the girl's dirty black hair, she suddenly wanted to cry. She fought back the tears and looked over at Luke.

He stared at her for a telling moment. His hands and arms were bloodied and so was his Kevlar vest where he'd carried the boy into the helo. His face was taut, his eyes unreadable as he listened intently to the boy's heart.

Shakily, Megan remained by the girl, her fingers wrapped around her limp hand. There was little else to do but monitor at this point. The metallic odor of blood hung in the cabin. The female crew chief medic with the flight was from the Air Force. Her dark green one-piece uniform had a Black Jaguar Squadron patch on one shoulder and an American flag on the other. Somehow, knowing this woman worked for BJS, Megan felt they had the best personnel for this particular mission of mercy. The shaking and shuddering of the helo increased as it gained altitude.

If they could reach Bagram and the children remained stable, it was a testament to their training and being at the right place at the right time. Briefly, Megan glanced across the helo to see how Luke was doing with his charge. For a moment, their gazes met and locked. Luke's eyes burned with a tenderness that shook her soul deep.

"It's all good news," Luke assured Megan as they exited Bagram hospital after releasing the children to the surgical staff. They walked far enough apart so as not to draw attention to themselves.

The sun was high and it was near noon. Megan took a deep breath and nodded. "Thank God." The minutes between the medevac landing and rushing the children through the emergency room of Bagram had been a blur. She'd calmly given the child's stats to an awaiting surgical nurse. Each child had been swarmed by knowledgeable and highly trained E.R. staff. In moments, she stood watching the gurneys bearing the children rushing away and disappearing out of swinging doors for surgery. She'd wanted to cry, but this wasn't the place to let go.

Megan moved aside, feeling numb in the aftermath. And terribly alone. Her heart and mind focused on the mother back at Lar Sholtan, who had no idea if her children were alive or dead. War was brutal, and it sickened Megan.

A wave of nausea hit her hard. She asked an orderly where the bathroom was. He pointed through the same doors the surgery team had gone through.

Megan bolted down the white, tiled hall, looking for the restroom, when Luke reappeared. His tense face lightened when he spotted her.

"You okay?" he asked, coming up to her.

"No. I'm sick…."

Nodding, Luke gripped her arm and led her down the hall. "Here…go on in…"

Without a word, Megan ran into the empty, quiet

bathroom. Her stomach churned. She pushed open a
door, choked and retched violently into the toilet bowl.
Tears squeezed from her eyes and she sank down on
her knees, hugging the commode as everything came
up. Her vision blurred and her nose ran. Her mouth
burned with acid.

Megan didn't hear Luke come in or push the door
open. She just felt someone's hand firm on her shoulder.
A paper cup filled with water appeared in front of her.

"Here," Luke said near her ear.

Hand shaky, Megan took the cup. Tears continued to
run down her cheeks as she cleaned up. When she was
done, Luke placed a second cup of water in her hand.
Wordlessly, Megan drank. The water tasted so clean.
Her nostrils were still filled with the odor of blood.

Luke knelt down beside Megan, his arm across her
shoulder to comfort her. "It's all right," he said in a low,
unsteady voice. "Kids always get to us…."

Shutting her eyes, Megan leaned wearily against his
tall, strong body. Sobs worked up and out of her chest.
Anger, grief and shock pummeled her. Luke said nothing as she buried her face against his neck and jaw. He
was warm, alive, caring, and right now, that was what
she needed to offset the terror of the past hour.

Luke closed his eyes, feeling Megan's body shake
with sobs. He felt helpless, knowing it was tearing her
up to have seen the children so badly injured. And for
what reason? He shared her rage, her sense of helpless-
ness in the wake of a war that didn't care about col-
lateral damage—civilian casualties. He couldn't tell
her it was going to be all right, because it wouldn't be.
Good people died. Children's lives were destroyed. Just
holding Megan helped him to control his own grief and
shock over what had happened this morning. She had

been strong, professional and caring and had saved a child's life.

Megan stopped crying and clung to him, her hand opening and closing against the shoulder of his uniform, as if to transfer the pain outside herself. Leaning down, he pressed a kiss to her mussed hair. "It's good to get it out," he said in a rasp. "We all cry for the kids. It sucks, Megan. I know it does…."

Luke's deep voice was balm to her broken heart. Slowly, Megan lifted her head and stared up into his narrowed eyes. His arm was supportive and right now she needed his strength. His face blurred for a moment as fresh tears spilled. "Oh, Luke, I—I'm sorry. It rips me apart to see a child hurt in any way…."

"I know, I know." He gently pushed damp strands of red hair away from her wet cheek. "It's okay. We aren't robots." Cupping her jaw, Luke looked deeply into her marred eyes. "We cry for them, Megan. It's all we can do. That and pray they live. It's a pretty damn helpless feeling at times like this."

His hand was rough against her cheek. Closing her eyes, she leaned into his palm, absorbing his care. "Th-thank you…"

"Come on, let's get you upright," he urged and helped Megan stand. He opened the door and led her out into the brightly lit washbasin area. She appeared unsteady and Luke kept his hand on her elbow. Pulling some paper towels from a nearby dispenser, he turned on a faucet. "Cold towels help," he told her.

Their fingers met and touched as Megan took the dripping paper towels from him. She leaned her hips against the sink and pressed the cool towels to her hot face. The tears stopped and the cold water felt good.

Luke released her elbow and she heard him turn on the faucet and then shut it off.

"Feel like some more cold water?" he asked.

"Thanks, Luke. You didn't have to do this." She dropped the wet towels in the wastebasket and took the paper cup. "I hope no one comes in. They'll be shocked seeing a guy in here...."

He smiled, his eyes hooded, as he observed Megan. Leaning up against the door, he made sure no other woman would unexpectedly enter right now. Megan was so distraught. "The first two tours I was over here in the Kandahar area, I heaved my guts out every time a kid stepped on an IED." He saw her look up, a flicker of surprise in her stormy eyes. Luke thought he saw relief in them, too. "I wondered if I'd ever get over my reaction. No one ever called me a coward or weak because I got sick afterward. I finally understood it's just my emotional reaction to trauma. In the States, we don't deal with limbs being blown off by IEDs. I'd had medical training on it, but I never realized what it would do to me, personally, until I saw it happen here in Afghanistan."

"You make me feel better," she admitted, her voice hoarse. There was such tender concern in Luke's face for her that all Megan wanted to do was walk into his arms and be held. There was something about this man that was healing to her heart, her soul.

Luke opened his arms. "Come here, Megan. Let me just hold you?"

He didn't need to ask again. She set the cup down on the sink, took an uneven breath and walked those few feet into his arms. As he drew her close, a ragged sigh issued from her lips. Megan buried her head beneath his jaw, soaking up the care radiating from him. He rested his cheek against her hair and she relaxed completely against his strong, unwavering body. Hearing his heartbeat slow and strong beneath her ear, Megan let go of the lingering stress. There was something calming about Luke.

"You're okay," he rasped against her hair, the strands tickling his cheek. He felt Megan surrender fully against him. Hotly aware of her breasts pressing against his chest, her hips melded against his, Luke fought his own desires. Right now Megan needed a sanctuary of safety, not a lover. This morning had been a traumatic welcome to Afghanistan. He bussed her hair and whispered, "You're safe, Megan. I'll always be here for you...."

Melting into his body, his arms making her feel as if nothing could ever harm her again, Megan heard the slight tremor in his huskily spoken words. There was so much to Luke she wanted to explore. She nuzzled beneath his chin, absorbing his male scent, cherishing the strength of his body protecting her. Nothing had ever felt so right. His lips were against her hair, placing small, chaste kisses here and there.

The minutes trickled away and Megan closed her eyes and allowed herself to be held. Finally, her stomach stopped roiling and the jagged emotions subsided. Luke smoothed away errant strands of her hair. Every grazing touch sent wild tingles racing through her. Megan realized she was over the initial shock when she felt a powerful desire to kiss Luke as if this were her last moment on earth. Megan's eyes flew open over the sudden realization. This man had shown her nothing but kindness, humor, strength and understanding.

Luke released her as he felt a shift of energy around Megan. She eased out of his embrace and reluctantly stepped away. He saw chagrin in her eyes. Smiling a little, he held her gaze. "At least you have some color back in your face."

Touching her cheek, Megan felt the heat and knew she was blushing. She managed a soft smile of thanks. "Luke, you're good medicine. Thank you."

He forced himself to remain relaxed, his hands at his sides. It was the last thing he wanted to do. The idea of kissing Megan, cherishing her lips, giving her all the feelings he held for her in that one contact, ate away at him. How many nights had he dreamed of kissing her? Loving her? Exploring every inch of her slender, strong body? But he could tell Megan was fragile. "I'll send you my bill once we get back to the company," he teased.

Megan slid a hand through her hair. She turned and looked in the mirror for the first time. Her hair was filled with dust that had been kicked up by the mede-vac helicopter at Lar Sholtan. She felt the grit of it on her skin. Turning, she noticed the humor banked in his thoughtful hazel gaze. "I'll always be there for you, too, Luke. You can count on it."

"I never doubted that, Megan. You're loyal, you care deeply and you're incredibly strong." He wanted to say so much more, but it was the wrong time and place. "I'll bet you'd like to get a shower. They're located in the basement of the hospital. They have towels, soap and washcloths available. I'm going to clean up myself." He looked down at his bloody desert camouflage blouse.

"That sounds wonderful," she murmured, taking the rubber band out of her hair and allowing the strands to swing free around her shoulders. She saw a hungry expression on Luke's face. And just as suddenly, the look was gone. There was something sensual about a woman's hair, she realized. For a moment, Megan wanted to feel his fingers threading through her hair, touching her, loving her....

Luke eased away from the door and pulled it open. "Come on, follow me...." He wished they could be alone. He wanted to shower *with* Megan, to run the soap lovingly across her body, to erase the blood and trauma once and for all. Somehow, this morning's experience had ripped away all pretense of how he felt toward Megan. It could have been one of them who had stepped unknowingly on that IED. And one of them could be dead, instead. The urgency to take her, to love her, made him dizzy for a moment. Never had he wanted a woman the way he wanted Megan.

Luke met Megan on the surgery floor. He'd gotten cleaned up and dressed in a fresh set of utilities first. They'd agreed to meet here to see how the children were doing. He had just talked to the head surgery nurse when Megan stepped off the elevator. Her hair was damp and clean. She had on a new set of clothes as well and they were a bit big for her slender form. There was life back in her eyes as she approached.

"Good news," he said. "Their surgeries are going well and they're stable."

Relief flooded Megan. She halted, closed her eyes for a moment, her hand pressed to her breast. "Thank God..."

"Those kids will live. I just finished speaking to Captain Hall. He'll send word to the mother of the children." An ache grew in him as he saw Megan's eyes widen with joy and tears. How easily touched she was. She seemed to trust him enough to show her real feelings. He felt an incredible happiness threading through him.

"Wonderful," Megan whispered. She smiled up at

Luke. "We did good work out in the field, and this is the result."

"It is," he agreed. He pulled the utility cap from his back pocket. "I thought we'd go check into our TDY rooms and get something to eat afterward. Are you at all hungry?"

Turning, she walked with him to the bank of elevators down the hall. "Oddly, I am. It's crazy, isn't it? One moment I'm upchucking and the next I'm hungry." Megan added in a lower voice, "Over in Iraq I was the same way."

Luke stood near her as they waited. "I was wondering how you survived Iraq."

"One day at a time," she said grimly. "Just like I will here."

Nodding, he understood only too well. "Did you have friends there who you could go to?"

"Yes," she said. "There were a number of us women at the combat support unit medical facility and we all bunked together. It was easy to get off a shift, go there and cry our hearts out to one another. No one can hold that kind of horror inside them."

The doors to the elevator whooshed open and Luke gestured for her to enter first. When the door closed, he pushed the button for the first floor. "I lost track of the times I went to hide in a supply tent to cry."

Reaching out, Megan shyly slid her hand into his. His hands saved a little boy's life. Squeezing it, she whispered, "I'm glad to know men cry, too."

He absorbed her unexpected touch. Returning the squeeze, he released her hand. "It's an occupational hazard, but it isn't one that will kill us."

Megan smiled a little and nodded. She walked at his

shoulder through the lobby. She placed her utility hat on her head before they walked through the large doors.

The wind was warm because Bagram sat on the desert floor near Kabul, the capital of Afghanistan. Outside, the wind was breezy, hot and dry. Megan pulled off her soft cover for a moment and pushed some strands of hair off her face. Settling it back on, she asked, "Where are the TDY barracks? I've never been to Bagram before."

Grinning, Luke said, "You're in good hands. We'll go get our rooms at the temporary duty barracks and then hit the chow hall.

"Lead on," Megan said.

The TDY barracks were for military personnel who were coming and going from the massive air base. She was assigned a small room on the first floor. Just the luxury of knowing tonight she had a hot shower raised her spirits. There were several sets of women's utilities in the closet. Megan found a dark green T-shirt and quickly pulled it on. She allowed her hair to swing around her shoulders and put her light camouflage jacket on over the T-shirt. Now she could take off the jacket when she was hot.

Megan looked forward to being with Luke. *Finally.* How badly she wanted to get to know him. Heart racing with anticipation, she left her medic pack in the room, grabbed her soft utility hat and made her way toward the lounge. Megan wasn't prepared for the look he gave her when he saw her. Standing tall, his broad shoulders thrown back with natural pride, he appealed completely to her yearning heart. The fact that Luke was single was far too tempting. As Megan stepped forward to meet him, she tried to remind herself of the reasons not to get involved with this handsome Navy medic.

Luke was careful not to be anything but professional toward Megan as she walked up to him. Despite the baggy clothes, nothing could hide the soft sway of her hips or her long, long legs. When his gaze settled on her mouth, heat throbbed unexpectedly through his lower body. Her shining hair lay across her shoulders like a gleaming cape. An ache centered in his heart. He'd been too long without a woman. But he didn't want just any woman. He wanted quiet, gentle Megan.

"Ready to eat?" she said.

"Let's go," he invited, gesturing toward the front door.

Outside, the day was hot and Megan could feel the burning sun on her exposed hands. Bagram was a massive air base—a helicopter and jet base as well as headquarters for all the military branches. Luke pointed down a narrow street.

"Would you like regular chow or something more exotic like pizza?"

Melting beneath his boyish grin, she said, "Pizza? Really? Wow, I'd love some!"

"Great minds think alike. Come on, I know the owner of this little pizza joint. He's one of the good guys."

Megan saw how popular the little restaurant was. There was a line of men and women outside it, waiting to order a pizza to go. Luke pulled out a chair for her to sit on beneath one of the red umbrellas. There were several small, round tables covered with red cloths and shaded from the burning sun. He disappeared around the rear of the building. What was he up to?

Megan waited fifteen minutes to find out. When Luke reappeared, he had a large pepperoni pizza in one hand and a huge pitcher of Pepsi in the other. A look of triumph was written across his face as he placed the pizza on the table.

"You forget, I'm a scrounger," he told her in a conspiratorial tone, pulling out napkins, knives and forks from his pocket.

"You are incredible," Megan said, the fragrance of the cheese and freshly baked bread making her stomach growl.

Sitting down at her elbow, Luke smiled. He picked up the napkin and laid it across his lap. "Thank you. Go ahead, eat all you want. Afzal is the owner. We go a long way back with one another." He hooked his thumb over his shoulder. "He's a stand-up guy."

"And he makes pizzas?" Megan bit into the wedge and groaned with pleasure.

"Yep. Afzal was born in America and came back over here when Bagram was built. He loves America and Americans. He wanted to do something for the war effort to help us, so he went through channels and got permission to create his pizza restaurant here on-base."

"Wonderful." Megan sighed. The cheese and pepperoni melted in her mouth. "Thank you."

Luke gave her a wolfish smile. "Do you realize we have the rest of today here at Bagram? We'll go over to Supply and get our medical stuff for the return trip, but that will only take an hour. And we get to sleep in real beds with real sheets. We don't have to go back until 0900 tomorrow."

The look in his eyes sent her heart pounding for a moment. "I feel like I'm in a dream and I'm afraid to wake up."

"I can keep this dream alive for both of us, Megan." He lowered his voice and held her gaze. "How would you like to go into Kabul later with me? I have a friend who has a home outside the city, a safe place. And I'm welcome there at any time. I can call him and let him know we're coming in for the night."

Megan's eyes widened as she considered his idea.

Luke could see the gold flecks deep in her eyes. "This has to be mutual, Megan. I can't tell you how much I've wanted time away with you. I want to know a lot more about you. What do you think?"

Megan's heart began to pound in earnest. "I want the same thing. Ever since I met you there's been something about you that touches my heart, touches me...." She shrugged, giving him a helpless look. "It's tough to put into words."

"I know." He stopped himself from reaching out to grip her hand. "This is your call, Megan. I'm not asking you to do something you don't want to do. But there's a hunger in my heart I can't ignore. I've never been drawn to anyone like this. Ever." Digging into her widening eyes, he asked the most important question of all. "Do you want to come with me?"

Chapter 7

Before Megan could answer Luke's question, a long wail of a siren began. Everyone sat up and took notice.

"What is it?"

Luke scowled. "Bagram is on lockdown." Twisting around, he glanced toward the airstrip in the distance. "That siren means one of our patrols or a drone spotted enemy activity somewhere outside the base. When that happens, it means no one comes or goes from the base."

Her stomach became queasy and she stopped eating. There was more activity; Humvees sped toward the airstrip.

Luke focused on Megan, who suddenly went pale. Her eyes were dark. "Feeling sick?" he asked.

"Yes, it's hitting me again. One minute I'm fine and then…"

"Would you like to take a walk? Maybe that will help."

"Yes, I'd like that." Megan stood and Luke gestured for her to walk down the street filled with personnel. The siren finally stopped screaming and her nerves settled down once more. She was grateful Luke was at her side.

They came upon some empty picnic tables at the end of the block. "Let's go there and sit down," Megan suggested.

"Sure," he murmured.

Sitting down opposite Luke, she rested her elbows on the roughened wooden surface. She forced a smile she didn't feel. "I'm really okay. I just have to let my body work through what it saw earlier."

"It's normal," he agreed. Her hair glinted in the sunlight, the strands turning copper and burgundy. Luke wondered how soft they would feel between his exploring fingers. And explore her he would. "Kid tragedy affects everyone. You can't sit there and cry when you're trying to save their lives. You have to stuff your emotions down in order to think through how to help them."

Rubbing her face, Megan said, "Exactly."

"Generally, I have the same reaction as you and it lasts about twenty-four hours."

"I try to go off by myself afterward because I know it's coming." Megan looked up at the blue sky dotted with white clouds. The *thunk, thunk, thunk* of Apache helicopters could be heard off to the north of them, near the airstrip. The loud sound blotted out the quiet. Pulling strands of hair away from her face, Megan said softly, "I have no way to shield myself from a wounded person's pain, from the pain loved ones are going to feel."

Luke looked around and made sure there were no prying eyes. He leaned across and placed his hand over hers for just a moment. "Don't feel embarrassed about this, Megan. Hell, I've cried until my throat hurt so much I was hoarse the next day. The stuff we do, the things we see, we can't escape. Nor can we ignore it."

His hand felt comforting and warm. "Thanks. Where I was in Iraq, I worked in an E.R. outfit at a base camp. None of the doctors or nurses showed their feelings. I sucked it up, too. After my shift, I would go back to my tent. Me and my roommates would cry where we couldn't be seen or heard." She unclasped her hands and squeezed his. "It's nice to be able to admit this to you. Thanks for understanding, Luke."

He had to remove his hand. Someone would inevitably see them. He pulled away, wanting to hold Megan. That's what she needed, Luke realized. But there was nowhere to go for that kind of privacy on a locked-down air base. He quelled the desire eating away at his heart. "I'm here for you, Megan. It's better to talk this stuff out than try to hide or ignore it. This morning, you saved that little girl's life because you were able to think above the fray and do what had to be done."

Giving him a wry look, Megan said, "I'm not battle hardened like you, Luke. You go out on Marine patrols almost every day where there's every chance a bullet could cut you down. Or the enemy can fire a rocket or grenade launcher at you. I haven't been in those situations."

"And I don't ever want you to be," he said, his voice deepening. "I think Captain Hall was right to keep you at the village or our compound. Out there—" he gestured to where they were stationed "—it's no-man's-land. The enemy hates us. No one is safe."

Wistfully, Megan studied his serious features. The desire for her burning in his eyes was clear. "Life is always dangerous to us in some way, don't you think, Luke? If not physically, then emotionally." She smiled. "Humans are always putting themselves in the line of fire when they get into a relationship. There's no assured outcome. And although it isn't life-threatening on one level, it can really injure us."

"No question," Luke agreed, his voice becoming a rasp. He recalled his contentious marriage to Hope. Both had been severely wounded by the situation. It hadn't been anyone's fault, but his emotional wounds were deep. "For a while, after the divorce, I thought I would die of a heart attack. I literally felt pain every day in my heart."

"It was grief." Megan saw the way his mouth tightened.

"Yes."

"Wounds of war. Wounds of love." Megan opened her hands and looked around the area. "Since Iraq, I've come to the conclusion that humans are always putting themselves out there in dangerous lands. It might not be like it is here at Bagram or at Lar Sholtan, but we're doing it in other ways. After my relationship in Iraq, I understood the other threat to my emotions and my heart."

"And when I asked you back there if you wanted to go off-base with me to spend the night at my friend's villa, I saw you hesitate. Now I know why." And could Luke blame her? He gave her an apologetic look. "I'm sorry for asking, Megan. I was out of line."

"War distorts things." She couldn't deny that she wanted to reach out and touch Luke. He had beautiful, rugged hands. It was those hands that had saved the life of a little boy this morning. *Healing hands*. What would it be like to have those calloused hands moving across her skin? Exploring her? A shiver of yearning coursed through her. Their situation was impossible. But it didn't stop her from wanting to kiss him.

"No question," Luke murmured. "When you're in a dangerous, threatening environment like Iraq or Afghanistan, you suddenly realize you can die at any moment. And then life becomes very precious and intense."

"Is that what is happening to us?" Megan tilted her head and looked deep into his eyes. "Is that why you asked me to leave with you earlier?"

Grimacing, Luke said, "I don't really know. I like you, Megan. A lot more than I should, I guess. When I see you smile, I feel an incredible happiness here." He touched his chest. "When I'm away from you, I'm worrying about you. That village is not safe. The enemy can come and go as they please. I worry they'll see you and either kill or kidnap you."

"And so we're drawn to each other. My concern is why. Is it the danger of dying? Or is there something more underneath substantial to this situation? Something to build on?" she asked.

"All good questions," Luke agreed, giving her the hint of a smile. "They should be asked and honestly answered. I wasn't looking for someone, Megan. I'm still getting over losing Hope. I never want to put another woman in my ex's place. It wasn't fair to Hope and I idealistically thought that our love for each other was enough to see us through the tough times." His mouth turned downward, his voice suddenly a rasp. "It wasn't."

"I never thought for a moment after I met you, Luke, that you were chasing me. I know the difference." Megan saw him lift his chin and intently study her. "I didn't come into this company looking for a relationship. My focus was on being a good role model for General Stevenson's initiative. I don't want to fail her. I didn't want to be drawn to you, but I was. And now I fight myself every time I'm around you." Giving Luke a rueful look, Megan said, "I see you do kind things for people every day. You care for others, and as a field medic, you're selfless. You'll put yourself between a bullet and a wounded Marine without ever thinking twice about it, Luke. You're a hero in my eyes."

Her words struck him deeply. Luke dragged in a breath. "I didn't know if what I felt for you was mutual. Thanks for letting me know."

"It is mutual, but there's nothing we can do about it. I'm not willing to jeopardize my career, Luke. I can't."

"I agree with you completely," he said. Smiling sadly, Luke added, "That doesn't mean I don't care for you, want you or want to spend time with you, Megan."

"I feel the same."

"Can we be depressed together?"

She grinned and laughed. "Never lose your sense of humor."

Warmth penetrated Luke's heart as he absorbed her smile. "My mother always said I was a jokester."

"She's right." Megan felt some of the heaviness melt away from her heart. "But I love your jokes. You don't do anything to embarrass anyone, you're just funny. You make people laugh in a very dark situation."

"Black humor."

"Oh, I can do black humor with the best of them," Megan said with feeling. "When things get crazy in the E.R. and we're avalanched with injuries coming in, it saves all of us."

"We all feel that way," Luke admitted. Brightening a little, he said, "Do you feel better? I see some color back in your cheeks."

"Amazingly, yes. Thank you." Megan's voice lowered with feeling. "Maybe it's you, Luke. You're good medicine for me."

"Hey," he said ruefully, "whether we like it or not, we're into each other, Megan. It's not a bad thing. Just bad timing."

"I'll second that." Seeing merriment come to his green-and-gold eyes, she said, "But there's nothing that says I can't appreciate you from a distance or enjoy your company."

He rubbed his hands together and grinned. "Good, because I'm not going to stop liking you, Megan. Maybe we can hang out on-base. Captain Hall wants me to get some things for his men. Plus, I'm going to raid the hospital supply department for Lar Sholtan. We need some things for the villagers and we might as well make the most out of being here."

Happiness flowed through Megan. As badly as she wanted to kiss his smiling mouth, she resisted. It was pure torture since she had a feeling he'd be a great lover. "Yes, I'd love to trail around with you. I've never seen a scrounger in action." She met his smile.

"Prepare to be amazed!"

The next morning, Megan flew out of Bagram with Luke. On board the CH-47 transport were two pallets of scrounged supplies covered with netting. The loadmasters had tightened them down to the deck so nothing could fly around within the helicopter. Luke seemed to know everyone at Bagram. He'd gotten an impressive amount of food, clothing, drugs and vitamins for the village. And everyone she'd met during his day-long scrounging mission had liked the field medic. There was nothing to dislike about Luke, in fact. As they sat together on the nylon-webbing seats in the noisy CH-47, Megan simply absorbed being near him.

When they landed just outside the compound, a group of Marines were on hand to help the loadmasters remove the boxes from the CH-47 as soon as possible. Megan rushed into the compound, directing the Marines carrying the medical supplies to the dispensary building near HQ. It was nearly noon before she and Luke had parceled out and arranged all the supplies, medical or not. And best of all, Luke had boxes of frozen pepperoni pizzas sent to the Navy chow hall chief. There wasn't a Marine who wasn't looking forward to pizza tonight, all thanks to Luke.

Shortly after noon chow, Megan caught up with Buck, who was over at the C.P. "Buck, are you going into the village sometime today?"

"Sure. In about an hour. Why? You want to come along?"

"I would," Megan said. "I got an update on the two children at the hospital before we left this morning and I want to go tell the parents how they're doing."

Buck nodded. "That's mighty fine of you to do that, Doc."

The grizzled Marine's praise pleased her. Most sergeants, the ball bearings of any company to keep it running in the right direction, were usually all-business. The thoughtful look in Buck's eyes, however, told Megan differently. "I try to put myself in their place. Their children are hundreds of miles away and there's no phone to talk to them. I'd like the same consideration if I were in their shoes, wouldn't you?"

"Yes, I would," Buck said, giving her a slight smile. "So, any supplies you want to bring over there with us for your clinic?"

Megan handed him a list of the boxes and numbers so they knew which ones to load into the Humvee. "I do. Thanks. What time?"

"1400."

"I'll be there. Thanks, Buck." Turning, she hurried out of HQ.

Buck seemed to notice Captain Hall listening to their conversation. The C.P. was empty except for the two of them. The radio chatter was constant. He walked over to his desk and sat down.

"She's turning into a real asset," Hall said.

"Yes, sir, she is. Pretty, smart and savvy. And she's a damn good medic, too. She's as good as Luke is."

Hall's brows fell and he stopped working on a report. "I worry for her, Buck. I don't think she realizes the dangers of working in the village."

"No safe places, sir, that's true. But I saw her in action out there yesterday morning when those two tykes got legs blown off by that damned IED. She's all-business. And frankly, my men are seeing a difference in the men in the village since she's been here."

"Oh?"

"Yeah, it's like the wives of the village have surrounded Doc Trayhern and they like her. I believe Mina Khan is leading the charge on this one. They *want* Megan there. She's doin' good work with the women and tykes. She's improving their lives by the day, and they're grateful."

"Good to know, but do you think Timor Khan is going to stop the next Taliban or al-Qaeda operatives from waltzing through his village?"

"No, sir, I don't. But I think Khan just might be more firm with them and tell them to leave us alone."

Snorting, Hall said, "That would be damned nice. A pipe dream, Sergeant."

"Yes, sir, probably is. But—" he picked up a paper "—you never know. I've been over here on four tours now. And I think I know the Pashtuns a little better than you, sir. If you show consistent loyalty to them, they'll return it in kind."

"Oh, *Lokhay*," Hall muttered, not disguising the frustration in his voice.

"Pashtuns are people with hearts and feelings, sir. While they haven't bestowed *Lokhay* on our company, my gut tells me that Mina Khan is close to giving it to Doc Trayhern."

"Well, that'd be a first," Hall said, scribbling his signature on a report. "Because if they ever bestowed *Lokhay* on her, it means the whole village would not only protect her, but go to war against the enemy to keep her safe." He shook his head. "I've never seen that happen."

"I think that's what General Stevenson is after," Buck said, thoughtful about the idea of placing well-trained American military women in the villages. "And right now my men see a positive difference in the way the male villagers are treating us. It's a start."

"Yes, that's all it is." Hall scowled and looked toward the open door, letting air into the squalid structure. "We know Gholam is the local Taliban leader. And thanks to Trayhern, we know where he lives. She's gotten us useful intel."

"Oh," Buck said softly, "I think over time, having a woman like Doc Trayhern here is going to switch things up a lot. For the better."

Megan finished telling the mother of the two children the good news. The mother wept with relief. Her husband, one of the farmers, was not home, but Mina was at her side, smiling through her tears. The small mud home smelled like goat dung, and the family was barely eking out an existence. The dirt floor was hard packed and one very thin, old Persian rug lay at one end.

"There's even better news," Megan told the mother, releasing her embrace. "Luke, the other medic, has already set up an appointment with an NGO that is going to supply your children with prosthetics. They're going to have a leg to walk around on."

Mina clapped her hands. "Allah be praised! Please thank Luke for his help. In the past, when one of our children or one of our husbands was wounded by an IED, no one did anything. Oh, the medic would come and they would save their lives, but you see how many of our people hobble around on wooden crutches."

"I saw that. And when Luke and I got a chance to go to Bagram, it was a high priority to get the NGOs involved to help your village." Megan sat down on the Persian rug as the tearful mother offered them tea. Mina sat down next to her.

"And what does that mean for all of us?" Mina asked.

"It means that the NGO will be sending out a team to fit and measure the rest of your villagers who have lost legs over the years. They're going to pay for the prosthetics. Everyone will have legs to walk around on."

Mina sighed and wiped more tears from her eyes. "This is almost too much good news...too much." She gave Megan a warm look of gratitude. "I wish they'd had a woman in every Marine company that has been out here. Since you've come, so many things have changed for the better." Gripping Megan's hand, she whispered in an unsteady voice, "Thank you, dear friend. Thank you...."

* * *

By the time Megan arrived back at the compound with Buck in the lead Humvee, it was chow time. Dusk was setting in, the sky pink along the horizon of the mighty Hindu Kush Mountains. It looked so beautiful and serene, yet Megan knew as she climbed out of the vehicle that the mountains were alive with roving bands of the enemy. And they lived to kill infidels, whether American or European. It was a sobering reality. She sniffed the air.

"Pizza!" she called out, grinning over at Buck.

"It shore is! I've been dreamin' of it all day long. Let's saddle up and get to the chow hall or there won't be any left for us."

As she entered the busy chow hall, Megan spotted Luke at their usual corner table. She waved to him and he waved back. Getting in line in back of Buck, Megan saw the power pizza had on the company. The Marines were devouring it like a starving wolf pack. The laughter and noise were higher tonight, much more so than on other nights. She moved through the line, and the cook put half a pizza on her tray. She thanked him and threaded her way through the packed confines to find a seat opposite Luke.

"Happy group," she noted, sitting down and smiling over at him. "You're the most popular guy in the company right now." She spread the paper napkin across her utilities and picked up a steaming wedge of pizza.

"Hey, that's what scroungers are. We make life better out here on the frontier," he said as he chortled. How beautiful Megan looked. Her face was soft and open. He liked the soft sprinkling of pale freckles across her nose and cheeks. Her red hair was once more in a ponytail, and nothing could hide the joy in her sparkling blue eyes.

"In my heart, you're *my* hero, Luke. The looks on these guys' faces is priceless. Everyone is homesick and you were able to give them a gift, a memory of better times." The words *I love you* nearly tore out of her mouth. It would have been an unfortunate slip. Shocked, Megan gulped. Where on earth had that come from? Shaken by her own impulses, she dodged Luke's warm gaze and forced herself to concentrate on eating her pizza. Her heart tumbled with anxiety and hope. For now, she had to keep this burgeoning secret to herself.

"You okay?" Luke asked, wiping his hands off on the napkin. "The pizza taste okay?" Or maybe she was still upset over the injured children?

"Er...yes, the pizza's fine."

"You're surprised about something?"

Flicking a glance across the table at him, she saw he was truly concerned. Panic ate at her. After their talk at Bagram, she couldn't let Luke know her growing feelings for him. "It's nothing," she managed. "I'm okay."

Luke looked around the noisy chow hall and grinned. "I think everyone's okay tonight. A momentary respite from war."

"Pizza is powerful," she managed in a joking tone. And then she met his merry gaze. "Have you told them you brought chocolate, vanilla and strawberry ice cream for them, too?"

"No way!" He grinned mischievously and leaned forward. "Listen, if these grunts knew there were fifty gallons of ice cream, they'd have torn the lock off the freezer and eaten it in a heartbeat. Fortunately, the chief put a guard on the refer—just in case." He chuckled.

Megan laughed. "Surely, someone knows about it."

"Yeah, Chief Gustafson, the head cook, knows. When we were unloading the stuff out of the helo, I pulled him aside. I told him there were three cardboard boxes that I'd written *fish sticks* on so that he'd know there was ice cream in them."

"You're a real fox, Collier."

"A scrounger's middle name," he agreed, and drowned in her husky laughter. The ache to touch Megan's smooth cheek, to follow the curve of her jaw and trail his fingers down her slender neck, ate at him. Luke sat back and wiped his mouth with the napkin. "It always pays to be a fox."

Joy filtered through Megan as she ate her pizza. Never had she heard so much laughter in the chow hall. Her heart warmed because all these men had loved ones at home. They missed them as much as she missed her own family. This wasn't a place where pizza could be found. Giving Luke a tender look, she said, "You're one of a kind, Luke, and I'm really glad you're here with me."

Luke nodded and didn't say much. Marines sat on either side of them. Her praise was enough under the circumstances. "Hey, let's take the gummy bear vitamin boxes over to your clinic tomorrow morning. The kids are gonna love 'em."

"I've already got the boxes stacked over at Mina's house. Buck helped me bring all the supplies into my clinic today."

"Those kids…I wish I could see their faces tomorrow morning when you start handing out bottles of gummy bear vitamins. Those kids will *want* those vitamins every day, without fail."

"No joke. I'm going to have to tell the mothers to

hide the bottles somewhere or they'll want to eat them all in a day's time. Every kid loves candy and sweets."

Chuckling, Luke agreed. "I'll be holding a clinic in the other part of the village tomorrow for the fathers and sons." Children age six and under were always taken by the mothers to Megan. Children who were seven and up were split up. The sons went with fathers to start learning how to till the soil, grow food and find wood for the fire. The girls stayed at their mothers' sides, wearing a head scarf for the first time in their lives. They would learn the intricacies of home and hearth.

"I'm sure my clinic will be the talk of the village by nightfall," Megan said.

"You'll be the go-to gal for gummy bears, no doubt. You'll be an overnight sensation."

Grinning, she said, "And if it wasn't for you haranguing that chief at the hospital supply depot, we wouldn't even have gummy bear vitamins to hand out." Her heart opened as Luke looked suddenly shy. Megan began to realize he didn't see what he did as special. But it was. Scroungers worked behind the scenes and without orders for the things they wanted to get. It was a military black market, for sure, but every company had such an entrepreneurial individual. Luke had given the story of the children of Lar Sholtan to the fifty-year-old medical Navy chief and he'd softened the man's heart. In the end, Luke was given enough boxes of gummy bears to keep every child in this village in vitamins for a year. And Megan knew those vitamins would make a difference.

Luke was a true hero. Megan's heart soared with sudden, nearly overwhelming desire for him. The only luck she had had was being assigned to his hut. She might not be able to kiss him, share her growing love for him, but at least she was *near* him. It was enough under these dangerous circumstances.

Chapter 8

"Stay safe out there!" Megan called as Luke opened the door. Dawn had chased away the night. This morning, he was scheduled to go out with a search-and-destroy team to scour the east slope of the mountain. It was a daily and dangerous job because the enemy hid among the thousands of large gray boulders. By day they hid from roving Marine patrols and by night, they fired grenades into the compound. Last night had been no exception, and Megan had spent half the night huddled in one of the many bunkers along with other Marines. She felt a twinge of sadness. Had it been three weeks since they'd shared that day at Bagram? Since then, Megan had settled into the rhythm of the company.

Luke turned, medic bag slung over his left shoulder. "Promise." Megan looked tired, shadows beneath her eyes. But who didn't? She had yet to wrap her hair into a ponytail. The urge to slide his fingers through that crimson mass was real. No one else was in their hut, and it would be easy to do. Yet at what cost? Neither was willing to push the relationship because of the circumstances. Giving her a half smile, he asked, "Are you staying in the compound today?"

"Yes. I'll be holding clinic at 0800." Megan sat down on the cot and pulled on a pair of clean, thick green socks.

"Wish I could be with you."

"I do, too. Please be careful out there, Luke...."

"Always." He saw the Marine squad assembling near the gate and the two Humvees. "Are you going to see Mina today?"

Shaking her head, Megan pulled on her boots. "No, she's gone across the mountain to Jabbar Gholam's village to talk with her friend Tahira. Her husband sent two of his soldiers to protect her. She said she'd be back in a week. I guess the way across the mountain is rugged and hard."

"Not to mention over ten thousand feet in nothing but boulders, gravel and scree." He made a face. "And that's where we'll be today, hunting Gholam's soldiers."

An unusual coldness crept through Megan. She sat up and gave him a tender look. "I'll keep you and the guys in my prayers today."

He blew her a kiss. "Good thoughts count. See you later."

Megan felt the warmth in the house disappear after Luke left. She busied herself with her pack, forcing her mind on the clinic. As she hefted her pack across her left shoulder, she wished she had kissed Luke goodbye. Megan hurried out the door and shut it, the chill seeping into her jacket. The noise of two Humvees filled the air. They left the compound.

Another Marine squad was mounting up in a truck, and two more Humvees went to search the road to the village for IEDs. It was always dangerous work. Looking to her right as she headed to the small clinic near HQ, she noticed Luke's squad in Humvees heading across a flat plain toward the massive rocky slopes of the mountain to the east.

Would Gholam's soldiers be up there waiting for them? *Yes.* Captain Hall had verified Gholam was working with al-Qaeda operatives—fellow Pakistanis. He was now on the wanted list. Hall felt the tribal leader was responsible for the attacks on the compound. He had planned for weeks to find and kill him.

"Hey, Doc!"

Halting, Megan turned toward the call. A short, stocky young Marine, a private first class, trotted up to her. On his jacket was his last name: James, R. "Yes?"

"You holding clinic this morning?"

"Headed that way. Why?"

The Marine fell in step with her. "Doc, I've got one hell of a toothache."

"No dentist here, but I'll see what I can do." Field medics were trained across a broad spectrum of medical and dental issues.

"Is there a dental team scheduled to come out here?"

She saw him rub his swollen left jaw. "No, but I can make the request to Captain Hall after I examine you."

"Could you? Because this sucker's been hurtin' me for five days now."

Megan felt for him. The clinic door was locked. She fished the key out of her pocket and pushed the wooden door open. There were three other Marines waiting in line.

Luke had the clinic laid out very well. She quickly

got out of her jacket, kept the Kevlar vest on and pulled a crinkled white jacket over her shoulders. In no time, the Marines had stepped inside. Another Marine, Marty, a lance corporal, appeared. He nodded in her direction and then took a seat at the front behind a desk. The lance corporal would log in each Marine patient—name, rank, symptoms—and keep things in order.

Looping the stethoscope around her neck, Megan grabbed a blood pressure cuff and gestured to James to come and sit on a chair next to a gurney.

"I know the drill," James said with a lopsided grin. He took off his jacket and exposed his burly right arm so she could wrap the blood pressure cuff around it.

"Good to know," Megan answered with a smile. She held a hand thermometer and placed a clean plastic glove over the tip. After James sat down, she pressed it gently into his left ear. She wrote down the temperature, then took his blood pressure and listened to his heart and lungs. Hands covered with protective gloves, Megan leaned closer and gently examined the right side of his jaw.

"Hurt?" she asked.

"It might if Doc Collier was rootin' around," James said, glancing up at her. "But a woman's touch definitely makes it feel better."

Megan was used to such teasing. "Open your mouth, James," she instructed. Peering into it, she saw how swollen the gum had become around the rotten molar. As she pressed her gloved fingers against the whitened gum line, she saw discharge ooze from the gum. "That has to hurt," she said in apology. Megan removed her fingers. "Relax, James. Close your mouth." She picked up a clipboard, writing down her examination. Next, she wrote out a script.

"Man, what's that awful taste in my mouth?" James complained, rubbing his jaw and scowling up at her.

"Discharge, James. You've got an abscessed tooth that needs to be pulled. I'm going to put you on some serious antibiotics, give you a sick chit and you're going to take the day off."

"Okay, but are you gonna pull it?"

"No," Megan said, handing him the script. "But I am going to call in a dental team. The antibiotics will help you a lot. You're running a fever, too."

James nodded and kept gently massaging his jaw. "I feel like it." Brightening, he said, "It's really nice to have a woman medic around here. Thanks." He got up and moved to the front desk. James handed the prescription to Marty, who would fill it for him.

Megan walked back to her desk and picked up the radio. She called Lieutenant Speed on it and requested he get a dental team to fly in as soon as possible. Megan knew the dental teams were located at Bagram. She looked up to find five more Marines waiting patiently in line to be helped. It was going to be a busy day. There were one hundred and forty men and plenty of medical ailments could crop up among them. Grateful to be busy, Megan didn't want to worry about Luke out on the hunter-killer patrol.

Just then, Captain Hall entered the clinic. Everyone snapped to attention.

"At ease," Hall said, taking off his helmet. His gaze fell upon Megan. Walking over to her where she was examining another Marine, he said, "Good morning, Doc. How's clinic going?"

Megan wondered if the C.O. was checking up on her. She was never sure Hall really wanted her with the company. "Fine, sir. No problems."

Grunting, Hall looked around, a pleased look coming to his face. "Need anything?"

Grateful for his concern, Megan said, "Yes, sir. We need a dental team flown in here ASAP. I've got a Marine with a badly abscessed tooth and I already made the request to Lieutenant Speed."

"Okay, I'll see what I can do to hurry it through channels. We've been needing a dental team out here since we arrived two months ago."

"It would be a good idea to get them in here," Megan stressed.

Hall smiled a little and tapped his jaw. "I got a tooth that's on the fritz, so I'm behind your request."

She smiled in return. "Is it abscessing, sir? Do you want me to look at it?"

Shaking his head, Hall put the helmet back on his head. "No, I lost part of a filling, is all. I'll be okay."

"Yes, sir." Megan watched the tall, broad-shouldered officer stride out of the clinic. She had found out from Luke that Hall was a Navy Annapolis graduate, or ring knocker. He had the walk of a leader, there was no doubt.

Megan finished at the clinic a little before noon chow. She walked over to HQ. Most of the Marines were out scouring the countryside. About fifty remained within the compound to protect it from attack. Entering HQ, she saw Hall leaning over his X.O.'s desk, intently discussing something on a map. The radio chatter was intense. Frowning, Megan felt suddenly fearful. She heard the voice of Buck Payne come over the radio.

"Red Robin One, this is Red Robin Two. Over."

Hall grabbed the radio. "Red Robin One. Over."

"We've spotted at least ten Taliban heading up to

a cave about a thousand feet above us. All armed and on foot. Three are carrying grenade launchers. Over."

"Have you cleared the area below you? Over."

"Roger that. We've also cleared our flanks. Over."

"Engage, Red Robin Two. Over."

"Confirmed, Red Robin One. Out."

Megan saw Hall's face deepen with worry as he placed the radio on the wall shelf. He looked up and saw her standing there.

"Doc?"

Quickly moving forward, Megan handed him the results of her clinic. All the information on each man she'd seen would be placed in a computer. "Here's the list, sir."

"Thanks, Doc. Dismissed."

Megan nodded. "Yes, sir," she said, and left the HQ. She worriedly glanced up at the mountain to the east. She couldn't see anyone, but she saw a Marine sniper lying on the flat roof of another building within the compound, his scope aimed up at the slope near the snow line. Judging from the tension in several other Marines' faces, there was danger somewhere up there.

There was a sudden *whummmp* from the mountain. It echoed loudly across the valley. Gasping, Megan could see, even from this distance, a frightening amount of rock and dirt flying high into the air and down the slopes. What was it?

"Doc, you'd better get inside," James told her, pointing toward a bunker.

"What's going on?" she asked, trying to keep the anxiety out of her voice.

"There's gonna be one helluva standoff up there. Listen, you need to get to safety, okay?"

Megan nodded jerkily, adrenaline starting to thread

through her veins. Another huge explosion reverberated off the mountain. Marines were running for the compound walls and the four towers, rifles in hand.

Captain Hall emerged from HQ, binoculars trained on the slope high above them. His mouth was thinned. Megan turned and headed toward him.

"Sir? What's happening?"

Hall let the binoculars drop to his chest. "Firefight," he said grimly. Lifting a radio, he made a call requesting two Apache helicopters to come in and help the Marines on the mountain.

Watching the firefight, Megan squinted, hand shading her eyes. She could barely make out flashes of muzzle fire but couldn't hear the actual fight. Only the giant dust clouds hanging in the air above the area were proof they were engaged with the enemy. "What's going on?"

Hall pointed upward. "The Taliban is holed up in that cave. Sergeant Payne is dropping bags of C4 explosives into it to get the enemy to give up and come out. Those were the two explosions you heard."

"That C4 won't do the trick," Lieutenant Speed said, moving to stand alongside Hall. His hands were on his hips, his eyes narrowed on the firefight. "They'd rather die in hell and go to the promised heaven with their rewards waiting for them."

Gulping unsteadily, Megan had seen firefights before. And sometimes she had been caught in the midst of them. This one, however, was different. Luke was up there with the Marines. Her heart began to thunder in her chest and suddenly she realized just how much Luke really meant to her. It was one thing to have someone you cared for in combat. It was completely different to see it happening in live time and not on some television video on a news network. "What's going to happen, then?" she asked the grim-faced lieutenant.

"The Apaches are on their way. At that point, we'll order the squad out of the area and let the combat helicopters bury those bastards once and for all."

The radio at Hall's side exploded with yelling and screaming. Hall listened intently. "We're taking casualties," he warned his lieutenant.

Oh, God. No. Megan nearly whispered the words, tension thrumming through her. She knew Luke would be right in the middle of it. He was without protection and would be exposing himself in order to reach any wounded Marines beneath the heavy returning fire from the trapped Taliban. How she wished she could be at his side! She heard Captain Hall order Payne and his squad to retreat. He asked how many were wounded.

"Three, sir. One is—" More explosions followed.

Fingers pressed against her throat, Megan stopped a cry from escaping her mouth. The two Marine officers were completely focused on the slope of the mountain. They became even more somber.

"Sir," Megan said, turning to Hall, "can we call in medevac?" She knew it could not land up there on the slope where the firefight was taking place, but it could land down here, just outside the compound. At least she could prepare and help when the wounded were brought down off the slope.

"Yes," Hall said, gesturing to his lieutenant to make the call to Camp Bravo, the nearest CIA base that had a medical detachment.

Megan wanted to do more, but couldn't. Within twenty minutes, two heavily armed Apache combat helicopters appeared over the horizon. As they drew near, Megan wondered if they were from the Black Jaguar Squadron. She got her answer when Hall called the lead pilot and a woman's cool, steady voice answered.

While she was hanging on every word of the radio calls, it was apparent to Megan the Marine squad was out of the area where the Apaches would send in their Hellfire missiles.

"Cover your ears," Hall warned her.

Automatically, Megan pressed her hands to her sensitive ears and opened her mouth. That way, her ears would equalize any blasts and her eardrums would be protected. She saw thick white smoke belch from beneath the stubby wings of the first Apache as the missile was fired. There were thunderous, booming sounds echoing across the entire valley. The earth vibrated and shook powerfully around them. Megan had seen Apaches in action over in Iraq, but not this close. She wondered how the Marines were handling being close to those destructive missiles fired into the cave.

The second Apache swung in and fired off two more Hellfire missiles into the cave covered by huge, billowing dust clouds. Megan closed her eyes for a moment, wishing fervently for an end to all wars. There *had* to be a better way! Opening her eyes, she blinked back tears. The Apaches swung over the compound, their heavy rotors puncturing the air and hurting her ears.

Automatically, she lifted her hand and waved to them. They were close enough to see the two women in each cockpit. Megan could swear one lifted a gloved hand and waved back to her.

"Here comes medevac," Hall warned her sharply. "They'll land over there." He pointed to a huge, circular area at the south end of the compound. It was free of rocks and pebbles so the blades wouldn't kick up the gravel and hurl it skyward, injuring anyone standing nearby.

"Here comes the squad," the lieutenant called, pointing toward the lower gravel slope.

The dust swirled from two Humvees hightailing across the flat plain toward the compound. They would arrive in less than a minute. The medevac landed, the rotors sending up huge, billowing clouds of red dust flying in all directions, blotting out the helicopter.

Megan knew she'd be of more help to the struggling squad than waiting at the helo. Racing out the open gates, she tore across the road and headed directly toward the two Humvees that slammed on their brakes. Marines piled out of them. As she drew close, she saw to her horror that the three Marines were seriously injured. One had a leg nearly torn off. Shoving all her emotions deep down inside her, Megan spotted Luke helping to carry a wounded Marine out of the second vehicle. The entire front of his uniform was bloodied. She wasn't sure if he'd been hit or it was the blood of another Marine. He was holding a dressing to the other unconscious Marine's bloodied head.

Their eyes met for a second.

"Megan, keep that tourniquet tight on the other Marine's leg!" he yelled hoarsely.

Nodding, Megan shifted and spun to the right. Buck Payne and another Marine carried the third unconscious man between them. Their faces were grimy and covered with dust, sweat creating trails through it. Payne's eyes were black with rage as they hurried forward.

Megan spotted the tourniquet. It had come loose! Buck ordered the Marine to be laid on the ground. Falling to her knees next to the unconscious man, she quickly tightened the tourniquet in order to stop further blood loss.

"Hold it tight," Payne ordered her. "Hold on to it until we can get him on board the medevac."

Megan quickly moved as they hefted the Marine off the ground. She kept her hand tight on the strap. They moved in unison like a crab scuttling crosswise. She saw the other Marines from the squad. They were exhausted and the stress was clearly etched on every face. All of them had rips and tears in their trousers caused by the sharp, cutting stones.

They entered the swirling dust cloud, the rotors on the medevac always turning. They were a target and had to keep the blades moving at liftoff speed. Battling the gusts of wind, the dust blinding their sight, they managed to move each Marine into the medevac. Megan worked with a medic on board to stabilize the man who had almost lost his leg. The moment she'd placed the IV in the unconscious man's arm, the crew chief medic threw her a thumbs-up. Megan immediately climbed out of the helo and quickly escaped out of the roiling dust cloud. Very soon, Luke and Sergeant Payne came running out of the cloud, coughing, tears running down their dirty faces.

Within seconds, the medevac lifted off. More dirt and dust blew into the air. Megan turned and walked away, covering her watering eyes with her hands as she stumbled toward the gate. As the helicopter lifted vertically in the sky, the dust finally ceased. Megan turned to find Luke. He was coughing deeply, bent over and holding his chest with his hand. Moving over to him, Megan slid her hand across his back.

"Luke? Are you okay?" she called, leaning down, her face near his. She saw the dirt and dust in his hair, cloaking his bloodied utilities. His hands were bloody. What had happened up there?

"I'm okay," he gasped, straightening. Looking into her anxious blue eyes and seeing the care burning in them for him, Luke felt some of the horror slip away from within him. Just her one gentle touch on his back momentarily eased his shock.

"Your hands look like they went through a meat grinder. They have to be looked at. Come with me to the clinic. I'll get you fixed up."

Luke looked around at the other Marines in his squad. They were all dragging their butts, exhaustion plainly written across their tense, dirty faces. Reassured the rest of his men were all right, he turned to her. "Okay, let's go."

The clinic was closed and Megan opened it with shaking fingers. Adrenaline was still coursing through her. Luke looked like one of the walking wounded.

Opening the door, Luke stumbled in and went directly to the sink in the rear of the house. Megan had added chlorine to the water to ensure that it was free of bacteria. Luke dipped his bloody, cut hands beneath the faucet and ruthlessly scrubbed them with antibiotic soap. The entire basin was splattered with his blood and pink soap.

Megan held out a towel to him. "It looked rough up there," she murmured.

Taking the towel, Luke could feel pain beginning to seep into his hands. Adrenaline anesthetized wounds, making them numb for a while until it wore off. "It was."

"I'm so sorry about those Marines." She searched his darkened gaze and thought she saw tears in his eyes for a moment. Just a moment. He quickly wiped his hands on the towel, turning it bloody.

"It was a helluva fight," he told her wearily, allowing her to lead him to the chair next to the table. Luke noticed she already had her gloves on and had laid out all the medical items she'd need.

"Sit down," Megan urged gently, guiding him to the chair.

Sitting next to him, his first hand resting on the desk, Megan quickly assessed the many cuts. "How did you get all of these?" Some were one or two inches long. She carefully moved each of his fingers.

"Nothing's broken," he told her, leaning back, closing his eyes. Luke felt helpless and angry. "The three Marines got nailed with a grenade launcher fired from inside the cave. It blew them into the air. I saw the one Marine's leg nearly ripped off. I had to crawl between the cave and the squad to reach them."

Megan shook her head and filled a needle with lydocaine. "I doubt you'll feel this. Your flesh is so torn up...but this will deaden your hand so I can stitch the longer cuts closed." She swabbed his hands to kill any infection.

Nodding, Luke saw a bottle of water she had thoughtfully set nearby. The cap had already been removed. He grabbed it and eagerly gulped down the entire pint. He looked down at her as she placed antibiotic in the longer cuts. He ravenously took her in. Head down, strands of red hair falling against her temples... Luke needed her in this traumatic moment.

Without thinking, he lifted his other hand and slid it beneath her chin. He brushed his mouth against hers, not caring one bit if someone entered the clinic. All he wanted, all he needed, was Megan. She represented calm in a world gone mad around him. He could have died out there on that rocky slope this morning. Bullets had been screaming around him like a pack of angry hornets attacking him as he crawled to the injured and unconscious Marines. He'd been hit twice, but the Kevlar vest had saved his life. Now he'd have huge purple welts where the bullets had landed.

Her mouth was incredibly soft. Luke could taste sweetness. It was life, he realized, as he deepened their kiss, their mouths clinging hungrily to each other. Her breath was chaotic, and he felt her surprise. His fingers were numbed and he wanted desperately to feel the softness of her cheek and jaw. Strands of her hair held the faint scent of citrus in their strands, and it cleared the metallic stench of blood away from his nostrils.

He wanted to bury himself within her, to feel her soft, gentle arms around him as a counterpoint to the violence he'd just survived. Luke felt her melt against his searching mouth. *Oh, God, just give me peace. Peace.* Her lips slid along his, her moist breath pumping life into his tense body.

Suddenly, reality returned. If anyone saw them kissing, both of them would get court-martialed. Luke released her as suddenly as he'd taken her.

Megan sat back in shock as she stared at Luke. The predatory look in his eyes burned into her. She was at a loss for words. The suffering she saw in Luke's face rocked her. She wasn't prepared for the amount of grief she saw twisting through him.

"It's going to be all right, Luke," she soothed. "You're all right. You did the best you could. I want you to sit back. Relax. Just start taking some deep, slow breaths. You've been through hell, but you survived...."

Chapter 9

Dizzied and in shock over the sudden kiss, Megan stared at Luke. His face was grim, his eyes burning with need for her. The silence in the clinic was deafening. Her hands were enclosed around his. "Luke…" she whispered, anguish in her tone.

Luke couldn't stand the agony in Megan's expression. Her lips were parted, gleaming from their shared kiss. She hadn't pushed him away. If anything, she'd *wanted* contact with him as much as he had with her. "I'm not going to apologize," he told her in a rough tone. "I don't know what happened, Megan. One second I was caught up in the emotions of the firefight and the next…" His voice fell. Swallowing hard, he held her gaze. What did he see in her eyes? What was she feeling other than shock over his unexpected kiss? "No excuses," he added. "It's my fault. I did this. You didn't."

Looking toward the door, Megan whispered, "Luke, if we'd been caught—"

"I know. Captain Hall would throw the book at us. Something just came over me, Megan."

Shaken, she released his hand and finished stitching up the worst of the injuries on his left hand. "It's war," she said. Picking up some gauze she gently dabbed the cuts on his hand. The lydocaine had taken effect and she closed a two-inch cut on the back of his hand. Her voice trembled. "It's the damned war."

"This isn't your fault. This isn't about strength or weakness, Megan. It's about the stress of war and how it emotionally affects all of us. The firefight made me aware of my feelings for you. When you think you're going to die…" He raised his gaze and looked toward the low ceiling for a moment. "You get real clear with what's important to you." His eyes met hers and he said hoarsely, "I was up there scrambling in those rocks, the bullets flying around me. I wasn't sure if I could reach the Marine with the leg wound or not. All I could think about, all I could see, was your face, Megan. I just held it in front of me as I crawled and got to his side. When I started dragging him backward toward a huge boulder that would give us cover, I kept you, your incredibly blue eyes, in front of me." He shrugged wearily. "I didn't think we'd make it to safety, but we did."

Megan forced herself to focus on the stitches. "I hate war."

"So do I. So do most people. I don't know why civilians think we like war. We hate it. We're in the middle of it."

"We do our duty," Megan said as she stitched up two more long cuts. "We serve because we want to help not only the Marines, but the people of this village. We're trying in our own small way to help heal a terrible situation that doesn't have any clear answer."

Even though Luke couldn't feel her hands on his, he felt better simply because she was helping him. "There are no simple answers to war," he agreed, wiping his mouth.

The door opened and Sergeant Payne entered. "There you are. You doin' okay, Doc?"

Megan smiled up at the sergeant. "He looks like he's been crawling over cut glass, Buck."

Payne came over, scowled and studied Luke's hands, which were now stitched up. "Yeah, it was bad up there," he growled.

Megan wrapped each hand with a dressing. "It sounded awful to us down here. I couldn't see you, but we could see the explosions and dust." She glanced up at the sergeant. The man's face was dirty and sweaty. "Are you doing okay, Buck? Do you or any of the other Marines in your squad need medical attention?"

"No, we're okay. Doc Collier exposed himself to get to my Marines. He's the one who took the risks." Clapping Luke on the shoulder, he said, "Well done, Doc."

"Thanks, Buck." Luke held up his newly wrapped hands. The white dressing looked out of place against his dust-ridden uniform. "Good as new."

Nodding, Buck glanced over at Megan. "I'm very glad the Cap'n isn't letting you go out with us on these missions."

"I'm not complaining, Buck." She made an effort to smile, but failed. "We're short two medics with this company, anyway. At least with me around, you have two."

"Yes, and every one of us is *very* glad you're here." Buck gave her a grizzled smile. "Kinda nice to come back here and see a woman's face. New and different, for sure, but nice. I gotta get back to work. I just wanted to see if our Doc was okay."

"He's fine. I'm giving him a sick chit for twenty-four hours." When she saw Luke open his mouth to protest, her voice became firm. "Twenty-four hours, Collier. And don't argue or I'll write down forty-eight hours."

"She's gotcha by the short hairs." Buck chortled.

Luke nodded. "Yeah, it's the right thing to do," he said, studying his neatly wrapped hands.

"Get some protective gloves on them," Megan told him, getting up and putting away the medical supplies. "And I want you on antibiotics."

"I can get them," Luke said, standing as Buck disappeared out the door. They were alone once more. Turning, he saw Megan putting the supplies away in a small plastic box. "I wish we had time to talk," he told her apologetically.

"Me, too, but that's not going to happen. Now I'm worried about Taliban retaliation."

"Yes," he said, moving over to the locked drug cabinet. It was awkward finding the key in his pocket, but eventually, Luke got it.

"What happens after you have a major firefight?" Megan asked.

"Generally quiet for a day or two, and then, according to Hall's predecessor, the Taliban sneaks close and lobs grenades into our compound to get even. They're great on revenge."

Wrinkling her nose, Megan went to the sink and washed her hands with the antibacterial soap. "Great. Something to look forward to."

Luke took out a bottle and filled it with seven days'

worth of antibiotics. He then shut and locked the drug cabinet. "Did you have close combat like this in Iraq?"

"Not quite like this. Sometimes we got grenade attacks, but it's nothing like here." She looked around the neat, clean clinic. "Here, you're under threat and stress twenty-four hours a day. It never lets up."

Luke popped a pill into his mouth and washed it down with some bottled water. "Welcome to the land of post-traumatic stress disorder. Almost everyone will have symptoms by the time we leave here." He capped the bottle and shoved it into the large pocket of his utilities. "How did clinic go this morning? Were the grunts happy to see a woman instead of me?" He grinned.

"It went well. I had ten Marine patients."

"Hmm, that's a lot." Luke walked over to her but kept his distance. "Half of them probably came just to get your touch and care." He held her luminous gaze. How badly he wanted to kiss Megan once more. He'd tasted her soft and cherishing lips. "I don't blame them."

Megan made a sound of frustration. "Yes, some of them had some really lame excuses as to why they were showing up at clinic. I understood. When I worked in the rear at the medical facility, I saw how much a woman's touch meant to the men who were wounded. There's a magic that happens."

"It happened between us." Luke reached out and briefly touched her shoulder. "I didn't kiss you because I thought I was dying up there, Megan. I kissed you because I've been wanting to kiss you ever since we were at Bagram. We share something good. Do you feel it?" He waited because he was fearful of her answer.

"No, it's not just you," Megan admitted in a halting voice. She shrugged. "I'm afraid, Luke. I've got this same pattern with you as I did with that officer over in

Iraq. War is no place to try and establish a relationship. I worry we're drawn to one another for all the wrong reasons." Megan gave him a frustrated look. "I—just need time."

"I'm going to give it to you," he said. "No more stolen kisses. The next time, Megan, if it's mutual, that's fine. But I'm not going to initiate a kiss like I did just now. Okay?" Luke saw instant relief replace the worry in her gaze.

"Good," she whispered. "Because I'm still adjusting to all the demands on myself out here. I know I'm not safe in that village. I have a lot on my mind when I'm working with the mothers and children. I worry about a Taliban soldier coming in and shooting me point-blank in the head."

Luke hurt for her but remained where he was. "I understand" was all he could tell her in a quiet voice. "You're on the front lines now, no longer behind them."

"I was trained for this," she said a little more strongly. "And I accept it without reservation." Her voice fell. "I—I just didn't expect to meet or fall for you, Luke. Relationships were *not* on my mind when I volunteered for this experiment. And I want to carry my part of the load and *not* mess it up for the other women. General Stevenson warned us as a group not to get into a personal relationship out here." Mouth quirking, Megan said unhappily, "And I agreed with her. We all did. Now, I'm messing it up and there's no *way* I'm going to hurt this experiment because I'm attracted to you."

"That's where you need to be," Luke agreed. "We can't get distracted."

"Or worse, others wounded or killed." She stared at him.

Grimly, Luke nodded. "Agreed. I'll be responsible

from here on out, Megan. I promise. I'll appreciate you when we work together, but no more stolen moments."

Relief swept through Megan. "Good…thanks." She looked at her watch. "It's chow time. Let's go eat, because tomorrow afternoon, my cousin and her husband are flying in. And I've got to get ready for clinic in the village tomorrow morning."

"Mina, that's wonderful news!" Megan reached out and hugged the woman. Just as Megan opened up the women's clinic at 0800, Mina had ridden in on a very tired bay horse, all smiles. She had been gone five days and had first stopped to share the good news with her husband. Gholam had agreed to allow the boys and girls of the villages beneath Timor Khan's rule to be educated.

With a laugh, Mina hugged her back. They stood in the clinic with the line of women and children waiting patiently for Megan. "This is a great day for our people," she said, pushing dark hair away from her cheek. She smoothed the green silk scarf across her head. "Now, we must have tea and talk after you close the clinic."

Looking at her watch, Megan said, "Yes, I think I can. Sergeant Payne is driving over to pick me up at 1300…I mean, 1:00 p.m." Her cousin Emma was flying in at 1500 and she wanted to be back at the compound to meet her.

Nodding, Mina said, "I'll have your favorite tea waiting for you in our house." Her eyes sparkled with happiness and she reached out and squeezed Megan's arm. "Thank you for *all* your help!"

For the rest of the morning, Megan walked on air. Luke had bet Megan a box of chocolates that Gholam would never concede to educating both the boys and girls of his village. Luke now owed her that box and her mouth watered just thinking about it. By noon, she had completed her medical duties. Closing and locking the door to the clinic, she walked next door to Timor and Mina's home. She stepped inside and was surrounded with the fragrance of lamb and delicious spices filling the air. She hurried up the stairs to the second floor and saw Mina in a dark brown robe with a gold scarf across her head.

"Just in time!" Mina said, gesturing for her to sit down at the table.

"Busy day," Megan said with a smile, pushing the scarf off her head so that it lay around the shoulders of her uniform.

"And a good one." Mina poured the fragrant tea and sat down. "On my ride back here, I had many days to think, Megan. I know the four widows are helping you, but we need a way for them to make money in order to feed their children. The people of the village give what they can, but I was wondering if you had any ideas that might help. I know that Khalid Shaheen has a charity and he and your cousin donate educational supplies and teachers."

Nodding, Megan sipped the hot tea. "Funny, I was thinking about this very same thing, Mina. My cousin, Emma Shaheen, said that they're enlarging a new program where women who want to learn to knit and crochet can create scarves, cloaks and sweaters for their worldwide catalog. Emma said they're selling the wool goods these women create on the web. They're being bought so fast they can't keep up with the demand. The women who do the work get eighty percent of the money."

Mina's eyebrows rose with surprise. "We are thinking along the same lines. What will it take to teach the widows? They, in turn, can teach the other women in our villages."

"Yes, it's a good plan. From what Emma was saying, someone teaches the women to knit. And they only have a few teachers and they're in high demand. There are a lot of villages in Afghanistan waiting for these instructors to fly in and teach them." Mina frowned. "But I know how to knit and crochet. I could take some time and teach them myself. I could get the patterns from Emma and they can start making them sooner."

"What about the wool?" Mina asked, worried. "We don't have many sheep. We have goats and cattle."

Sipping the tea, Megan said, "Let me talk to Luke. Maybe he knows where we could lay our hands on the supplies we need."

"He is an amazing person," Mina agreed. Her expression grew merry. "And you two are well suited to one another."

Megan wanted to tamp down any romantic suggestions. "We do work well together. And we're both field medics and we share a love of helping others."

Mina shrugged and said nothing, but the knowing smile remained on her face. "And how much will this cost us? Do you know?"

"I don't. I'll ask him tonight."

"And don't forget to tell him he owes you a box of chocolates."

Laughing heartily, Megan said, "Oh, not to worry. That's the *first* thing he's going to hear about when I get back to the compound."

Megan's spirits lifted as a CH-47 bearing Emma and Kahlid Shaheen arrived midafternoon. The helo landed, throwing up dust in all directions. Hall had ordered Marines to be on guard for against Taliban soldiers lobbing grenade launchers at the helo on the ground. To Megan's surprise, her family members brought a lot of supplies with them. In minutes, Marines gathered to help the two loadmasters clear the pallets out of the belly of the bird. Then, the helicopter pulled up its rear ramp and promptly took off. Out of the billowing dust clouds walked red-haired Emma and her tall, handsome Apache combat pilot husband, Captain Khalid Shaheen. He wore a dark green U.S. Army uniform and she wore a light blue one, denoting her civilian status.

Hurrying forward, Megan opened her arms as Emma rushed toward her.

"Hey!" Emma said, hugging her. "It's so good to see you, cousin!"

Laughing, Megan released Emma and grinned. "You two are a sight for sore eyes! That's smart of you to get that helo out of here. You must have had a backup crew?"

Emma pushed her hair away from her face, her helmet tucked beneath her left arm. "We have two BJS women pilots at the controls."

Khalid came over and hugged Emma, as well. "Good to see you, Megan. How are you hanging in here?" He smiled as he released her.

"By our fingernails," she joked.

Khalid scowled and studied the mountains around them. "This is a very dangerous place for all of you," he agreed.

"Come on, Captain Hall is waiting for you," Megan urged, grasping Emma's hand. "The C.O. asked that Luke Collier, our other medic, be present, as well as the X.O., Lieutenant Speed, and Sergeant Payne."

"The more the merrier," Emma said, slipping her arm around Megan's waist. They quickly moved from one end of the compound to the other.

Inside HQ, Hall shook Emma's and Khalid's hands. There were enough chairs for everyone to sit around the rough-hewn picnic table that served as their strategy area. Megan felt good that she was placed next to Luke. When Emma and Khalid noticed his bandaged hands, they simply nodded a hello to him. The C.O. and X.O. sat at either end with Buck Payne seated next to Megan. A lance corporal served them hot coffee in tin mugs. In the background, the chatter of radios was nonstop. Megan almost felt soothed by the sound. There were two more squads out patrolling the area.

Hall had a notebook and pen in front of him. He focused on Emma and Khalid. "Thanks for taking the time to fly out here. What can you do for us?"

Khalid leaned forward. "The pallets we've brought in today, Captain Hall, contain wooden desks, textbooks and supplies for the children of Lar Sholtan." He grinned. "We added some boxes of candy, of course."

Hall smiled and nodded as he scribbled notes. "Sounds good. What else?"

Emma took over. "Captain, a *jirga* must be convened with Timor Khan and the other elders. "You *must* make it clear that the education is for boys *and* girls. If the *jirga* wants only boys educated and not the girls, we'll refuse to help. You will provide information about the services we'll give to the village through our charity. If the *jirga* approves, we will have a male teacher fly out here once a building is found for a classroom."

Megan sat back, silently agreeing. The Taliban wanted no girl or woman educated. It was dead wrong. By educating the women, they would have a chance to throw off the shackles of imprisonment because they would realize a bigger, better world was out there.

She glanced at Luke. He'd changed clothes, his face was scrubbed clean and his hair was dark and still damp from a recent shower.

Her heart swelled with a powerful emotion that caught her off guard. He was a true hero, a man who had selflessly put his life on the line to save wounded Marines. She'd just received information from Bagram via radio that all three Marines would live. One Marine had lost his leg. That, she'd expected. At least he had his life, and Luke had given him that chance. A fierce new emotion flooded her. How badly she wanted to love this heroic medic. He was a self-effacing man, never talking about how he risked his life for others. She'd heard Buck talking to Captain Hall about putting him up for a medal.

Lieutenant Sean Speed spoke up. "I'll see to it Timor Khan gets a *jirga* together in the next few days, if possible."

Khalid nodded. "Good. You'll have a lot of material to present to the elders. I'm hoping they won't knee jerk on the girls being educated, as well."

"Makes all of us," Hall growled.

"And," Khalid said, "there are some boxes the Marines are going to like. They have come from America through our charity. Different women's groups in the States have been baking cookies for about two weeks. They call it the Cookie Surge."

Payne grinned and rubbed his hands together. "Hey, that's pretty decent, Captain Shaheen. I know my men will like them. Thank you."

Hall beamed. "Hell, Buck, you better put a guard on

those items or we're going to have a hundred and forty Marines tearing into those boxes and chowing down."

"Yes, sir, I already thought of that," Payne said. "Of course, I have to be concerned about the guards filchin' the cookies, too."

Emma laughed. "Not to worry, sergeant. Each box contains one dozen cookies. With a hundred and fifty boxes, each Marine will get a box."

"Mighty smart of you, ma'am," Buck said. "I just can't let word get out about these cookies."

Everyone agreed with laughter.

Megan saw Emma studying Luke and then her from across the table. There was curiosity in her eyes. Megan desperately wanted to talk to her about her feelings for Luke. Maybe she would have some words of wisdom on how to handle this attraction that was eating through her.

"What's going on between you and Luke?" Emma asked as they walked slowly around the compound after the meeting.

"God, am I *that* obvious?" Megan groaned.

Emma smiled gently at her. She raised her hand and touched Megan's shoulder. "No, it's nothing obvious, but, hey, you're my cousin. And we've got the same blood running through our veins."

"I'm trying hard to *not* let anyone know I like Luke."

"You're doing a better job of it than he is." Emma laughed as she released Megan's shoulder and they continued their slow walk.

"I don't know what to do, Emma. I never came out here on this assignment to fall for a guy. I mean, I really believe in General Stevenson's idea."

"I know. I didn't expect to be drawn to Khalid, either." Shrugging, Emma said, "It just happens. It's not like you or I were looking for a man."

"No," Megan said, frustrated. "But we're in a 24/7 wartime situation. This relationship can't escalate."

"Right on. You have to just put it on hold." Emma cast a quick glance over at Megan, who walked with her head hung, worry in her face. "Your secret is safe with me."

"Do you think your husband knows?"

"Doubtful." Emma laughed. "You know how men are. He's smart and I love him dearly, but guys just do not see the subtle signs and pick up on them like a woman does."

"I hope you're right," Megan said, worried.

"But it has to be a special hell on you, cousin."

Halting, Megan lifted her head and stared at the mountain to the east. She told Emma how Luke had risked his life to save three Marines. Her cousin's freckled face reacted grimly as she finished the story. "I stood down here knowing there was a firefight going on. Luke was up in the thick of it. That's what field medics do—we risk our lives to save the guys around us. It's part of our job." Opening her hands, Megan whispered, "But damn, Emma, I found myself wanting to cry. I could *feel* Luke. I swear, I still can. And I knew the danger he was in. For a while, I thought he was going to die." She cocked her head and stared over at her cousin. "Am I crazy, Emma?" She touched her heart. "I've *never* felt for a man like I feel for Luke. And on top of it all, I could feel him, his emotions and the danger he was in. I stood there feeling so helpless...."

"You know, there's a real psychic streak that runs through the Trayhern family. It's alive and well in you, Megan. Your dad has always had strong psychic intuition. More so than Uncle Morgan. My mother has it real strong and so do I."

"Do you feel Khalid when he's in trouble?"

"Every time," Emma deadpanned. "And you're right—it's a special hell to feel the man you love is in danger or trouble. And I'm sitting back at the villa in Kabul or I'm out at Camp Bravo when it happens. He's an Apache pilot, Megan. He's always in danger. The Taliban would love nothing more than to take down one of those combat helos."

"I know," Megan said sadly. She reached out and squeezed her cousin's hand. "How do you handle your psychic premonitions?"

"Not well," Emma said, squeezing her fingers. "I want to cry. I want to scream. If I'm at Camp Bravo, I run over to Ops and listen to the radio chatter, trying to find out where Khalid is flying and what's going on. It's worse when I'm at our home in Kabul. I have no way of knowing. I have to wait, and that's a special hell for me."

"It's awful." Megan glared at the mountain. "I've never experienced this before. Luke could have been killed." She pushed her hands through her loose hair. "It's hard enough liking the guy."

"You 'like' Luke? Or you love him?"

Megan looked up at the blue sky. Her heart contracted with fear. "I can't love him, Emma. You know about my history with relationships."

"I do." She turned and stared out across the valley. Megan joined her. Lifting her chin, Emma looked over at her cousin. "You just met, but you know, when I saw Khalid, I instantly fell in love with him. I fought it like a tiger, but no matter what I did, I couldn't avoid it. Love just happens, Megan."

"It can't happen here," she insisted, pointing to the red, dusty ground beneath their boots.

Emma snorted. "I don't think you have any control over it. I tried to hate Khalid, but in the end, I surrendered to the fact I love him. I didn't want to love anyone in a war zone. Who does? They can get killed in a heartbeat. I'd lost my first love to a war. I simply did not want to fall in love with Khalid because he could get killed, too."

"He still can," Megan reminded her sourly. "So how do you handle this, Emma? My emotions are all over the place. I can't allow my feelings to interfere. It's not fair to everyone else. I'm here to save lives, not lose them."

"When we had to fly together, I focused my mind on my job. I know you do that, Megan. It's just in the off-hours, the time when nothing is happening, that's the hard part."

"I have no one to talk to. I don't dare."

"No, you don't dare." Worried, Emma turned and looked at her cousin. "Listen, you have me. I'll be out here at least once a month if the *jirga* approves the education for their kids. We can get together." She placed her hand on Megan's slumped shoulder. "Trayherns stick together. I'm here for you."

"He kissed me this morning," Megan said, giving her cousin an anxious glance. "It was driven by Luke nearly losing his life, I know that."

"Listen to me," Emma said in a stern undertone. "It's going to happen. You are in a war zone. And because you love one another—"

"I don't love him. I can't."

Emma shook her head. "Look, I played the same head game with Khalid. I told myself it was an infatuation. It would be here today, gone tomorrow. I avoided using the word *love* like the plague. But the truth was, I loved Khalid. And there wasn't a damn thing I could do about it."

Tears jammed into Megan's eyes. She turned away so no one could see her. Emma's hand was on her shoulder and she tried to choke back a sob. Frustrated that tears leaked out of her tightly shut eyes, Megan angrily swiped them away. She fought for control. "This is all wrong!"

Gently, Emma reassured her. "Love doesn't realize you're in a war zone. It just happens. You and Luke are aware you're attracted to one another. And you're doing the right thing by putting a lid on it." Patting her shoulders, she added softly, "You're both strong people. You'll do the right things for the right reasons. And one day, this mission will be over and you'll get shipped back stateside, where you can pursue how you feel toward one another. That's as good as it gets."

Sniffing, Megan lifted her head. She took one more swipe and brushed the rest of her tears off her cheeks. "You're right," she said, her voice rough with unshed tears. "I didn't come out here to fall in love with Luke. And that's what I feel for him if I stop lying to myself, Emma. I do love him. The feelings for him just double every day. We sleep together in the same hut. I see him all the time except when he's out on a mission. I just feel so torn up inside…I wish the pain would stop, but it won't."

"It's not going to be easy." Emma placed her hands on her hips and looked around the busy compound. "Our helo will be coming back in about ten minutes and we've got to saddle up. "You got it under control?"

"Of course." Megan lifted her head and took a deep, ragged breath. "I'm a Trayhern. We might be emotional saps, but when it comes to duty, we'll be there toeing the line. Don't worry, okay?"

"You'll be okay," Emma said, "because you are a Trayhern."

Megan smiled. "Thanks for being here, Emma. I'm sure going to look forward to those monthly visits from you."

"Me, too," Emma said, reaching out to touch her shoulder.

Megan recalled the conversation with Mina and asked her cousin about the knitting and crochet teachers.

"We're in flux on this program," Emma said. "We're really strapped for finding women teachers who will fly around to different villages to teach the women who want to learn."

"What if I taught the women of Lar Sholtan?"

"That would be helpful, but right now Khalid is having problems finding the needles and wool."

"What if I could get Luke to scrounge them up? Would you bring the patterns with you the next time you fly in? Maybe together, we can jump-start the project here?"

Emma brightened. "That would be great. We're shorthanded, too. I'm juggling so many balls up in the air right now. Our education charity has taken off and I'm always scrambling. Khalid is going to hire an assistant, but that hasn't happened yet."

"I hear you," Megan said, nodding. "I'll stay in touch with you on this, then. If Luke can find the supplies, I'll call you."

"Great, because it's a terrific program, Megan. We just are suffering right now from lack of people to carry it forward."

Hugging Emma, she said, "You're amazing. Thank you."

"It's what we do for one another. Women stick together." Emma heard the helicopter coming in and saw a black speck up in the sky. "Speaking of tough women, I want you to meet Captain Aylin Sahin. She's from Istanbul, the first woman in the military to be taught how to fly an Apache combat helo. She's a force to be reckoned with." She grinned widely. "I thought I was hell on wheels as a combat pilot, but Aylin put all of us to shame."

"She's Turkish?"

"Yes. Her father is a general in the Air Force, and he got her into this program because she's been flying since she was sixteen. Women there are leading the charge for being in the military even though it's a Muslim country. I want you to meet her, if but for a moment."

"I'd like that." Megan turned and saw Khalid coming out of the HQ. Luke was with him and so was Sergeant Payne. Her heart skipped a beat as she gazed a bit longer at Luke. To everyone else, he looked like just another Marine in the company. But he wasn't. He was a true hero. And her hero. Overwhelmed by her emotions, her love, Megan felt her heart open wide to this man. She admired his broad shoulders and how he walked with confidence born from experience. His face was ruggedly handsome and she vibrantly recalled the unexpected kiss they'd shared earlier. She had to look away. No one could know how she felt. He couldn't know she was falling in love with him. Not now. Gently, Megan tucked those secrets away. She had a job to do here and she was going to make General Stevenson proud of her.

Sacrifice was something Megan understood by being

in the military. And now she was going to put her love on hold. No matter what happened, she had to treat him like she would anyone else. A new strength flowed through her as she stood and watched the CH-47 hover and begin to land within the compound. Grateful for Emma's presence, words and experiences, Megan knew she was strong enough to handle anything that this valley could throw at her. Anything.

Chapter 10

Megan stood back as Captain Aylin Sahin stepped out of the CH-47. It was an hour before sunset, the sun dipping behind the western mountains. Emma had been right about the Turkish Apache combat pilot: she was not only beautiful, but formidable. There wasn't much time. Her red-haired cousin slipped into the pilot's seat of the massive transport helicopter.

For a moment, Megan appreciated the tall foreign pilot. Most combat pilots were under six feet, and Sahin fit those guidelines—just barely. The olive-green one-piece Army flight suit and Kevlar did little to hide her statuesque figure. Most of all, the Turkish pilot exuded confidence. Megan couldn't get close enough to see much else as more supplies and boxes were swiftly unloaded from the rear opening of the CH-47 by two loadmasters. Tension thrummed through the air.

Luke came up beside Megan. "Who is that?"

"Captain Aylin Sahin. She's the Turkish pilot who flies with the Black Jaguar Squadron. It's an all-woman squadron formed by General Maya Stevenson."

Nodding, Luke tried to ignore Megan's nearness. "She looks powerful."

"Right on. I wouldn't want to meet her up in the air, would you?"

Chuckling, Luke watched the pilot reenter the rear of the helo after the last pallet had been removed. "No, she looks like an eagle."

"Emma was telling me her last name in Turkish means 'falcon.'" She gave him a warm look. "You're pretty astute, Collier." She saw him grin.

"Sometimes."

"How are your hands doing? Are you in much pain?"

He lifted his bandaged hands encased with latex gloves. "I take ibuprofen and they're fine. I'd like to get rid of the dressings, though. The grunts are giving me hell about wearing them."

"Hey, you're cannon fodder on that one." She laughed. "Do they call you Mittens, I wonder?"

"Yeah," he said as he chortled, "and worse. Things I would never repeat to you."

"Well," she said drily, "tell them you're lucky you're not pulling an exam to check their prostate today."

He doubled over with laughter, hands on his knees for a moment. Straightening, he said, "You have a wicked sense of humor." He felt his heart expand with joy as she smiled wide. Her eyes sparkled. It was one more reason to like her.

"Yeah, I think it comes with the territory, don't you? We see so much suffering, deal with so many trauma-tized men, women and children, we have to blow it off somehow."

"You're right. You picked that philosophy up real fast in Iraq, I bet?"

"Yes." Megan glanced over at him. Every time she met his warm gaze, an ache began in her lower body. Luke affected her deeply, though he couldn't know it. Still, Megan allowed herself to feel the pleasure and happiness he stirred within her.

"They're taking off," Luke warned her.

Both of them quickly walked away as the rotors whirled faster and faster, stirring up the dust clouds once again. They headed for the clinic. A number of Marines were carrying boxes of supplies into the clinic's open door.

"What's on your agenda for the rest of the day?" he asked.

"Being company medic. You can't work with those hands. At least, not for twenty-four hours."

Grimacing, Luke nodded. "You're right. I feel helpless and I don't like it at all." He brightened. "Hey, I just heard from some of the grunts who came to your clinic this morning. They had nothing but praise for you."

"That's nice. Do you think they said that because I'm a woman?" Giving him a slight grin, she added, "I don't think they go around talking about you in the same way."

Luke chuckled. "The guys like having a woman around. It reminds them of home, their spouses. And you have to admit, a woman's touch is nice in a grungy, godforsaken place like this."

Megan couldn't argue. "Well, looks like we got about six Marines waiting to see us." She slowed her stride as they reached the door. The Marines had brought in all the boxes from the helicopter. Megan thanked each of them. Some were bashful. Others grinned. Some blushed. It might be odd for Marine companies not to have women in their ranks, but over in Iraq, she was used to having men and women working around her at the forward medical facility.

Luke did what he could to help Megan. His wrapped hands felt like bulky oven mitts. It was frustrating in one way, but in another, he got to see the young Marines react to her beauty and kindness. When he held clinic, the Marines were coarse and macho. Today, as he moved some medicine around in the cabinet, he witnessed them being docile, smiling and even hesitant. Megan's natural beauty, her sweet smile and gentle touch turned these warriors into plowshares right before his eyes. Luke enjoyed watching the interactions. He knew the power of touch. And when someone was sick, that touch could make all the difference in the world. The rough-and-tumble Marines were on their best behavior toward Megan, even though she was completely professional.

Within an hour, the clinic was empty. Luke came over and sat at the desk where she stood. "Any serious ailments today?"

"No, little stuff. Allergies, upset tummy and a migraine."

"I like days like this," he said wistfully, looking toward the opened door. "Nothing critical."

"I know what you mean. When I was in the forward medical base, we always got Marines and Army soldiers who were horribly wounded. It was insane and stressful. I liked it, but some of the other nurses and doctors didn't. I think best when all hell is breaking loose around me."

Luke gave her an admiring look. "That's why you're

a field medic. We operate under fire—under life-and-death situations."

"It's different being out here," Megan said, turning and sitting on the gurney opposite Luke. For a few minutes, she just wanted to share time and space with him. That much they could do. As she saw the desire banked in his eyes, she knew he was remembering their earlier kiss. So was she. Megan had to keep moving her gaze from his strong mouth up to his eyes. That mouth had sent bolts of heat through her. He knew how to kiss. He knew how to pleasure a woman.

"Are you unhappy that Captain Hall isn't allowing you to go out with the squads?"

She shrugged. "Not really. I think I can help hold down the fort here when you go on patrol. I mean," she said, gesturing around the quiet hut, "we're short two medics. You're working triple duty and there's no one to go out on patrol except you. And I really worry for you out there. You're exposed every day to firefights." It upped his chances of being wounded or killed, but she bit back that logic.

"Listen, you can't worry about me. I was here in Afghanistan for two years before this. I was going out on Humvee patrols and foot patrols in Helmand Province every third or fourth day. None of the Marine companies has enough medics. So many of them have been wounded or killed in the line of duty. He smiled at her. "I've survived two tours without any wounds." And then added sourly, "Except for these mitts on my hands. Really, can't you remove them?"

"No way," she growled. "I'll remove the dressings tomorrow morning and see how they're doing. You know all those cuts have to be protected from the dust and dirt around here. You'll wear the dressing until those cuts close. Sanitation isn't lost on you, Collier."

"You're such a spunky little thing," he teased, melting beneath her gaze.

"Wimps don't join the military." Megan sat up and rolled her shoulders to get rid of the tension in them. "I'm a Trayhern. And just because I didn't elect to become an officer in the Navy after graduation doesn't mean I'm wimpy."

"No, you're courageous," Luke told her, giving her a long, hard look. "If you were a nurse officer, you could have had a cushy, safe job in a hospital or medical unit far behind the lines. Instead, you chose to become a field medic and get out there on the front lines where combat is guaranteed."

"I wanted my time to count. I wanted to do something to help others." Slipping off the gurney, she pulled the stethoscope from around her neck and set it on the desk. There were plenty of boxes to be opened and supplies to be put away. Luke could assist, but with his hands bandaged, he would need her help.

When they were done putting away the supplies, they walked over to the chow hall. Dusk was deep on the horizon and Megan saw the last of a pink watercolor wash outlining the massive peaks west of the valley. It was a beautiful but deadly scene. Inside, they got their food and found a table with several other Marines. Luke sat opposite her at the end of the table.

"Hey," she said, buttering the roll, "I need your help on another project."

"What's up?" Luke treasured the moments with Megan. He didn't care where the time was spent. Getting to be with her was what counted.

Megan told Luke about the idea of teaching the widows of the village and any other women who wanted to learn how to knit and crochet. She filled him in on Emma and their project. Megan stirred the spaghetti on her aluminum tray with her fork as she talked between bites. The noise in the chow hall was always loud. She noticed the Marines nearest to them were politely listening. Megan didn't care if they overheard the conversation. After all, Luke was the company scrounger.

Shrugging, Luke said between bites, "I've been asked to get a lot of things, but never knitting and crocheting needles." Grinning, he saw her face scrunch up with worry, so he said, "I'll see what I can do."

"What about yarn?"

"I don't know yet, but let me scout out some possibilities."

"You can really do this?"

His heart expanded beneath the hope in her husky voice. More than anything, he absorbed her respect of him. "No promises, Megan, but I'll make some calls from HQ and see what I can find."

"I don't think there are many knitting needles to be found in Afghanistan," she said.

Chuckling, Luke said, "No, I don't think so."

"Hey," the Marine private next to Luke said, "my sister is a knitter. She makes all kinds of things. And she's the president of her local knitting club."

"Good to know," Luke said. "But I think I have to go after bigger fish than your sister, Bates."

The young Marine with short brown hair grinned lopsidedly. "Well, if you're going to scrounge that kind of stuff, how about a Nintendo 3DS for me?"

"In your dreams, Bates," Luke growled. "You know they aren't allowed here."

Shrugging, the blue-eyed Marine grinned. "I can ask."

"That you can," Luke agreed, then smiled over at Megan. He saw the tenderness in her eyes—toward him. He'd give anything to kiss her once more. But that just couldn't happen.

"Hey," Bates said, "we're holding a Texas Hold'em tournament over at my hut. You coming over to play?"

"No," Luke said. "Got some calls to make."

Megan knew Luke was well liked in the company. Most medics were seen as demigods among the Marines. They saved lives. She had seen Bates yesterday for a fever. He looked normal tonight. "Luke is going to show me how to play Scrabble."

Bates rolled his eyes. "Scrabble?" He stared over at the medic as if he'd suddenly grown two horns in his head. "You'd trade that kids' game for poker, Collier? What's got into you?"

"Now, you know I hold Scrabble tournaments, Bates. Just because there's no money involved doesn't mean it isn't a good competition." Luke patted the young Marine on his thick shoulder. "Just think, you could improve your language skills in English."

"I'll take a poker game and let the aces talk to me." Bates turned to Megan. "You're in trouble," he warned her. "This dude thinks a monthly Scrabble game lifts our company's language skills and our spirits."

Brightening, Luke said, "Well, I'm changing some of the rules, Bates. At the end of this month, I'm going to hold another tournament. And there's no money involved, but I managed to get my hands on an iPod that has a thousand songs in it." The Marine's eyes lit up in response. "So, if you're the winner, you get the iPod. How about that?"

Bates was clearly excited about the possibility. His face glowed with the idea of winning the iPod. "Can anyone enter?"

"Of course." Luke preened. "Captain Hall likes the idea. He says it improves everyone's English because Scrabble is about words and word building."

"I like your giving away an iPod. I'll tell the guys tonight at the poker tournament."

"Bet you don't have an iPod to give away, do you?"

Grinning, Bates slapped Luke on the back. "No, I don't. But we use pennies. You're still invited." And then he looked over at Megan. "Do you play poker?"

Megan shook her head. "No. Not one of my strong suits, Bates."

"Well, you're invited."

"Thanks, that's very sweet of you, but I think with an iPod for a prize, I'm going to let Luke show me the finer points of Scrabble tonight. I could use a thousand songs." If Megan could read the Marine correctly, he'd finally decided to offer her an invitation out of duty. No need. She was sure if she showed up in a crowded hut with forty Marines, they would bristle. Such tournaments were a way for the men to blow off stress, and their cursing would turn the air blue. If present, she would have a decidedly dampening effect on them. Poker had unique healing abilities.

Bates nodded. He wiped his mouth with the napkin and eased up to his feet. "I'll tell the guys, Doc."

"You do that," Luke said, grinning.

Megan watched the lanky Marine leave. She smiled fondly over at Luke. "How did you get an iPod?"

"Trade secret," he murmured, digging into the green beans on his tray. "Scroungers never give up their sources."

Laughing, Megan said, "So, you're really are going to teach me Scrabble after you make your secret phone calls over at HQ?"

"Sure. Want to?"

"You bet. I want to win the iPod. I lost mine in transit between Iraq and here. I love music and really wouldn't mind having one."

Luke set the Scrabble board on the table. There were no windows in the hut, so he used a small battery-powered lantern with just enough light to shed upon the immediate area. Megan sat down on one side of the table and he on the other. "Now, you have to draw seven square tiles from this black bag." He held it up for her. "Place those squares toward you on the wooden rack so you see the alphabet letter on it. Don't ever show them to anyone else."

Megan loved the glimmer of competition in his eyes. If anyone came back from the poker game, they would find them playing a harmless game. That would not arouse suspicion. "Okay." She took the bag and pulled out the tiles. Setting them on the rack, she asked, "Do you think your contacts can get the knitting needles or yarn?"

"Maybe," he said, frowning. "I don't normally get orders like yours." He picked his tiles from the bag and set it aside.

"I think you're amazing, Luke. Everyone loves you."

"Oh, I think *love* is a little strong," he protested with a chuckle. "The guys know I can usually come up with what they need. And I like doing it. Anything to make this year survivable."

Megan nodded. "Now what?"

Luke handed her the bag. "Pick a tile. Then lay it

faceup on the board. Whoever has drawn a letter closer
to *A* gets to go first."

Their fingers touched as Luke handed her the bag.
Megan felt like a thirsty sponge, absorbing the unexpected and momentary touch. "Okay," she said, choos-
ing one.

Luke chose a tile. "Let's turn them up." He laid his
on the table. In the lantern light, Megan's face was shadowed. When she'd come back to the hut, she'd released
her ponytail, her hair falling softly around her features.
The light emphasized her large eyes, which were filled
with intensity. As his gaze fell to her mouth, he felt himself go tight with longing.

"Ah, I got a *C!*" she crowed, pointing to his tile that
had an *R* on it. "I go first?"

"Indeed you do," Luke said. "Create a word with
your tiles and lay it here, in the center." He pointed to
the many squares on the colorful board.

Luke watched Megan's brow furrow as she studied
her tiles. The way her mouth compressed for a moment
sent another wave of longing through him. He'd never
felt as he did for Megan, and it stymied him. What was
love? He thought he knew because of his love for Hope.
But this was different. Very different. He saw her give
him a triumphant look and she laid down four letters.

"Love?" He almost choked on the word, shocked.
Was Megan reading his mind?

Shrugging, she said, "Hey, I got a bunch of conso-
nants and only two vowels. What do you want me to
do?" She gave him a competitive grin.

He studied his tiles. "Okay, I just thought you were
teasing me." He glanced up to see her reaction. Megan
eyed him sadly for a moment. And then she brightened.

"It's the only word I could make, Luke. Sorry."

"I'm not sorry," he soothed. "I like what we have. Even if we can't get too close, we can be grateful to see each other every day. These grunts won't see their loved ones for a year, and that sucks."

Glumly, Megan agreed. "War does nothing but cause pain and suffering."

"No disagreement there." He laid down his tiles and created the word *van*.

Megan picked four more tiles from the black bag. "My heart bleeds for the people of Afghanistan. They're caught between their culture, this war and us."

"By the way," Luke said, "did you talk to Mina? I heard she got back to the village."

Megan leaned forward and smirked. "I almost forgot! You owe me a box of chocolates, Collier!"

Sitting back, he laughed. "You're kidding me!" How beautiful she was in that moment, the merriment in her eyes, her cheeks growing pink. He wanted to sift his fingers through her red hair but stopped himself from going there. "Really? The Taliban leader gave her the go-ahead to have the children taught?"

"Yep," Megan said, aching over his smile. "Pay up. I really am looking forward to those chocolates, Luke. How soon can you get them here?"

Groaning, he set the chair back on two legs, smiling. "Who woulda thunk? This teaches me not to bet with you, Trayhern. You're dangerous." Her eyes grew lustrous and Luke felt as if he could read her mind in that moment. She was dangerous to his heart and his body, and he found himself melting beneath her sultry look. He laid down the word *not*.

"Hey, I don't bet unless I think I can win." She chortled. Picking up her tiles, she laid them down to create the word *tame*. "Anyway, I love chocolates and I can't tell you how much I'm looking forward to getting a box of them from you."

"Well," Luke warned, setting the chair down on its four legs, "this will take some finesse. You know it gets over a hundred degrees during the day around here. I have to find some way to get the box of chocolates packed in dry ice so they don't melt into an unidentifiable blob by the time they reach you."

"I love See's candy," Megan hinted broadly, meeting his grin. "I especially love the coconut smothered in dark chocolate...."

"Now you're making me hungry."

Megan laughed softly. "Hey, I'm not trying to bust your buns, Collier. I just thought you'd like to know my preferences in case you can get exactly what I want."

Her teasing, husky voice rifled through him like sweet candy of another kind. Luke enjoyed her brashness, and his heart expanded with quiet joy. "Well," he said, "I'll see what I can do to rescue my good name as a scrounger for the company."

"Really," Megan said, getting more serious as she picked more tiles from the bag, "I'd much rather have you get the needles and yarn for the widows in the village."

Luke studied his tiles. "Not to worry. Scroungers can get anything." He created the word *error* on the board.

"This I gotta see to believe." She enjoyed the glimmer in his hazel eyes, which had taken on a gold tone in the low light.

"I deliver."

"I bet you do."

"Shall we get back to Scrabble and not wander off into forbidden territory?"

"Oh, I thought that's where we were."

"You're a real tease, Trayhern. You know that?"

"And you have such a way with words, Collier." Megan plunked down the next word, *tart*.

"It's hell keeping my hands off you," Luke said.

"I know. Same here."

"I wish we could get sent TDY to Bagram."

"Won't happen. We're shorthanded. No company can afford to have both its medics leave for TDY at the same time."

Luke nodded. He laid down the next word, *roar*. "So, were you a precocious child growing up, I wonder?"

"My mother would tell you I was a wallflower in comparison to my twin, Addy."

"What did you do as a wallflower?" He was hungry to know about Megan.

Shrugging, Megan pulled more tiles from the bag. "I was always the one reading, writing and drawing. I wasn't into sports like Addy was."

"You weren't competitive?"

"I'm competitive, just in a different way. I was quiet, like my dad." Her voice grew soft. "My mom says Dad and I are like twins. And yet he was a U.S. Coast Guard officer and skippered a ship. He saved so many people's lives during the course of his thirty-year career. My dad is a real hero. By his actions, he showed people what he was made of. I really like that about my dad. I'd like to think I came from the same mold." She laid down the word *tor*.

"It's called walking your talk." Luke raised his head and held her softened blue gaze. There was such strength in her at that moment. It was nothing obvious, but he could feel her confidence. Maybe it was that steel Trayhern genetic core he sensed.

"Absolutely. I'm not one to boast or tell other people about myself."

"We're opposites," Luke said, a smile curving his lips. He laid down the word *base* on the board. "In my family, I was firstborn. Julie, my sister, came three years later. I was always restless, talkative and curious. Julie is more introspective, introverted and quiet."

"Like me. I bet Julie and I would get along like a hermit crab in a shell." She laughed. "Did you get along with Julie?"

"We're close. I'm an extrovert, and I was into everything and everyone, and had an insatiable curiosity about life. Julie was very happy to remain in the background, take classical piano lessons and ballet and be in shadow status."

Pleased, Megan said, "Well, I'm not a pianist, although I have a decent voice. I love to sing when I'm alone." She saw the joy in his eyes. "Only in the shower," she warned. "I don't sing in front of anyone."

"Pity. You have a beautiful, cultured voice and I'll bet you're an alto."

"Yes, I am. My mother is a great singer, too. She sings in the local church choir. I always loved going to church because I got to sing."

"You ought to tell the chaplain. He holds services every Sunday and the grunts sing. I'm sure they'd like an angelic voice like yours added to it."

"Oh, no," Megan said quickly. She laid down the word *barter* on the board. "Remember? I'm shy. I like living in the background. I don't like being out front or drawing attention to myself. I prefer to just quietly do what I do best."

"Well," Luke said, his voice lowering with feeling, "I wish I could give you my attention."

Remembering his hard, searching kiss, Megan hesitated and was held enthralled by his dark look. Her throat went dry and she couldn't think of anything to say. Without thinking, she reached over and grazed his hand with the dressing on it. "I know. So do I."

"This is a special hell on earth," Luke muttered. He wished he could have felt Megan's fingers, but the thick dressing and latex gloves prevented it.

"It is." Her voice softened. "But we have to persevere, Luke. If what we have is right and good, it's going to not only remain strong, but grow. My dad always said the test of time proves everything." Megan gave him a tender look. "And we're trapped in this together. Neither of us likes it, but we're adults and we'll accept it."

"I don't like being an adult. I'm like a kid trapped in an adult body."

Giggling, Megan said, "Oh, you may say that, Collier, but in my eyes, you're a real hero. You proved that the other day." Stopping herself from reaching out, Megan tucked her hands in her lap as she saw his eyes turn predator-like. Only, it was a man wanting his woman—in all ways.

Chapter 11

Where had a month flown? Megan had just handed out three different knitting patterns to ten women from the village. The sun was in the west, hanging above the sharp granite peaks. Hurriedly, Megan gathered up her supplies, waved goodbye to her protégées and opened the door to the street.

"Do you have a moment?" Mina called from the door of her home.

Megan didn't see the Humvee that Sergeant Payne and his men were using to come pick her up. "Yes, hold on." Megan spoke into the radio attached to the epaulet of her uniform. She called Buck and told him where to pick her up. Turning, Megan hurried back up the street to where Mina stood in her dark purple robe and scarf.

"I haven't seen you for a few days," Megan said by way of greeting as they went inside the home. The hundred-degree July heat was baking the valley.

"We've all been busy," Mina said. She went upstairs to the kitchen. "Come, I need to talk to you about something. It won't take long."

As she set her medic pack on a chair near the table, Megan noticed the teapot, cups and some sweets on a plate were already prepared. Mina seemed distracted. Megan wondered what was up as she sat down facing her at the table. "This is really nice. I love your sweets!"

Mina smiled. "I must say, it was very kind of you to share the box of chocolates that Luke gave to you. The women of my village have never tasted coconut and dark chocolate before."

Grinning, Megan held up her cup while Mina poured the tea into it. "It was a lot of fun. I liked winning that bet from Luke."

"You've been very, very good to us, Megan. And so have Luke and Captain Hall." Mina placed the teapot on an old, frayed pot holder near her left hand. "Now we have a teacher, we have a classroom and our children are expanding their minds. You come in twice a week and hold clinic, and so does Luke." She picked up her cup and sipped the steaming tea. "Timor and I have never seen our people so happy." Her eyes grew moist as she regarded Megan. "And I believe it is because of you. You are a woman in a man's world, and you are a positive force of nature who has come into our lives."

Feeling heat spread across her face, Megan gave her a sheepish look. "There are many people coming in to help your village, Mina. It isn't just me. I'm a tiny cog in a bigger wheel. It's true, my cousin Emma and her husband, Khalid, have done a lot for you. They are devoted to helping the villages along the border. They know how important it is to educate your children."

"True, true," Mina said. Her brows fell. "But you,

Megan, are like an angel who guards this village and our people. I'm not the only one who sees this. Timor holds you in high regard, too."

"That's wonderful," Megan said, surprised. She rarely saw the leader of the village because he was constantly riding from one of the four villages beneath his leadership by horseback to another. He was gone two weeks out of every month with his leader duties. Mina had a part-time husband as far as Megan was concerned. And when Timor was gone, Mina was in command. The people of this village loved her, and Megan could see why. She was an educated woman who adored her people as if they were her own children.

"Before Timor left to ride to the other three villages this morning, we had a very deep and important conversation," she murmured. Setting the cup down on the porcelain saucer, Mina folded her hands. "My husband and I are in total agreement about this."

Stymied, Megan tilted her head as she drank the tea. "What agreement?" She saw the Afghan woman's face become somber. Her full lips were pursed. "You need to go to Captain Hall," Mina began in a whisper, "and tell him Jabbar Gholam is coming over the eastern mountain to attack your Marine Company two days from now."

Megan sucked in a quick breath. "Oh, no."

"Wait," Mina demanded holding up her hand. "Timor and I agree you need the information to stop him. There is a warlord in Pakistan who has paid millions of dollars to raise an army of four hundred al-Qaeda soldiers who are coming across the border as I speak. They are gathering at Jabbar's village on the other side of the mountain. And then, tomorrow night at midnight, they are coming across on goat trails to attack your compound at first light."

Fear shot through Megan. She studied Mina's serious features. "A-are you sure, Mina?"

"I would stake my life on this, Megan. You must inform your captain. You must do something to drive back their attack."

Megan's heart raced with more fear. It would be a hundred and forty men against a massive enemy force of four hundred. Swallowing hard, she asked, "Why are you telling me this?"

Mina wrapped her slender hands around the fragile teacup. "Timor and I respect what the Americans are doing for our people. And he has already sent a messenger to Jabbar warning him and this Pakistan warlord not to attack the Marines. Our runner just returned this afternoon with the answer. Jabbar says he must attack. It cannot be stopped." Reaching out, Mina touched her hand. "Megan, you are like a daughter to me and Timor. The people of the village think you are an angel sent by Allah to protect us. We cannot, in good conscience, allow you or the Marines to be murdered by al-Qaeda."

Anxiety sizzled through Megan. "Okay, I believe you." She suddenly stood. "This isn't much warning. I have to get back to the company, Mina."

Rising to her feet, Mina nodded. "I understand. If Captain Hall wants any more information, I will be available to help. I know the route Jabbar is taking over the mountain. There are many trails. You will need to know which one he's taking."

Megan's mind ran in a hundred directions at once as she considered the information. "Yes, Captain Hall will absolutely need to know that."

Mina pulled a piece of folded paper from her pocket

and handed it to Megan. "Timor drew a map. We hope your captain will know where the attack is coming from." She sighed heavily. "We are sickened about the loss of life of all concerned."

Megan took the paper and opened it up. It was a very clear and detailed map of the east mountain. "I hate war," she muttered, stuffing the map in the pocket of her utilities.

"Yes," Mina said wearily, giving her a weak smile. "Life is precious. It should be honored, loved and cared for. Not brutally ripped from us. You need to go, my friend."

Picking up her pack, Megan went over and hugged Mina. The woman was tall and thin. Often, she had seen Mina give food from her home to the widows, who had so little. As a consequence, Mina was close to starvation. She always brought over MREs for Mina and the poor of the village so they wouldn't starve. "I'll be in touch. Thank you."

Luke sat beside Megan as Hall called in his sergeants for a strategy session. Within ten minutes, the sergeants arrived and sat down around the table. Knowing how anxious she must be, Luke wanted to reach out and hold her hand. Of course, he couldn't. Her beautiful mouth was compressed. Her hands were two knots pressed into her lap. If only he could tell her it was going to be all right, but this was a serious attack against the Marine company.

Hall launched into the details given to him by Megan. On a wall map, he outlined the trail that Timor had drawn to show the movement of the enemy at midnight. His voice was grim. "I've been on the radio with Bagram Air Base, Camp Bravo as well as Kabul.

We've got a drone specifically assigned to watch the east mountain. We'll be getting Apache combat helicopters provided by the Black Jaguar Squadron out of Camp Bravo. There will be B-52s coming in to drop five-hundred-pound bombs first on the mountain after the enemy is confirmed on the path." He tapped the map. "Heavy bombing is going to destroy a lot of them. After the bombing phase, we're sending in the Apache helicopters to finish them off. All the while, there will be a drone flying high above and we'll be receiving real-time info from Kabul headquarters at Bagram Air Base."

He turned and studied the attentive group. "Air Force jets will be on standby at Bagram in case there's any cleanup that the Apaches don't finish off. By the time dawn comes—" he tapped the watch on his wrist "—bodies are going to litter the slopes. There should be no one alive. And we're sure the enemy will run back over the mountain. If they do, the Apaches will meet them on the ridge and cut off their escape route. No one is returning to Pakistan."

"Sir," Buck asked, "what about the local militia leader, Gholam? He's got a village on the other side of that mountain. Can you bomb it back into the stone age, too?"

"No," Hall said. "One of the things Timor Khan requested of us was not to bomb Gholam's village." With a grimace, Hall added, "This is a political decision, Sergeant. Timor Khan has to live with this Taliban leader in his backyard. Khan is afraid if we destroy his village, the Pakistani warlord will launch another attack against us with his help. If, on the other hand, we merely destroy the al-Qaeda assault and leave the village alone, it sends a positive signal to Gholam. If he leaves us alone, we'll leave his village alone."

"Maybe Gholam will die," Payne said.

"Maybe. I don't know. I do know Khan is adamant we leave that village alone, and we will."

Clenching his fist, Payne drawled, "I'd like to get my hands on that bastard. He's done a lot of damage on this side of the mountain to us and Lar Sholtan."

Hall shrugged. "The Taliban isn't going away, Sergeant. It doesn't matter whether Gholam dies or not. Someone else will take his place. Khan feels Gholam can be worked with to a degree. He agreed to allow a teacher to come in and teach the boys and girls of Khan's villages."

"Sir," Luke asked, "where does the company come into this operation?"

"After sunrise and after all the aircraft and helicopters have finished with their work, I'll be sending two platoons up on the mountain. You'll be going with them, Doc." Hall pinned Megan with a look. "And you'll set up the clinic for casualties if there are firefights up on that mountain."

"Yes, sir," Megan said. A lump formed in her throat. Oh, God, Luke would be in the thick of it—again. She tried to sound unemotional and confident.

"There will be five medevacs on standby at Camp Bravo, a thirty-minute flight from here if we need them," Hall told her.

"Good to know."

"You don't anticipate firefights, sir?" Buck demanded.

"I expect something after that mountain is bombed, Buck. If there's no resistance, you need to capture the casualties, give them medical aid. On the dead ones, search for any maps and information our intel guys can use."

Nodding, Payne muttered, "There's gonna be fights. Guaranteed. These fanatics, if they could, would pick up their weapons and kill us even after they're dead."

A soft chuckle rippled around the table from the other sergeants. These battle-hardened vets had spent two, three or four tours in Afghanistan and knew the territory and the enemy.

"Lieutenant Speed and I are going to work throughout the night, and you sergeants will have orders for your platoons come tomorrow morning. I want everyone on the same page. This is a major engagement and it's the first time a village leader has turned over information like this to us. We're going to make sure their back is broken and Khan's villages along the border are safe."

"I want you to be safe out there," Megan whispered to Luke. They stood alone in their hut, darkness surrounding them. In less than thirty minutes, the B-52s would begin their bomb drop. She'd hurried over to the hut to retrieve her medical pack and walk to HQ. Everyone was gathered there because the drone far above them was sending live feed into Hall's laptop.

Luke risked everything and walked over to her. He could barely see her eyes and the worry banked in them. Outside, there was peak activity—platoons getting prepared for combat readiness. If the plans Hall made failed, there would be a bloody last stand at this compound. They could all die. And it pushed him to reach out and find her hand. He leaned over, his face inches from hers. "I'll be fine. It's you I worry about…."

His hand was strong and warm. Closing her eyes, Megan fought his powerful male nearness. "Luke, I keep fighting wanting you, wanting…more. I know it's wrong. But we could die before this night's over. Something could go wrong. I know that…I—"

His mouth curved across hers. Luke's breath was hot and moist against her cheek. Moaning softly, Megan said to hell with it. She threw her arms around his broad shoulders, pressed her body urgently against him. For a moment…just a moment, she wanted to drown herself, her heart, into Luke's mouth, hands and body. His fingers spanned her Kevlar vest, moved up to her shoulders and framed her face. He felt strong and confident. Megan thirstily absorbed the courage that came naturally to him. Lips moving against his, she breathed Luke into her body, starving for his touch, his kiss.

Luke felt dizzied by their spontaneous kiss. They stood in the dark of the hut, the air cold and chilling, the threat of death looming over them. Megan tasted of life, of honey, of promises fulfilled in his torrid dreams. Her fingers moved along his unshaven jaw and tangled in the short hair along his temples. The Kevlar and utilities were a wall between their yearning bodies. He moved his tongue across her lower lip. "I need you. I need you so damn bad I've never ached like I do now…." He plunged his tongue into her awaiting depths. Hearing her moan, her hips moving strongly against his own, Luke knew this could be the last time he'd ever have with Megan. Grateful for this stolen moment, he reluctantly tore his mouth from hers.

Megan moaned as she watched his narrowed eyes glittering like obsidian on a moonless night. She felt him tremble, his hands trapping her face, his eyes peering into her heart and soul. The words *I love you* were all but shouting in her head. Instead, Megan whispered,

"Come back safe and sound, Luke. That's all I'll ever need. Okay?"

Her emotional plea ripped through him. Luke felt his heart breaking with fear. Fear that he would die up on that slope. Sliding his fingers through her loose, silky hair, he leaned over and pressed small kisses across her wrinkled brow, her cheek damp as she cried—for them. For what could happen in a few hours if everything went wrong instead of right.

"I'll always be with you, Megan. Always." He lifted his mouth away from her lips, his gaze digging deeply into her. "You stay safe. I want to come back down off that mountain and see you here in one piece. No heroics, okay?"

"Oh, Luke…I want more time with you. I'm scared."

"So am I," he said huskily, grazing her cheek with his thumb. "We'll be scared together, Megan. We're connected here." He drew her palm against his Kevlar where his heart lay. "We're always in touch."

Swallowing against a painful lump forming in her throat, she whispered, "I never expected to get to kiss you again…."

"A stolen moment." He managed a pained smile, his finger beneath her stubborn chin. "There will be others. For now, we have to get through this night. One hour at a time. All right?"

"Yes, one hour at a time…."

Luke turned and left like a silent shadow. Megan was always amazed at his stealth, but then she found out he'd been with SEAL teams off and on in Afghanistan. On special missions where more than one medic was needed, he'd learned the art of stealth alongside them.

She touched her lips, knowing she had to get over

to the clinic and begin preparations she hoped they wouldn't need.

The night was dark and moonless. Megan stood outside the hut. She looked toward the unseen mountain to the east of the compound. If Mina and Timor hadn't given them the information, they would not know what was coming down a rocky path toward them right now. Her eyes adjusted to the blackness enough to see where she had to walk. She mentally thanked the courageous couple and continued toward the hut that would be her clinic to save lives. She prayed there would be no injured among the Marines. Tension was high. It felt as if the night would crack and shatter unexpectedly around her.

Luke stood inside the HQ huddled with a group of Marine sergeants. They watched and listened to Hall's laptop, which had the drone's real-time infrared pictures moving across the screen. Hall had projected the real-time video up on a wall so his sergeants could see what was going on. Luke stood silent, grimly watching an incredible number of soldiers skulking silently down across the slope. The mountain was twelve thousand feet tall, ragged-looking and nothing but rock and scree below ten thousand feet. The drone's pictures were so clear and sharp Luke could make out each man, the rifle he carried and the turban on his head. They were all bearded, and he saw most of them had a crisscross of bandoleers across their thin chests.

"We've got four hundred al-Qaeda on this side of the slope," Hall announced. He looked at his watch. "The B-52s will be on-station in five minutes." Glancing up, his taut face sweaty because the hut was stifling even at night, he growled, "Sergeants, take your men and get them into position on the walls and in the towers."

Luke moved aside as the four sergeants quietly left, rifles across their shoulders, faces painted with camouflage colors.

"Collier, does Trayhern have the clinic ready?"

"Yes, sir, she does. She'll stay there unless you need her elsewhere."

Hall nodded. "I'd give my right arm for two more medics right now."

He'd said it to no one in particular. Luke read his mind. The commanding officer was worried things could go wrong. No military plan ever went a hundred percent correctly. There were always accidents and screwups because humans and machines never functioned perfectly. He'd been in enough firefights and Taliban attacks to know Hall had a right to be concerned. This company of Marines was facing an overwhelming force. If the B-52 bombs went off target, it would leave a lot of them alive. And then they'd be like angry hornets, knowing they'd been set up for an attack, swarming down the mountain at the Marine compound. These men were fanatics and had no fear of dying.

Lieutenant Speed growled, "It takes ten Taliban to take down one Marine. If everything goes to hell in a handbasket, we're not outnumbered. We're even."

Grinning, Luke turned away so that worried Hall wouldn't see his smile. "I've been in situations similar to this," he told the X.O.

Speed looked up from the monitor. "And?"

"Marines kick ass, sir. No question."

Hall looked at them but said nothing, his mouth a thinned line.

"This is my first tour," Speed said. "That's good to know."

Luke knew this was Hall's first tour, too. It was clear

the C.O. was anxious as he watched the soldiers sneaking quietly down the switchback path that the goats used. "We were surrounded by six hundred Taliban in Helmand Province," he told them. "Two local Taliban leaders got money backing from probably the same warlord in Pakistan. We had two Marine companies dug in when they attacked. Only," he emphasized, "we had no warning it was going to happen."

Hall snapped a look across the table at Luke. "And?"

"It was an all-night battle, sir. The Air Force threw B-52s, fighter jets from Bagram at them, and the Army called every available Apache into the fight. When dawn came, we had five Marines dead, ten wounded, but we repulsed their charges. It was the single most damage done to the Taliban in that province." He met Hall's dark gaze. "And we only had four medics, sir. Not nearly enough. We were able to save lives that night."

"Glad you're here," Speed grunted. "Nice to hear this right now."

"Marines rock," Luke told them with a cool assurance. "Why do you think I like being with you grunts?" He gave them a teasing, wolfish grin. The Marine officers glanced at one another, smiled thinly and then nodded.

"Okay," Hall said softly, "here we go."

Lieutenant Speed quietly gave the order over the radio to the Marines that the B-52s had just begun to drop their load of bombs.

Luke moved outside. The air was cooler than inside the HQ. He listened but couldn't hear anything. The B-52s flew at forty thousand feet and could not be heard below. The bombs wouldn't be heard until they came closer to the drop zone on the darkened mountain. He'd seen B-52s drop their five-hundred-pound laser-aimed bombs before. First, the shriek of a whistle would be heard. And then the night would erupt into a hellish firestorm that would, if the bombs were accurate, take the lives of four hundred of the unseen enemy up on those blackened slopes.

He suddenly heard the piercing shriek of the bombs screaming through the night. Tensing, Luke stared hard at the mountain. Would the bombs hit their targets? If they didn't, all hell would break loose.

Chapter 12

When the bombs began hitting the mountain, Megan thought they looked like a string of fiery pearls dropping out of the black sky. She'd never experienced a B-52 raid before, and the ground shook, trembled and rolled continuously beneath her booted feet. She watched the fury of octopus-like arms of fire belching and leaping skyward. The red, yellow and orange arcs resembled a flower blossoming in the night. With each five-hundred-pound bomb landing, the ground continued to tremble. The booms reverberated across the valley like rolling thunder, hurting her sensitive ears.

As she turned, Megan's eyes had adjusted enough that she saw the Marines in position in the wooden towers above the compound. Lethal machine guns stuck out of each, aimed into the pit of night. All guards wore NVGs, night-vision goggles, which turned dark into green so they could spot anyone trying to sneak up to the compound. Tension thrummed through her as she gazed back at the mountain now on fire. The bombs kept coming. How many B-52s were on this raid? She had no idea. Yet the bombs seemed to be landing with deadly accuracy near the ten-thousand-foot line where year-round snow met scree and boulders.

Knowing Mina and her villagers were also watching this attack from their homes, she wondered how the woman was feeling. Mina had been anxious about giving her the information. And now it was killing a lot of Afghan and Pakistan men up on that mountain. Could she live with such knowledge? Megan shivered internally, arms wrapped around her body.

There was a lull. The last of the bombs exploded and the shaking stopped. The thunder finally rolled away, consumed by the thickness of the night. Now everything was still once more. Megan tried not to wonder how the enemy was fairing up on the slope. As badly as she felt for them as human beings, she also knew if they didn't stop this attack, they would all die in this compound by dawn.

The *thump, thump, thump* of Apache helicopters came into earshot. Megan turned and walked to the corner of the house, looking to the southwest. The Apaches were from the Black Jaguar Squadron. The thumping sound of the blades grew powerful, echoing between the mountains and the valley.

These helicopters had no flashing red or green lights. They were night predators of the finest sort. They had instrumentation and avionic night vision to see the infrared body heat of a human being or an animal.

The first two Apaches flew overhead. Megan looked up but saw nothing. The power of the helos was palpable. The air trembled around it. The Apaches would scan the mountain slope for warmth, indicating human life. And then they would begin their systematic destruction of anything still alive.

For the next twenty minutes, the mountain looked as if it were being assailed by red dots coming from the unseen combat helicopters. The red tracer bullets clearly showed where they were working. Megan stood transfixed. Because it gave her some protection, she remained with her back against the thick mud wall. The Kevlar chafed as it always did against her rib cage. It was a necessary protection.

"Megan?"

Luke's voice came out of the night.

Gasping, Megan jumped.

"Sorry," he murmured, appearing at her side, his hand on her arm. "I didn't mean to scare you."

"That's okay." Megan's heart thumped wildly in her chest. She could barely see Luke standing there, helmet on head, medic pack thrown across his broad shoulder.

Squeezing her arm, he whispered, "I just wanted to see how you were doing."

His hand dropped from her arm. Closing her eyes for a moment, she tried to steady her heart rate. "How is everyone?"

"Okay," he said in a low voice. Inches separated them. "I just got back from HQ. Those B-52s did a helluva job. They were right on target. Those Air Force boys know their stuff."

"It looked beautiful and deadly when they dropped. I feel sorry for those men. Maybe I shouldn't, but I do."

Luke nodded grimly. "Death is not why we're here. Medics see the world differently than a grunt does. Nothing to be ashamed of."

"The Apaches have been busy up there."

"Have they stopped the attack, do you think?"

"Captain Hall thinks so. The Apaches are communicating with him and Kabul at the same time. I think when dawn comes and we go up there, it's going to be a graveyard."

Shivering internally, Megan was grateful for his strong, steady presence. "I've never seen a B-52 raid before. It's awful. I wonder how Mina feels now."

"Probably torn up. She doesn't want bloodshed. By her giving us this intel, that's exactly what has happened."

"I feel so sorry for her...."

"That was your job. You made friends with her and she trusted you. General Stevenson made a good plan. You've become indispensable to Mina's village, and now she's protecting you and us against the Taliban and al-Qaeda."

"I wonder if she'll regret it tomorrow."

Luke shrugged. "I don't know. She sees what good you're doing for her people, for the women and children. Don't forget, Timor Khan also approved coming to us with this intel."

"Now I'm worried that if Jabbar Gholam has survived, he'll take out his revenge on Lar Sholtan." She searched Luke's face.

"Maybe. The enemies survive here in Afghanistan because of the villages accepting them with *Lokhay*. You feed the strangers who come into your village. I think Jabbar will think twice before taking revenge on Lar Sholtan."

"But he'll sure be wanting our heads. Literally."

"Yes. But he wanted them before this attack."

Megan didn't know how a man could hate so much that he would willingly kill men, women and children.

And that's exactly what al-Qaeda had done when its forces attacked the Twin Towers in New York City. War was not logical. It was fueled by hatred.

"You doing all right?" Luke asked. He studied her clean profile and noticed her lips were tense, as if to hold back emotions. How badly he wanted to protect her. He couldn't. Despite how he felt about Megan, she was a lot stronger than he'd realized. Megan came off as soft, gentle and quiet, but she had the Trayhern backbone of military steel.

"Yes. Just…mixed feelings, you know?"

There were tears in her voice even though he saw none in her eyes. "Medics live in a special hell," he agreed. "And tomorrow, when I go up there with those platoons, if I find a Taliban soldier alive, he'll be treated according to the Geneva Convention. It's my duty to try and save his life."

"Even though, if he has a chance, he'll try to kill you."

Sobering beneath her husky words, Luke said, "Yes. I can defend myself because I carry a weapon."

"I'm sure Sergeant Payne and his men will be watching your back like hawks." And how badly Megan wanted them to do just that! Her heart ached with tension and fear for his life. Without night-vision goggles on, no one could see her slip her hand into his, and Megan did just that. She felt the scars along the back of his hand. The stitches she'd sewn into the flesh of his palm were ridged but healing. Gently squeezing his long, strong fingers, she whispered, "I just want you to stay safe up there. No heroics like the other week, okay? Come back in one piece, Luke."

He lifted her hand to his lips and brushed his lips against her soft skin.

"Stop worrying. I'll be okay," he said. *Because I've got you to come home to. I love you.* He withheld those words he so badly wanted to share. These stolen moments fed his soul and soothed his yearning heart.

"I need to get back to HQ," he told her, regret in his tone.

"Thanks for visiting. It was nice, Luke…." Megan watched him disappear as quietly as he'd come. She forced herself to remain alert, even with her stormy emotions. The Apaches seemed to have completed their mission and were now flying back toward Camp Bravo. The night suddenly quieted.

It felt as if a heavy blanket or pall had been thrown over the area. Megan knew the Marines in the towers all had NVGs on and could pierce the darkness. They would remain on high alert until dawn. The radio on her shoulder crackled to life. Lieutenant Speed's voice came over it.

"All personnel, return to duty. Repeat, return to duty. Out."

Pushing away from the dirt wall, Megan took off her helmet and drew in a deep, ragged breath. The lieutenant's orders meant the assault on the enemy had been successful. She could go to bed. Her roommates would be coming to their hut.

She uncovered the leather flap to look at her watch: 0100. Dawn would come at 0530. Pushing the Velcro down on her watch to hide the faint radium light, Megan turned around and locked the clinic. She was grateful she wouldn't have to use it on this furious night of killing. She hurried across the flat, sandy soil for the unseen home where she could sleep.

What would dawn bring? Megan had never been on the front lines of combat before. And even though she had a year's training beneath her belt, this was all new to her. She felt destabilized.

Fierce night winds blew across the compound off the surrounding mountains. As she entered her home away from home, Megan's nerves bristled. She felt danger stalking them even though she couldn't identify what, exactly, it was.

This sense of instability, of turmoil, continued throughout the rest of the week.

Mina was depressed. The villagers had varying re-actions to the attack on the mountain. Megan heard the many remonstrations of the village wives who brought their children for help at the clinic. To Megan's relief, the platoons of Marines met no resistance. No one was injured, yet the carnage on the slopes was daunting.

The Marines knew the Muslim tradition of burying a dead person as soon as possible after death. The soldiers spent the day making cairn graves for four hundred deceased. It was a grim time for everyone. A Muslim chaplain from Bagram was flown in to help direct the Marines and pray for the souls of those buried.

"I'm worried," Mina confided over tea after the clinic closed. She studied Megan and frowned. "It has been five days since the attack and I've not heard from Tahira. I feel as if I should ride over there to see if she's all right. She's pregnant. I'm worried that Jabbar was killed in the bombing. She may need my help."

Megan nodded. "According to Luke, Jabbar was not found among the dead, Mina." She saw the woman's face show relief and then move into a fearful expres-sion. "They have a photo of Jabbar, and the Marines were looking specifically for him. They didn't find his body, so I'm assuming he's alive."

"That's good news for Tahira and the baby she carries."

"You seem frightened." Megan set the teacup down on the white china saucer. "What's wrong?"

"I worry about many things, my friend. Timor is on his way back to our village by horseback. Alone. He always rides his horse alone between all the villages he has responsibility for. I worry that if Jabbar survived, he'll know…he'll know Timor or I gave your Marines the information about the big attack." She looked out the dirty window for a moment. "I know Jabbar will blame Timor," Mina added in a strained tone. "Will he ambush him on the way home? Murder him in retaliation for working with the Marines?"

"Timor was found by our helicopters and was given the message of what happened on the mountain. He turned down the offer from the Marines to protect him from Gholam or his men. He felt he'd be safe. I know he's due back here in a couple of days." But Mina's worry seemed to escalate. "You still feel Gholam would attack Timor?" Megan asked.

"Yes. The Taliban punishes us swiftly if we work with Americans."

Megan reached out and touched the woman's hand. "Could I bring your concern to Captain Hall? Maybe something could be done to protect Timor."

"No…Timor knew the cost. This time, he put his people in front of his life. And he knows Jabbar could kill him."

More alarmed, Megan sat up. "What about you, Mina? Would Jabbar try to kill you?"

Giving a shrug, Mina said, "Maybe. I don't know."

"That's why the people are so on edge. I've seen it

in the women's eyes. The children are upset, too. They feel the threat."

"Yes, we're very agitated right now."

Frustrated, Megan said, "I'm going to tell Captain Hall. Maybe there's something he can do."

"Our village is surrounded by five-foot-high mud walls with only two entrances. Jabbar, if he's going to attack, must come in one way or the other. I think if Marines were in our village, that would infuriate him even more. We have men who have volunteered to stay awake and watch those gates. We're as safe as we can be."

Megan wanted to do more, but she had no ready answers. "I'm still going to tell Captain Hall, if that's okay with you."

"There's nothing he can do. We must wait. And watch…"

Megan was awakened by nearby explosions. It was the middle of the night. Everyone sleeping in the hut leaped up, alarmed. More explosions occurred, and the hut shivered. Bumping into one another, they grabbed their boots and shoved them on. Buck turned on a small battery-powered lamp.

"Something's under attack," he growled, reaching for his weapon and putting on his helmet. "But it's not us."

A sudden spasm of fear arced through Megan as she hurriedly grabbed her helmet and medic bag. Running, she followed the sergeant out the door. She skidded to a halt as she passed the house. In the distance there were explosions…in the village of Lar Sholtan.

"Oh, God," she cried out. "No!"

Luke caught up with her. "Come on, get out of the open!" He grabbed her by the arm and hauled her forward.

Megan ran quickly toward HQ. It was near dawn. There was bare light outlining the jagged peaks. Gasping for breath, she followed Luke. All the Marine sergeants were clustered and crowded into the office. Captain Hall looked as if he'd just awakened. The radios were squawking. Lieutenant Speed's voice carried over the tumult.

"Lar Sholtan is under attack!"

"Get the Apaches," Hall ordered.

"It's Gholam," Buck growled to no one in particular. "The bastard's attacking the village because they helped us stop that attack last week."

Megan bit back a sob. She was crowded into the confined space, glad to be leaning against Luke's strong body. "Can we help them?" she called out.

"Not until dawn," Hall said. "Sergeants Payne and Thornton, get your men mounted up on Humvees. Get that Stryker truck out in front to locate the IEDs. If Gholam is attacking the village, you can bet he's sure as hell mined the road to it with IEDs. Get moving!"

Megan stood there, eyes widening in terror. The people of the village had no way to protect themselves. Oh, some of the men had ancient rifles, but few bullets.

"Sir, I'm going with Sergeant Payne," Luke said.

"Yeah, get going, Doc," Hall said, harried by the different reports now coming in. He grabbed a radio and called Camp Bravo for Apache help.

It was going to be too late, Megan realized. Tears flooded her eyes as she recalled how terrified Mina was of reprisal. Pushing forward, Megan made her way to the table where the two Marine officers were intently studying the maps.

"Captain Hall," she called out, her voice strong and carrying above the radio chatter, "I'm going with Collier. Those people are going to need every available medic."

Barely glancing up, Hall said, "You're staying here, Doc. That's a firefight going on down there."

"Sir, I don't care. Those are people! They need help." She stared into his eyes. "I'm a medic. That's what I'm here for."

"Okay, get your butt out of here," Hall snapped. "And be damned careful, Trayhern. I don't need you getting nailed by a bullet or an IED."

"Yes, sir. Thank you, sir! Can you call in medevac?"

"We will once the attack has been pushed back," Hall told her. "Mount up!"

She hurried out of HQ. Running between buildings, she stopped and watched the village. She could hear gunfire. A lot of it. The explosions still rocked the area. Swallowing hard, Megan ran to the clinic and opened it. With unsteady hands, she packed more antibiotics, more dressings and bandages. After locking up the clinic, Megan ran as hard as she could toward the front gate of the compound.

In the bare dawn, a gray pall hung over the valley. She spotted Buck Payne standing next to the lead Humvee and went straight for it.

"Sergeant Payne. Do you have room for me?"

Buck turned and regarded Megan with a frown. "You going?"

"Yes. Captain Hall gave me permission." She was gasping, her heart pounding with fear.

"Okay, climb in. You hang close to me." He glanced toward the village, eyes narrowed on the firefight.

By the time they got to the village's blown gate, Megan could see everything. They had to stop twice for IEDs that had been hastily dug and planted along the only road to the village. Frantic to help, she peered out the windows as the Humvees crawled cautiously into the village. Many of the mud homes were burning. Fire lit up the dawn sky. Buck had his rifle locked and loaded. Everyone was on guard. Tension thrummed through the growling vehicle as they traversed the main dirt road heading toward Timor Khan's home.

Megan clenched and unclenched her hand. Her gaze locked on Timor and Mina's home, which appeared to be standing. People were screaming, some running alongside the Humvee, begging for help.

"Drop me at the clinic," Megan ordered the driver. "Get word out to the villagers that I'm here and can help."

"We'll drop both of you off there," Buck said. He told the driver to halt in front of the locked building.

Climbing out, Megan could smell the thick, choking smoke. A number of frightened people raced toward the clinic.

Buck ordered two of his Marines out of the vehicle. "Doc, you two are getting bodyguards. We don't know if Gholam is still in the village or not. His men could hide among the villagers and you won't be able to tell them apart. I can't let you remain here without protection."

"That's fine," Megan said, hurrying to the door and unlocking it. Glancing to the left, she noticed a family of four running toward them. In the arms of the terrified father was his unconscious young son. Luke pushed the door open and followed her in. They had no time to speak and instantly set up two aid stations in the room. Wounded, burned and injured men, women and children pressed through the doors.

Pulling on her protective latex gloves, Megan called

to the shocked villagers to line up. Very quickly, she and Luke moved through the twenty of them to triage the group. The children were crying and screaming. It was just like Iraq for Megan, when villagers would be wounded and brought by medevac to the combat hospital. She buried her emotions, focusing instead on saving innocent lives. Jabbar Gholam was a monster of another sort and more than willing to murder helpless, innocent people to get revenge. Choking on tears, Megan busied herself with saving lives.

Chapter 13

"Mina!" Megan called as she moved into the crowded medical clinic. Luke peeled off inside the door and went to one of the examination rooms. The place was overwhelmed with the injured and children crying over the attack.

Mina's eyes were filled with terror as Megan made her way to her side.

"Jabbar has struck," Mina said, quavering, standing beside Megan as she began to work over a young girl. "He's still here somewhere in the village. I'm trying to get my men to find him, but he's evasive." The woman straightened and looked at the two Marine guards standing alertly at the door to the clinic.

Megan's mouth tightened. "He's getting even. I'm so sorry, Mina. Have you been able to contact Timor?"

"No, it's impossible. He's on a circuit to his other three villages." Rubbing her forehead, Mina gathered her black robe more tightly around her body. "I don't know if Jabbar is waiting to kill him, capture him or what...."

Hearing the veiled terror in Mina's voice, Megan tried to focus her attention on the screaming child whose left arm and leg had been burned. "The Marines are in the village, Mina. Did Sergeant Payne get your permission to search for Gholam?"

"Yes, yes, he did." Mina anxiously watched the door. "They have a picture of Gholam. But he knows how to hide among us. I don't think the Marines will find him."

Megan glanced over and saw men and boys lining up to be helped by Luke. He was just as busy as she was. Megan quickly wrapped the child's reddened, blistered arm. "What is Gholam waiting for, then?"

"For Timor to return. He'll be on a rocky goat trail that only other Afghans know. It would be easy for Jabbar or his men to hide and attack him. I told Sergeant Payne the name of the village he's riding to right now. He said he'd try to find my husband to warn him about the attack."

Torn, Megan reached out for a moment and touched Mina's arm. "I just heard over the radio that Buck has called for an Apache helicopter to be sent to find him. They could easily spot him on the slope of the mountain and can tell us his whereabouts."

Mina bit her lower lip. "What if they don't find him?"

Megan knew that if they didn't, Gholam had found Timor himself, killed him and dispatched his body. More than likely, the horse would be saved and used by the Taliban. "God, I hope they locate your husband soon, Mina."

"How can I help? I've done everything I can for our people. I've told them to stay inside today. With Jabbar and his men sweeping through the area, there are people who are sympathetic to the Taliban. They will hide him from the Marines."

Grimly, Megan nodded. "Let's hope Buck and his men find him first." There was little else she could do or say. Mina left her side to talk to the parents and crying children to try and soothe them.

Glancing out the clinic door, Megan saw more and more injured people crowding around. She was glad Luke was with her. Buckling down, Megan worked without rest to help the wounded villagers.

As soon as the little girl was taken care of, a farmer, his face dark and in pain, sat on the gurney next. He was holding his bloody right hand. Megan turned and spoke into her epaulet radio. "Blue Boy One, this is Blue Boy Four. Over." She needed to call Captain Hall.

"Go, Blue Boy Four."

Hall's voice sounded grim. "Blue Boy One, we need medical backup here at the village. Can we get some medevacs in here? I've got forty villagers who are wounded. I have six cases that need to be flown to Bagram. Over."

"Roger, Blue Boy Four. I'll call. Out."

Relieved, Megan returned her attention to the thirty-year-old farmer. Megan knew the Marine retaliation had set the wheels of revenge in motion against these villagers. All these people wanted was to be able to grow their crops and get enough food for their families. She wanted to cry for them, but couldn't.

By the time noon rolled around, Megan and Luke had gotten the worst injuries stabilized. People weren't looking as worried or anxious as earlier. Wearily, Megan got a number of farmers to carry those who needed medical help at Bagram outdoors to the designated landing area. The medevacs would arrive shortly. Mina remained in the clinic with the widows as Megan led the men carrying the six litters outside the walls of the village. Luke got picked up by the Marines and was ordered to join the platoon for a patrol up on the slope of the eastern mountain.

There was a flat, clean landing area nearby. Megan spotted two medevac helos arriving, black dots against a blue sky. The sun felt good, easing the iciness she felt within.

When the first medevac helo landed, billowing yellow dust clouds erupted. For the next ten minutes, Megan worked with the crew to take three litters with injured on board. As soon as they were transferred, the door was shut and the helo quickly took off. Then the second medevac landed. The same hurry to land and transport the wounded took place.

The rolling clouds blinded Megan as the second medevac rose into the sky carrying the injured villagers. Choking and coughing, her eyes watering, she stumbled back. Once the litters had been transferred, the other villagers ran back behind the walls, no doubt aware that the American helicopters were targets of the Taliban.

Megan stood still, the clouds swirling violently around her. The blades of the helicopter made it impossible to see. She knew enough to wait as the helo lifted off. Good feelings threaded through her. They had been able to help those who had been severely wounded by Gholam.

Her heart and her thoughts turned to Luke in those moments. Was he all right?

The dust cleared. As she walked toward the walled gate, Megan glanced up at the mountain that had been on fire last night. The snowy peak thrust skyward into the light blue sky. Its blue granite flanks were so large and sprawling she couldn't see the Marine platoon that was somewhere up there. She said a quick prayer before trotting through the gate and hurrying to the clinic.

"We couldn't find Gholam in the village," Buck informed Megan. The Marine stood in the doorway of the emptied clinic.

"Is that good news?" Megan asked. She had two more men to examine and then she could go back to the Marine compound with the sergeant.

"I'm not sure," he drawled, studying the closed clinic door. "There are Taliban sympathizers here in this village."

"Mina was worried about that, too," Megan said, applying antibiotic to a man's right foot. Crouching down, she bandaged the wound. "Is the Marine platoon still up on the mountain?"

"Yeah."

"What have they been finding?"

"They're just keeping a presence on the mountain, that's all. It's a way to tell the Taliban we're here to stay. And if Gholam's still alive, it sends him a message he's not welcome on this side of it."

Megan grimaced. "I wish we knew where he was."

"Makes two of us," Buck said, resting the butt of his rifle on his left hip. "My gut tells me he's alive and well. Men like him are like starved wolves. They know how to survive anything."

"Is there any shooting up on that mountain?" She worried that snipers might be in place to pick off the Marines.

"No, it's quiet."

"That's good," Megan whispered.

"How about I come back at 1700 and pick you up?" Buck asked.

"That's fine. I've got two more patients." Glancing up, Megan pointed to several boxes in a corner. "The medevac brought me more supplies. I need time to unpack them and get them in the locked cabinets before I leave."

Nodding, the sergeant said, "Okay, I'm taking the two Marine guards I stationed here this morning and we're going to make one last search of the village for Gholam. We'll be back at 1700."

Megan finished helping her last patient and hurried to unpack the boxes of supplies. She had her medical bag sitting on the gurney next to the drug cabinet. Already, she'd refilled it with medical items. In a half hour, Buck would drive up in the Humvee.

The drugs were well packed. She automatically pulled morphine, several types of antibiotics and other medications and placed them in special compartments within her knapsack. Megan swiftly put the bottles back in alphabetical order on the shelves. *Done!* After locking the cabinet, she pocketed the key.

There was a sound behind her.

Frowning, Megan turned. And then gasped.

Standing in front of her, grinning, was Jabbar Gholam and two of his Taliban soldiers. Their weapons were pointed directly at her.

"You are Megan?" Jabbar demanded in Pashto.

Heart pounding, she stared into his black eyes. She recognized Gholam from the picture that had circulated yesterday. "Yes, I am," she returned in the same language.

His thin lips twitched beneath his fuzzy black beard.

"Come with us. Now." He pointed toward the rear door to the clinic. "And bring your medical bag."

Mind stunned with shock, Megan hesitated. Gholam was barely five feet five inches tall, thin and reminded her of a starving, angry dog. What should she do? What could she do? The rifles were pointed at her. She'd already put on her Kevlar, but her rifle was in the kitchen. Should she scream for Mina? It was doubtful the woman would hear her. And even if she did, Megan was afraid this dangerous Taliban leader would kill her, too.

"Pick up your bag," Gholam ordered impatiently.

"Where are you taking me?"

"You have no right to talk to me, woman." He jabbed a finger at her pack on the gurney. "Pick it up."

The icy rage in his guttural tone spurred Megan into action. "Okay," she said, grabbing the pack.

"Wear it."

Megan slid the straps of the medical bag across her shoulders. Terror moved through her. What was Gholam going to do with her? The eyes of the three men projected pure hatred. "Now what?"

"Come with me." Gholam gestured sharply toward the rear door.

Megan remained anchored to the spot.

"Move or I'll tell my men to shoot you where you stand."

The two soldiers prepared to shoot her.

"Okay," she said and headed toward the wooden door at the rear of the clinic.

Outside, the two soldiers grabbed her arms, hauling her toward a group of awaiting horses and two other soldiers. Shoved roughly, Megan was ordered to mount up on a scrawny bay horse. Her hands were tied tightly in front of her and she was attached to a long rope. It was handed to the leader. Gholam grinned unevenly as he moved his stallion close to the Megan's gelding.

"I hope you know how to ride, because we're going to move quickly." He glanced toward the opened gate that led out to the creek and valley. "One word, one cry for help, and the man riding behind you will shoot you in the head. Do you understand?"

Gripping the leather reins of the horse, Megan nodded. There were five men. Where had the horses come from? She didn't know. The sun was sliding behind the western mountains. Another man on a bay horse rode up beside her. He took out a curved knife and grabbed her shoulder, nearly unseating her. In seconds, he'd sliced the cord to her radio and ripped it off her shoulder.

"Let's go," Jabbar growled to his men. He turned his stallion around, laying his heels into the animal's flanks.

Megan was jerked forward as the gelding rapidly broke into a gallop. They made a mad dash though a back street of the village. Would anyone see her? Would they warn the Marines and let them know she was being kidnapped?

They rode hard out the gate, the horses pounding down a dirt road toward the slope of another mountain. Megan's mind whirled. Unfamiliar with the area, she could only cling to the saddle, her fingers entwined in the horse's long black mane. She hadn't ridden since she was a child, and the hard wooden saddle seat was harsh against her backside. Only the thin rope stirrups helped keep her on top of the fleeing horse.

Within fifteen minutes, the group was hidden by towering trees that followed the trickle of a stream between two larger hills. Gholam slowed his horse to a trot and they wove ever higher, the dirt path becoming narrower and rockier as they continuously climbed. Many times in the next hour, Megan nearly fell off her gelding as the animal slipped on the shale and loose gravel.

They rode into the night. Megan's hope of rescue died with the last of the light. Above, thousands of stars twinkled and observed her below. She had no idea where she was, only that the horses labored mightily along a path in the shadow of a mountain. The air had turned cold.

The soldiers never rested, and they whipped their horses to keep them moving. The animals were clearly exhausted, stumbling, their heads down as they labored up the mountain slope.

Where was she? She looked around, but saw nothing but darkness. By now, Buck must know she was gone. Would the villagers tell him what they'd seen? As she closed her eyes for a moment, tears froze on her lashes, the chill of the mountain well below freezing at this altitude.

Her legs were raw and she felt shaky as they crested a slope. For a moment, Jabbar halted. She saw he had night-vision goggles on. No one talked. The horses grunted and breathed heavily, trying to catch their breath from the brutal climb.

Megan turned to scan the sky. She couldn't hear any Apaches coming to rescue her. There were no lights far below in the valley. It was as if nothing existed in that moment—except her kidnappers.

Her mouth was dry. Her throat ached with unshed tears of fear. Thirsty. She was dying for some water. Yet no one in the group had any bottles or canteens on them. She wondered how the horses were managing in this situation. And then her heart turned to Luke.

Megan rubbed her eyes. She couldn't be seen crying. As she lifted her head, the Taliban leader kicked his horse and they started downward on an unseen path.

In her mind's eye, she saw Luke's rugged face, his eyes tender with love for her. More than anything, Megan regretted never telling him she loved him. Now it was too late....

Chapter 14

Luke stumbled, exhausted. Sunset was less than an hour away. Every Marine in the platoon was silent as they followed the goat trails down the mountain. The threat of retaliation never came, thank God.

A few scraggly groves of trees survived the massive B-52 bombing. Huge craters were dug, spewing debris, mostly rocks, all over the forbidding landscape. It reminded him of a barren moonscape. The wind was cold at this altitude and Luke had to get two of the Marines into their gloves because of frostbite. This was a harsh, unforgiving land.

Halfway down the slope, they moved onto an easier path, one used more often by the many goat herds. Sergeant Troy Archer gestured sharply for him to come up front. Moving carefully, Luke squeezed in and out of the line of Marines. Based on Archer's expression, something was wrong. Terribly wrong.

"What's up?" Luke asked, hurrying to catch up with the long-striding sergeant.

"I just got a call from Cap'n Hall. Mina Khan sent a farmer up to our compound to tell us she can't find Megan at the clinic."

Eyes widening, Luke exploded, "What are you talking about?" He knew there was worry about the Taliban still hiding in the village. His heart wrenched with terror.

"I don't know any more than this. The cap'n is sending a column of Humvees with Lieutenant Speed to the village right now." His mouth turned downward.

Luke felt as if someone had just hit him in the chest with a sledgehammer. For a moment, he couldn't breathe. "But she had two Marines protecting her."

"We've got to get more intel. I'm sorry." He clapped his hand over Luke's shoulder.

"Maybe…maybe Megan's made a house call? She's done that before with the elderly." Desperation leaked though his hoarse voice. Luke stared hard down at the village in the center of the valley. Two miles away stood their huge military compound. He noticed four Humvees on the road crawling along.

"We don't know," Archer said.

Shock rolled through Luke. He stopped and looked around on the surrounding mountains. What if Megan had been kidnapped? The Taliban would seek revenge for the bombing. Was this their retaliation? Wiping his mouth, he muttered, "I wish we had a SEAL team nearby."

Archer nodded and increased the speed of his stride. The path was wide enough for both of them. "Cap'n told me he was asking for a four-man SEAL team from Bagram."

"Then he thinks Megan was kidnapped," Luke said, his mind in chaos. "That she's with a group of Taliban going somewhere." He tried to stop the terror from eating him into oblivion, but people were kidnapped for two reasons in Afghanistan. Either for money and the person was returned unharmed, or they were kidnapped for political reasons.

He couldn't erase the possibility Megan had been kidnapped and would show up on a video being decapitated. His stomach clenched hard.

"Don't go there," Buck growled. "Just chill out. The SEAL team is on its way right now." He looked down at his watch. "They'll arrive about the time we get to the compound, an hour from now."

The SEALs were the only ones who had the ability to help in this situation. Luke knew from working with the Navy teams that they had the focus, lethal training and tracking ability that could make a difference in finding Megan. He wanted to run now. Run down this damn mountain, run to the village to find out from Mina what had happened.

"Luke!" Mina rushed forward as he appeared at the door to the clinic in the village. Night had fallen and she had lit several oil lamps in the room.

As he greeted Mina, he could see the tears in her eyes. "No one's found Megan?" he asked. He'd been listening to all the radio exchanges on the mountain. The farmers and Marines were scouring every place within their walled village.

"No. I'm so sorry, Luke!" She rushed over and sobbed. "Lieutenant Speed and the Marines have searched every home in our village. Megan has not been found."

Grimly, he looked around for signs of a fight. Everything seemed in order. "Did any of your villagers see anything?"

"No, not that we know of."

"What do you think happened?"

"I think she was kidnapped. She was here by herself the last hour. Sergeant Buck took the two Marines to continue looking for Gholam in our village. We both felt sure she would be safe for that hour." Sobbing, tears leaked from her eyes. "I was wrong. I know you love her and she loves you." Looking around, Mina pulled the dark red scarf up over her hair. "I should have told Sergeant Buck to allow them to stay. If they had, this wouldn't have happened." There was real sorrow in Mina's voice.

But he didn't have time to comfort her since he was crazed over Megan's disappearance. Luke saw a small, thin farmer come in the door. Behind him were Lieutenant Speed and two other Marines. None of them looked happy.

"Good that you're here," the lieutenant said to Luke. He pushed the farmer forward into the clinic. "You speak Pashto. Ask this bastard what he knows. Another family gave this dude up. He saw what happened." Speed glowered at the defiant farmer, who stood in a dirty white turban and dark clothes.

Luke moved forward, wrestling with his own emotions. The look on the farmer's face was one of hatred toward the Marines. Luke had seen this look too many times before. Before he could open his mouth, Mina stepped forward. She squared her shoulders, lifted her chin to an imperious angle and kept her gaze on the farmer.

"What did you see?" she demanded.

"Jabbar Gholam and his soldiers came in here," the farmer said in a gloating tone, pointing his finger toward the door. "They took the American infidel with them. Out the back door."

Luke's heart lurched in his chest, but he remained motionless. Mina was doing the hard work and he was grateful.

"Where were they taking her?"

The farmer frowned, as if considering not speaking, but Mina moved closer to him, her gaze angry. Finally, he spoke. "As you know, my lady, Lord Gholam's wife, Tahira, is pregnant. She is having problems and he came over here to kidnap the American woman medic because only she can work with another woman under Muslim law."

Some of Luke's terror abated, and he jerked a look toward Mina, whose expression conveyed surprise and relief. He waited for Mina to ask the next question.

"And that is the only reason he kidnapped Megan?" she demanded.

The man screwed up his face in a sneer. "The Marines have killed hundreds of our people! I do not know Lord Gholam's plans. I only know he needed medical help for his wife."

"Thank you," Mina said, then turned to Luke. "This is good news. I thought Jabbar took her as an act of revenge for the bombing."

Luke heard the lieutenant order the Marines to take the farmer away for more questioning at the compound. Speed came back and stood with them, a worried look on his face.

When the three of them were alone, Mina spoke in English to them. Giving Speed the information, she added, "I just finished a visit over there and Tahira is in her eighth month of pregnancy. She isn't well, but the old woman who helped the women of the village died two months ago. They have no other midwife."

Speed rubbed his jaw. "So is this not an act of revenge against us?"

Mina wrung her hands. "I don't think so. Jabbar is ruthless. He's unpredictable and cruel. The only people he loves are his beloved wife and his two sons."

Luke dragged in a deep breath. "This isn't good. Megan is skilled in all types of emergency medicine, but she's not a specialist in pregnancy issues. Jabbar doesn't know that. And it puts Megan in danger."

"She's in danger, anyway," Speed muttered, pacing the floor.

"Lieutenant, as long as Tahira is alive, he won't kill her. That is my opinion."

Luke cursed to himself. "Mina, do you know what's wrong with Tahira?"

Sorrowfully, Mina shook her head. "I do not. She only said she was uncomfortable and bleeding a little."

"She's bleeding?" Luke asked, alarmed.

"Yes, a little."

"How long?"

"For the last two months. It's a small amount, though."

Luke knew Tahira was in serious medical trouble. There was little Megan could do to help her.

Speed drilled a look at him. "What does that mean, Doc?"

"It's called placenta previa. It's a condition that occurs usually in the last trimester of pregnancy. The placenta literally is being torn away from the wall of the uterus. She will bleed a little or a lot. And by the description, it sounds like Tahira's condition."

"What's the outcome?" Speed demanded, scowling.

"Tahira is a ticking time bomb," Luke told him. "If the placenta continues to tear away slowly, she may be able to carry the baby to near term. The real problem is when she goes into labor, the muscle contractions can quickly tear the placenta completely away from the wall of the uterus at a moment's notice. Tahira could bleed out and die in three minutes and her baby could die along within her."

"Oh, no," Mina cried, her eyes growing huge.

"Damn it," Speed snarled, pacing again. He stared at Luke. "Can you tell me how stable or unstable this woman is right now?"

Shaking his head, Luke muttered, "No way. I'd need a lot more information, sir."

"You got any ideas on how we can stop this from happening?"

"If we could get a medevac helo in there right away, Tahira could be flown to Bagram and monitored. They could do a C-section on her, get the baby out of there immediately. That way, both mother and child would be saved."

Rubbing his chin, Speed halted and looked down at his feet in thought. "And so Doc Trayhern is in a highly unstable medical event?"

"Completely. She can't tell if or when Tahira's placenta might rupture. The wrong movement could do it, never mind going into labor."

"And she'll know all this when she examines this woman?"

"No question," Luke said with grim certainty. Megan would realize the danger to Tahira, her baby and herself.

"This is not good," Mina whispered, shaken by the

information. "When I visited Tahira, she was very pale and feeling very tired."

"That's because she's been continually losing blood over several months," Luke said. "She's probably anemic, which isn't good, either. Was Tahira very active? Walking around?"

"No, she does nothing but remain in her home surrounded by many pillows and blankets. Jabbar visits her all the time when he's home. He's very worried."

Luke shook his head. "It's good she's immobile."

Mina wrung her hands, tears running down her face. "This is terrible! I know Jabbar's world revolves around his wife. If—if Megan can't help her or if Tahira dies… oh, Allah, he'll kill her."

Shutting his eyes for a moment, Luke felt pulverizing grief. He heard the lieutenant curse. Opening his eyes, he asked, "Mina, could you go over there? Could you help us?"

Mina wiped her eyes. "I will do whatever I can. You want me to convince Jabbar to allow the helicopter to take Tahira to Bagram?"

"Exactly." Luke looked over at the lieutenant, whose face was dark with worry. "Sir, could we allow a farmer from this village to carry a message over the mountain to Gholam from Mina?"

"Sure," he muttered. "Do it now, because Doc Trayhern is in a lot of trouble."

Luke said nothing, knowing just how dangerous the situation really was. He wanted to do something, but knew the messenger was the best idea for now. He couldn't just fly into Jabbar's village. The Taliban leader would blow the medevac out of the sky. No, the messenger was the only way.…

* * *

As dawn rose, Megan clung to the horse as it stumbled along the narrow mountain path. She could see Gholam in the bare light, and everyone slowed their animals. They had stopped once to drink water and get off the horses. She couldn't see anything but she could hear the low murmur of Taliban soldiers' voices. A soldier was always near her, a rifle on his hip, making sure she didn't escape.

Exhausted, her stomach clenched with hunger, Megan saw the path change. The horses grunted and scrambled and slipped up a steep, rocky hillside. As they rounded a corner on the slope, a small village of rock and mud came into view. It was tucked away within the maw of a huge limestone cavern. Bits of gray smoke came from some of the homes. Where was she? The wild mountains surrounded them at various elevations, all the peaks covered with snow.

The village had no wall, as many others she'd seen. There were about fifty homes. Dogs and small children were running around the wide, flat cave entrance. About a hundred goats were being herded by two older boys off the lip and down another thin trail. It looked like any other Afghan village.

The horses picked up their pace, no longer hanging their heads, but moving along as they neared the steep entrance to the mighty cavern. A number of older children, some older women, came out of their homes as the riders trotted across the flat ground toward the cave. Megan clung to the horse's mane, her butt numb from the beating it had taken perched on top of the animal's narrow back. Finally, they halted.

New fear worked its way up her spine as she saw Gholam leap off his sweaty, lathered stallion. A small boy ran up and took the reins of the animal and led it away toward a wooden corral to the left of the village.

"Get down!" Gholam snarled, waving his hand toward Megan.

Though her legs barely worked, Megan dismounted, her front hands tied, the ropes biting unrelentingly into her tender flesh. When her boots hit the ground, her knees started to crumple. Megan clung to the saddle to stop from collapsing onto the ground.

"Weak American infidel!" Gholam growled, halting and jamming his hands on his hips.

Glancing toward the angry leader, Megan noticed he wore a dark brown turban to match the obsidian color of his small, close-set eyes. His black beard fell to his chest. The long black vest hung to his knees, his rough woven cotton shirt and baggy trousers the same color as his turban. She chilled beneath the scorching look of disgust he gave her.

"Stand up!" he ordered angrily in Pashto.

Megan pushed up and locked her knees. Turning, she saw her medic pack being pulled off the back of the saddle by another soldier.

"Come!" Jabbar ordered, hooking his finger and pointing toward the village.

The soldier hurled the heavy medic pack at Megan. She caught it and moved her arms through the straps. The hatred in the eyes of the soldier made her stomach knot. She followed the leader, who walked with a noticeable limp.

Megan breathed hard as they hurried toward the cluster of huts. They were probably at ten thousand feet; the air thin. More people poured out of their hovels, staring as they approached. There was surprise in the villagers' eyes. Gholam charged like a bull, head down, limping quickly between the homes and down what seemed to be a narrow street.

A soldier ran ahead to a door painted red. He opened it and quickly stepped aside.

Jabbar turned and snarled to Megan, "Get in there. Stand just inside the door and do not move."

Nodding, Megan ducked because the door entrance was barely five and a half feet high. As she entered, she was surprised. The room contained a rare cast-iron-bellied stove. The hard-packed dirt floor was covered with Persian rugs. Light came in both windows, taking away the gloom. Standing to one side, Jabbar entered and shut the door. They were alone.

Jabbar looked up at her. "Get out of your medic pack. You're here to see my wife, Tahira. She needs medical help and you are going to fix her."

His black gaze drilled into Megan. The room was coolish for summer, but the cave sat near the ten-thousand-foot level on the mountain. Nodding, Megan said nothing and shed her pack, letting it drop to her feet. "I'm thirsty. I need some water first."

Jabbar reached over to a round clay pot with a stopper. "Get water out of there. Hurry!"

A chipped mug sat beside the pitcher on the spindly wooden table in the corner. She felt stiff and sore from the nonstop riding. She poured water and drank three glasses.

Jabbar was impatient, moving like a feral fox around the perimeter of the large room.

Megan picked up her pack and hefted it over her shoulder. Jabbar pointed to a closed door. She walked up to it, meeting him.

"You understand me?" he demanded, glaring.

Nodding, Megan decided it wouldn't be wise to pre-

tend she didn't know Pashto. If his wife was sick, she'd
have to speak to her in her language and Gholam would
know, anyway. "Yes, I understand."

Gholam's thick black brows rose in surprise. "So,
you speak Pashto very well." His eyes narrowed to slits.
"What are you? A woman SEAL?"

Megan's mouth twitched but she kept from smiling.
The curved knife in his belt and a pistol on the other
side kept her straight-faced. "I'm part of a group of military women who are here to help villagers wherever
assigned." She saw his eyes change to one of curiosity.

"And so you are a skilled doctor?"

Megan held up her hand. "No. I'm not a doctor. I'm
a trained paramedic." She doubted he knew the difference. And judging from the confusion in his eyes, she
was right.

"No matter!" he snapped. "My wife, Tahira, is in
the next room. She is very frail and sick. You are to
help her. Go!"

Megan watched the door open. Jabbar shoved her and
she lurched into the hall. The door shut. Standing in the
coolish hall, Megan heard nothing. Was this why Jabbar kidnapped her? To provide medical services? Some
of her fear abated as she slowly walked down the rug-
covered corridor. Exhausted from no sleep and hungry,
Megan forced herself to concentrate on locating Tahira.

At the first door on the right, she saw a very small
woman with black hair and dark brown eyes lying
propped up on thick pillows. There were many blankets beneath her black robes. Across her hair, she wore a
gold scarf, emphasizing her wan features. Megan halted
and tried to smile.

"Hi, I'm Megan. Your husband sent me to see if I
could help you. Are you Tahira?"

The woman sighed and managed a weak smile. "You've come.... Allah be praised. Yes, yes, come in. Mina talked so much about you. Thank you for coming. I know I am dying and you must help me...please...."

Chapter 15

Megan focused on Tahira. She doubted the woman was more than twenty years old. They married young in Afghanistan. "I'm an American Navy field medic," she told the woman in Pashto. She decided to leave out the fact that Jabbar had kidnapped her because Tahira appeared frail. Megan had no wish to upset her. "Do I have permission to touch you? I need to listen to your heart." She pointed to the woman's swollen belly. "And carefully examine you and your baby."

Lifting her long, graceful hand, Tahira sat back weakly on the pillows. "Thank you so much for coming. I am so grateful. Yes, yes, please…we have no one in our village any longer who can help me. I need a midwife."

Unzipping the medical bag, Megan quickly pulled the stethoscope across her neck and grabbed the blood pressure cuff. She donned her latex gloves. "Can you tell me what's wrong, Tahira? Why do you think you're dying?" Megan gently wrapped the blood pressure cuff around the woman's left upper arm.

Closing her eyes, Tahira whispered, "I am constantly bleeding from below. Our old midwife, Afsana, died two months ago. She had given me herbs that slowed the bleeding. Now I have no herbs and the bleeding is constant."

Alarm swept through Megan as she read Tahira's blood pressure. It was 70/50, far below the normal 120/80. Blood loss could precipitate such a reading. Nodding, she removed the cuff and set it aside. There was no sense in scaring Tahira. "How long have you been bleeding?"

Tahira sighed and pulled up her robe as Megan gently examined her belly. "For two months."

"And how many months along are you?"

"Eight months." She managed a partial smile on her full lips. "I think it is a girl. A very strong, big girl." She reached out and touched her exposed belly. "My silly husband thinks it's a third boy, but he's wrong." She laughed softly.

Megan nodded and carefully moved her hands across the woman's abdomen. She didn't like what she felt. The pad of cloths beneath her were spotted with blood. Easing Tahira's robes down and drawing a blanket up to her waist, Megan said, "Are you feeling weak?"

"Oh, always. I can no longer cook for Jabbar. I cannot take care of my two sons." Her voice turned tearful. "If not for the other women, my sons wouldn't be fed, either." Tahira held Megan's gaze. "Please, can you tell me what is wrong? Am I dying?" She reached out and gripped Megan's hand.

Megan squeezed the woman's elegant hand. It was

Beyond Valor

work-worn but beautiful. "Has your baby been active? Have you felt her move around a lot?"

"Oh, yes! She is most active!" Tahira took her hands and smoothed them across her swollen belly. "I know this is a girl because she is so different from carrying my two sons." Tahira smiled broadly up at Megan. "I think she is like you, Megan. You are a strong woman, too, or you would not be in the military."

Megan returned her smile. "Is it possible for you to be flown from your village to Bagram Air Base in Kabul? Because the help you need is there." She saw Tahira's face grow worried.

"Move? Fly? Why must that happen? Jabbar said he was going to ask a woman medical doctor to come and stay with me until I birthed my baby."

Keeping her voice gentle, Megan reached over and touched Tahira's shoulder. She was terribly thin, almost starving. Was there enough food in Jabbar's village? Tahira's pregnancy could have been harmed by lack of nutrition alone. "Listen, I must talk to your husband about all of this. May I come back and visit you later?"

"Of course. Jabbar said you would be in the room across the hall from me."

Megan wondered what other lies Jabbar had told his wife, but she remained mute. Getting to her feet, the stethoscope around her neck, she said, "I'll be back soon." Megan knew the man ruled his wife and children. She had to argue her case in front of the Taliban leader.

Outside the door, a soldier in the hall watched her. She walked toward him and told him to take her to Jabbar. He turned, went through the door and led her into another part of the house.

Jabbar was eating at the table when she entered.

"Get in here," he snapped, pointing to where she should stand.

The soldier pushed Megan forward.

The leader had a loaf of fresh bread and a bowl of thick soup with vegetables and meat in it. The hatred in his eyes scared her. Standing, her hands clasped in front of her, she knew her presentation had to be pitch-perfect.

"Lord Gholam, I've just examined your wife, Tahira. She's in great danger of bleeding to death. Her baby is turned." Megan used her hands to show him. "It's a breech birth, which means her baby is feetfirst to come out, instead of headfirst."

"So," he growled, ripping off another piece of the bread, "fix it."

"I can't," Megan returned with the same growl. "Your wife has been bleeding for over two months. The sac that contains your baby is pulling away from the wall of her womb. It's causing bleeding."

"Then fix it!"

"I can't!"

Jabbar glared at her. "Then you die. I will *not* allow an American infidel helicopter over here!" He sneered. "Do you think me stupid, woman? You could be telling me nothing but lies! It's a ruse to allow infidels into my village and then they will kill everyone."

"I'm a medic. I'm trying to save lives, not take them!"

"One more word out of you and I will punch your face in so you can never speak again!" Jabbar made a sharp, angry gesture toward the soldier standing with his rifle drawn. "Get her out of here!"

Jerked by the soldier, Megan was escorted unceremoniously back to the hall. The guard pushed her savagely and she nearly fell. Catching herself, she heard the door shut behind her. As she breathed hard, Megan forced herself get hold of her escaping emotions. She couldn't go back to Tahira shaken and scared. The worst thing she could do would be to upset Tahira. Megan moved quietly down the hall and knocked softly on Tahira's door.

"Come in...."

Megan entered and smiled. Tahira looked a bit better. She saw a tray with food and a pottery urn filled with water. "I'm back," she said, closing the door. "It must be lunch."

"Yes, it is time to eat." Tahira gestured and said, "Come, there is food here for you. And water. You must eat to keep up your strength."

Megan came and sat down, her legs crossed. "Have you eaten?"

"Oh, I do not feel like eating." She gave Megan a weary smile. "I know I should. Afsana was always chiding me and saying I had to eat to keep up my strength and drink much water to replace the blood loss."

"She was right," Megan said, picking up the vessel and pouring water in both cups. "Your midwife was very wise. I would tell you to do the same thing." Megan was touched by the woman's smile as she handed her the cup. "So, drink?"

Taking the cup with both hands, Tahira wrinkled her nose. "I'm not thirsty."

"It doesn't matter, Tahira. Look at it this way. You're drinking to keep your little girl alive inside you. Any food you eat, you are feeding her, too."

"Really?" Her arched brows rose. "Truly?"

"Truly," Megan answered, drinking the water from her own cup. Her stomach grumbled because she was starving. There were bowls of steaming couscous and fragrant-smelling lamb on another platter. "The more you eat, the more strength you give your body to repair itself." She took the cup from Tahira after she finished drinking from it. Handing her the bowl of rice after placing some vegetables and meat across it, she added, "Eat and feed your baby."

Heartened, Tahira took the bowl and the wooden spoon. "You are wise like Afsana was."

Megan sat there eating beside the woman. She tried not to gulp the food. "Afsana was a very wise woman."

"She took care of my husband's village for forty years." Tears came to her dark eyes. "I miss her so much...."

"Midwives out here on the frontier would be worth their weight in gold," Megan agreed. She reached out and touched Tahira's drooping shoulder. "Honor her by eating a lot and drinking at least one cup of water an hour?"

Tahira nodded and obediently began to eat. The silence cloaked them. Megan could hear nothing outside the thick rock and adobe walls of her small bedroom. Her mind revolved around her dilemma. Without quick medical intervention, Tahira could suddenly bleed out and die. And if she died, Gholam would gladly kill her.

"It was so kind of you to come and help me," Tahira said after she finished eating. Handing Megan the bowl, she smiled up at her. "I told my husband that Mina loved you and that you were the right woman to come and help me. I so appreciate you agreeing to come and be with me."

"Mina is a good person," Megan agreed. She finished off the rest of the food that Tahira didn't want to eat. "Did Mina suggest I come here to help you?"

"Oh, no," Tahira said. "I decided to tell Jabbar about

it. He is so worried over me. We sat here crying in each other's arms a week ago over my condition. When I told him what Mina had said, he got the idea to ask you to come over the mountain from her village to ours."

There was such innocence in Tahira's face and voice that Megan understood she really didn't know about Jabbar's kidnapping her. "Well, I'm glad to help."

"Mina was so excited that you had set up a medical clinic in her husband's village. She praised your work. You have helped so many, Megan." Reaching out, Tahira gripped her lower arm and looked deeply into her eyes. "Truly, you are an angel of mercy sent by Allah. I pray for you, Megan, because you are a strong, good woman."

"I'm a medic," Megan said, her voice off-key. "My life, my heart, is devoted to saving lives."

"You speak as a Sufi," Tahira said with a sigh, releasing her arm. She lay back, suddenly weary. "Rumi would say you live your life through your heart's eyes." She moved her head and looked at Megan. "Do you know of Rumi?"

"Yes, I love his poetry. I was introduced to him in college. When I read his first book of translated poems, I fell in love with him."

Pointing to the corner where there was a small stack of books, Tahira said in an excited tone, "All my books are Rumi's poetry! Perhaps you will read them to me? Afsana would often read to me when I was having trouble sleeping." Her lips moved into a sad smile laced with grief. "Afsana would sit where you sit. She would choose a book and read Rumi's words to me. I would immediately fall asleep!"

"Then would you like me to read to you tonight?" Megan asked.

Tahira sighed and smiled. "We are sisters of the heart, Megan. Truly, you are an angel."

"Why don't you try and rest now?" Megan suggested. She got up and picked up the tray. "I'll take this away."

Moving into the hall and quietly shutting the door behind her, Megan spotted the frowning soldier. She took the tray up to him and asked where to put it. The guard glowered at her and opened the door. As Megan moved into the room, she spotted a young farmer from Lar Sholtan by the name of Bahraam. The farmer's eyes widened in surprise when he saw Megan. Jabbar was standing nearby, reading a piece of paper delivered by the farmer.

"Take the tray," Jabbar ordered his soldier. "You." He pointed at Megan. "Stay where you are."

She met Bahraam's dark eyes. He looked very tired. Why was he here? His face was not filled with hatred for her, but, rather, worry. Her gaze moved to Jabbar, who was reading the paper. What was going on?

Jabbar turned to her. "This is from Timor Khan. He is telling me that you have *Lokhay,* that you are protected by him and his villages."

Stunned, Megan felt her mouth drop open. She saw Gholam's face grow angry. "What?" She'd never heard of any Afghan village extending *Lokhay* to an American. It meant that if Jabbar harmed her in any way, Timor and his many villages would, quite literally, go to war against Jabbar.

The Taliban leader shoved the letter back into Bahraam's hands. "Tell Lord Khan I will think over his request. You tell him she is an infidel! I think it's foolish he gives her *Lokhay!*"

Megan tensed as the farmer gripped the note. The

young man was taller than Gholam. She had cared for his wife and three children.

"My Lord Gholam, Timor Khan will accept only one answer. That you understand she is under his protection. You must agree to that."

Snarling, Gholam hissed, "Watch your place, boy!" And he held up his fist, waving it in Bahraam's sun-burned face.

The farmer drew up his shoulders, chin high. "If you threaten me, Lord Gholam, you threaten Lord Khan."

She was watching *Lokhay* at work. Stunned by what had happened, Megan remained motionless. Gholam moved around the room like a caged snow leopard. What would he do?

"I need her help," he snarled at Bahraam. "You will *not* take her from me. She is here to help my wife!"

"We had no understanding of this," Bahraam began. "You kidnapped her, and that goes against *Lokhay*."

"Don't you think I know that?" Jabbar roared. He came and punched the farmer in the chest with his finger. "How did I know you extended *Lokhay* to this infidel?"

"You know now. We are Pashtun and you know, even though you were born in Pakistan, that we have a fifteen-hundred-year-old set of laws that govern our people. *Lokhay* gives Dr. Megan protection and you need to return her to our village."

Megan was amazed at the farmer's stubborn audacity and grit. Gholam looked as though he wanted to slit the farmer's throat. Would he release her back to Bahraam? Her heart sped up as she waited for her fate.

"You tell Lord Khan I'm keeping her here! I will not harm her. She's here to tend to my wife, Tahira. When Tahira has birthed, I will bring her back to you."

Hesitating, Bahraam, asked, "Is this your word to Lord Khan?"

"It is."

Megan wanted to speak up, but didn't dare. She knew how much the Taliban hated women. Bahraam gave her a questioning look.

"Is this so, Megan? Are you staying of your own free will? Mina Khan said you were taken without your consent."

"Do *not* speak to this infidel!" Gholam shrieked, coming at the farmer, his curved knife drawn. He held it up to the face of the farmer. "She has *nothing* to say!"

"She does, my Lord Gholam," Bahraam answered quietly, staring back at the Taliban leader. "*Lokhay* gives her the right to speak."

The Taliban soldier backed down. He sheathed the curved blade in his belt.

"Megan?"

Clearing her throat, she told Bahraam the situation. She made it simple so that the information could be carried back to the village. Knowing that Luke was there, she was sure he would be involved in finding her.

The farmer looked at Gholam. "If your wife needs help such as this, why do you not allow it?"

"Because," Gholam snarled, impatient, "it could be a trick! The Americans just murdered four hundred men! They want *me!* They would stop at nothing to kill me!"

Megan looked at Bahraam. "Is it possible Captain Khalid Shaheen could fly over here? He is Afghan. And he has a charity that flies sick men, women and children from any village along the border to Bagram Air Base for advanced medical help." Anxiously, Megan glanced at Jabbar. Some of his anger abated. Pressing on, she

added, "If Lord Gholam would allow Captain Shaheen
to fly in here, I could go with Tahira."

"This could be a trap!" Jabbar yelled.

"No, my Lord Gholam," the farmer said, holding
up his hand. "I have met Captain Shaheen. She speaks
the truth."

Heart pounding, Megan said in a pleading tone,
"Lord Gholam, your wife is in grave danger of dying
any moment. I know you love her. And I know you love
her sons. Please, you must believe me when I tell you
I don't have the equipment or skills needed to save her
life if she starts bleeding heavily. It's important to get
her on a helicopter and to Bagram as soon as possible."
As she begged, Megan saw Gholam's anger dissolve.

"And what promise do I have that if you take my
wife, you'll return her and my child?"

"*Lokhay* is invoked," Bahraam intoned. "Her word
is her honor. Our villages and Lord Khan will support
her word. Your wife and baby will be returned to you."

Jabbar wavered. He stroked his thick black beard,
glaring at Megan and then at Bahraam. "I've never met
this Khalid Shaheen. I must look him in the eye. I must
see for myself that he is a man of honor."

"I will leave now," Bahraam said quietly. "And I
will ride over the mountain and give your words to
Lord Khan."

"Excuse me," Megan said, holding up her hands.
"Bahraam, we don't have that kind of time. Tahira is
in a medical emergency. I need Captain Shaheen to fly
here as soon as possible." She glanced over at Gholam,
who again had a murderous look in his eyes. Megan
added in a stronger, demanding tone, "I need your radio,
Lord Gholam. I know the frequency on which to contact Captain Shaheen. Your wife is dying. I know you

want her to live and so do I. But we must hurry her to the hospital. This can't wait a day or two. Please!"

Hissing a curse, Jabbar strode around the room. He halted, thought and then prowled some more. Throwing a glance at the farmer, he glared at her. Finally, he stopped in front of Megan.

"Very well." He jerked the radio from his belt, a Russian model. "You stand here right now and call Captain Shaheen. He must come *alone.* If I see anyone else in that helicopter when it lands here, I will destroy it. Do you understand?"

Megan took the radio. "Yes, I understand. He'll come alone."

"Could Bahraam ride back with us?" Megan demanded.

"Yes," Jabbar growled. "I know who he is."

Relief flooded through Megan. She didn't understand the Russian alphabet on the old, beat-up radio, but she fiddled with the dials until the right frequency showed up. Jabbar stood in front of her, arms across his chest. Glancing beyond him, she saw Bahraam's dark face filled with hope. If only the radio would work. If only it would reach Khalid.

Gulping, Megan gave it a try and made the call.

Chapter 16

Luke stood tensely within the HQ with the two Marine Corps officers and Timor Khan. The elder had ridden his horse into the compound to talk with Captain Hall about the situation regarding Megan's kidnapping. The radio jumped to life.

It was Megan's voice!

Startled, Hall picked up the radio, but his gaze shot to Luke, who stood near the entrance.

Luke listened intently as Megan explained the situation regarding Gholam's wife. Captain Hall seemed confused. He wasn't a medic, so he didn't understand the gravity of the situation. Luke was going to speak up, but Hall beat him to it.

"Come and talk to her, Doc," he ordered, thrusting the radio toward him. "I don't know what it all means."

Gripping the radio, Luke said, "This is Collier. Captain Hall wants me to speak to you about the medical issue. Over." He gulped, his heart beating in his chest to underscore his fear for Megan. She was alive! She seemed well, but he could hear the strain in her voice. After listening closely to her descriptions, he finally said, "One moment while I convey this to Captain Hall and Lord Khan." Luke understood that Gholam was at her side, listening to every word. He wanted the Taliban leader to know Timor was present.

"Sir," Luke said, holding Hall's worried gaze, "if we don't get a medevac out there right now, Gholam's wife can bleed to death and her baby will die."

"Okay, get Gholam on the radio. Ask him if we can send in a medevac that he won't shoot out of the sky."

Suddenly, Gholam was on the radio.

"You bring Captain Shaheen only with the medevac! That is all I am allowing! You infidel pigs could be lying to me!"

Luke translated to the captain. "Sir, we are going to need two pilots and I will need to go with them. Megan can't stabilize and care for his wife alone. Plus, I can bring other medical supplies we may need during transit."

"Tell him," Hall ordered, grim.

Luke replied.

The Taliban leader screamed into the radio.

Timor Khan, who stood near Luke, said, "May I talk to him, Dr. Luke?"

Hall nodded and Luke handed the elder the radio.

"Jabbar, this is Timor Khan," he said, speaking slowly in Pashto. "I am here with the Marines and Dr. Luke. I can vouch for all of them that they are only concerned for the welfare and care of your wife. You *must* allow them to fly in with two pilots and Dr. Luke. He is bringing medical supplies that will help your wife live, not die."

There was a long, tense silence on the radio.

Luke stared down at the table in emotional turmoil. He knew the life-and-death situation Megan was in with Tahira. Timor held the radio, his face unreadable. Hall appeared worried.

"No!" Gholam screamed into the radio. "You do as I say! One pilot. No other men on that helicopter!"

Luke saw Timor's sunburned face go dark with anger. Seeing a flash of annoyance in Timor's dark brown eyes, the leader held up his hand toward the captain.

Timor pushed the button and said with firm authority, "Jabbar, we have extended *Lokhay* to the helicopter crew and to Dr. Luke. Your wife is going to die very shortly if something isn't done. These men have only the care of your wife in their hearts. Now, you will allow them to take Tahira to Bagram. This is my final decision as leader of my tribe."

A bomb could have gone off in HQ as Luke saw Timor smile a little as he handed the radio back to him. Taking it, Luke waited. He had never heard of *Lokhay* being extended to Americans. He gave Timor a slight nod of thanks as they all waited.

"Very well," Gholam ground out. "Bring the medevac in here with two pilots and Dr. Luke."

"We will ask Captain Shaheen to pilot the medevac," Luke told him. He knew if another Afghan was involved, Jabbar would be far less trigger-happy.

"Get here as soon as you can. You call me on this radio when you come over the mountain."

"We'll be in touch," Luke promised. He signed off and handed the radio to Captain Hall. After relaying the conversation, the Marine officer looked relieved. Instantly, Lieutenant Speed called Bagram. They discovered Captain Shaheen was at Camp Bravo. That was a piece of luck. In minutes, they had a plan cobbled together.

Shaheen would fly with the Turkish woman pilot, Captain Aylin Sahin. That way, it would be a Muslim crew. That should allay Gholam's worries. They would pick Luke up outside the compound, flying in special medical equipment for Tahira.

Luke excused himself and ran to the clinic. Within a half hour, the medevac would arrive. Grabbing a number of Ringer's lactate IVs and drugs that might be needed, Luke felt his heart pound with anxiety. Even though Timor Khan had given them *Lokhay,* no one knew for sure if Gholam would really honor it or not.

He ran for his house to pick up his medic bag. As he hurriedly packed the items and zipped it shut, he desperately wanted to tell Megan he loved her. She had to know that.

Jerking the pack over to his shoulder, Luke hurried out the door and into the late-afternoon sunlight. He couldn't steady his emotions. He needed her to know she had become his life, that she was the only person he ever wanted to wake up to every morning. He wanted to love her, care for her and have a family with her. He trotted across the dusty compound toward the opening gate. This day had to turn out right. They needed this chance.

Luke saw Timor Khan standing outside HQ with his horse. He lifted his hand to the elder and silently thanked him for his help. He prayed Gholam would honor their agreement. Or else they were all dead.

* * *

Megan had Tahira on an IV of Ringer's lactate to keep her hydrated. Some color had come back to the woman's face as Jabbar and another soldier carefully placed her on a litter. They carried her gently out to the main room of the house. Megan held the IV in her hand and she saw Tahira looking at her husband, worry in her eyes.

"Jabbar, do not fuss. My husband, I want to live. I want our baby to live." She gripped his hand as they lowered the litter. "Thank you for doing this."

Megan watched Jabbar's angry face turn soft beneath his wife's cajoling voice. He picked up her hand, kissed it and pressed it against his chest.

"I would gladly die and go to heaven for you, beloved," he said, his voice gravelly and low with feeling. "Stop your worry." He took his fingers and smoothed out the wrinkles on Tahira's broad brow. "You are in good hands with this woman doctor. I don't like that she's American, but she is all we have."

Tahira gave her husband a pleading smile. "Beloved, she is to be trusted. I know it here, in my heart. She cares for me…for our baby. I feel good being with Megan."

The radio in Jabbar's belt went off. The leader got to his feet after releasing his wife's hand to answer it. Megan heard Captain Khalid Shaheen's voice. They were inbound and would reach the village in ten minutes. Relief tunneled through her as she listened to the exchange. She saw Tahira's face turn hopeful with the good news.

Jabbar ordered his two men out the door and he left with them. Megan remained at Tahira's side. She continued to hold the IV up. Megan had also given her some prednisone earlier. Often with this condition, the baby's lungs would begin to fill with water, and this drug would keep them clear. Tahira seemed at peace and closed her eyes, tucked beneath the colorfully woven blankets.

Megan tried to steady her heart. Luke was coming! Another kind of relief went through her because she knew he'd bring other lifesaving supplies. Just getting to see Luke made her feel that she was going to survive this. But Gholam was unreliable and she never knew from one moment to the next what the dangerous man might do.

Luke's eyes widened with fear just as the medevac landed. It kicked up clouds of dust in Gholam's village, which was hidden within a cave. Khalid Shaheen hissed a curse beneath his breath as Gholam and ten of his soldiers quickly surrounded the helo, rifles pointed at them.

The blades on the helo were still turning, and Khalid powered down, shutting off the engines. They couldn't afford to bring Tahira on board in the choking dust. The litter bearers would be unable to see where they were walking.

"What do we do?" Luke demanded, speaking into his microphone as he twisted around. The Taliban soldiers were at the door, hatred in their eyes.

"Stay put," Shaheen growled. "This is Gholam's way of establishing supremacy."

"Don't be so sure," Aylin muttered, sitting in the co-pilot's seat. "There's their leader." She pointed a gloved finger out the cockpit window. Her hand automatically went to the pistol strapped across the Kevlar on her chest.

Luke leaped back as Shaheen jerked opened the door.

Instantly, Gholam came inside, his lips drawn away from his yellowed teeth, his rifle pointed in his face.

"I want the woman pilot!" he snarled, jabbing a finger toward Aylin Sahin. "She stays here! She's my insurance you will bring my wife and baby back to me. Now move!" He jabbed the rifle barrel into Khalid's chest.

Luke remained crouched where he was. This was crazy!

"She has *Lokhay,*" Khalid said, glaring into the back toward the Taliban soldier. "You can't do this."

"Yes, I can. And I will." Gholam sneered into Shaheen's face and jerked his hand, indicating Aylin should come out of the cockpit.

The woman was one cool customer, her face expressionless, her gold-brown eyes narrowed on the soldier. It was the gleam in them that told Luke this Apache pilot wasn't the least ruffled by the threat.

"I'll go," Aylin said, unhooking her harness. She pulled the pistol strapped to the chest of her Kevlar vest and slowly placed it where Gholam could see it. "I'll play hostage," she told Khalid in English, derision in her tone. A slight, feral grin came to her lips for that moment. Pushing to her feet after taking off her helmet, she squeezed between the two seats.

"Put your rifle down," Aylin growled at the Taliban leader in Pashto. "I'll be your hostage, you pitiful excuse of a dog. What true Muslim man would hold a woman hostage?" she added.

Gholam's lips moved away from his teeth as he met and locked gazes with the woman pilot. He lowered his rifle and moved out of the back of the helo.

Luke watched the brave Turkish pilot. Her black hair was pulled back into a ponytail. For a moment, she was nothing but pure warrior, the look in her eyes lethal as she regarded the five Taliban soldiers outside the helo, all their rifles pointed up at her.

"Cowards," she muttered to Luke and Khalid. "What scared little boys they are, eh?"

Khalid barely smiled. "Be kind to them, Captain. They have no idea what and who you are."

Laughing huskily, Aylin turned, her hands on either side of the door. "They do not know the warrior Turks, do they?"

"No," Khalid said evenly, "and I hope they don't need to find out. Just stand down and be patient. I'll be back to pick you up. That's a promise."

"I'll take an Afghan's word anyday," Aylin called over her shoulder.

Luke watched Aylin walk like a graceful cat out of the helo. She moved away from the slowing blades, her head held at an imperious angle. The five soldiers scrambled and rushed to catch up with the proud, unflappable Aylin Sahin. Luke admired the woman. She was fearless, but then, that was what everyone said of her at Camp Bravo. She ambled into the cave as if she owned the place.

Khalid turned. "Luke, go ahead and prepare for Tahira. I have to stay with the helicopter."

"Roger that, sir." Luke quickly exited the helo, his medic bag on his shoulder.

Another Taliban soldier, a young, thin boy no more than fifteen years old, approached them.

"Take me to Lord Gholam's wife," he ordered the boy in Pashto.

The boy's eyes widened with surprise that Luke spoke their language. Bobbing his head, he quickly lowered his rifle and gestured for Luke to follow him. He trotted off and Luke followed on his heels.

Megan's eyes widened when Luke stepped through the door. In that split second, their gazes met. So much silently passed between them. Her throat closed with tears, but she gulped them back.

Luke smiled as he approached Tahira. Kneeling down on the other side of her litter opposite Megan, he softly introduced himself. The woman's face relaxed. Luke had a way with everyone. He had a way with her.

Quickly, Megan filled him in. Just as she finished, Gholam and two soldiers entered. The leader's eyes were dark with worry as his gaze flew to his weakened wife.

"I am fine, husband," she protested, waving her hand weakly. "I am being very well cared for."

Luke rose to his feet. "We need to transport her to the helo right now," he told Gholam in a firm voice. "No more waiting and no more games."

Glaring at the medic, Gholam ordered his soldiers to pick up the litter. They did so with great gentleness. Gholam opened the door and exited.

Luke moved to Megan's side while they came down the rocky hill toward the medevac.

"Are you all right?" he demanded, giving her a concerned look. Megan wore a scarf over her head, her expression strained. He wanted desperately to embrace her, kiss her, make love to her, but none of that was possible.

"I'm fine," she replied in English, holding the IV above the litter.

"Gholam's holding our copilot as hostage," he warned her.

"What?" Megan gasped.

"Shh, it's all right. They took Captain Aylin Sahin. She's from Turkey and I think you know her from Camp Bravo."

Nodding, Megan slowed as the men slowed. "Yes. You don't mess with her." They were going down a very steep embankment. She slid and caught herself. The soldiers were like goats and were able to traverse the slippery, graveled path with assuredness.

"Tahira is a ticking time bomb," Megan warned. "Is there a surgical operating team waiting for her at Bagram?"

"Yes." Luke looked up as they approached the helo, the blades now still. "All we have to do is get her there before she starts hemorrhaging."

"Right now she's stable," Megan said, giving him the blood pressure and pulse information.

"Good to hear." He hurried ahead and trotted up to the lip of the medevac. There was a special litter anchored to the floor. With the help of Gholam and the other two soldiers, they carefully transferred Tahira onto the gurney. Megan climbed in and knelt at the woman's shoulder, hooking the IV overhead. It left her free to help place the dark green wool blankets over her.

Gholam remained at the helo's door, his gaze pinned worriedly on his wife.

"I'll be fine, husband," Tahira called. "I am in good hands."

Reaching in, he gripped his wife's long, graceful hand. Kissing it fiercely, he rasped, "Come back to me, beloved. Bring our baby back with you. Life is not worth living without you…."

Tahira nodded, giving her husband a tender smile. "Pray for us, my husband. I know Megan will be calling you on the radio and letting you know how our baby and I are doing."

Megan was touched by the leader's sudden, raw anxiety and love he clearly felt for his wife. She met Gholam's eyes, which were filled with tears.

"I promise, I will call you, Lord Gholam. As soon as we land at Bagram, I'll be on the radio and let you know how Tahira is doing." Megan touched her heart. "I promise."

Glaring at her, Gholam said, "You had better! If I don't hear from you, I will behead that arrogant woman pilot! Understand?"

Megan gulped and nodded. Gholam wouldn't get near the Turk, but she didn't tell him that.

Gholam retreated and so did his soldiers. All rifles were now on their shoulders, no longer a threat.

"Let's turn and burn," Shaheen told them over the intercom. "Close that door and let's go!"

Tahira's eyes widened as the door shut. It became a murky darkness in the cabin, the medevac shaking and shuddering as the blades whirled faster and faster. Megan saw the woman's fear and she reached over and held Tahira's hand. She had never flown before, and Megan didn't want the stress to push her into starting contractions or hemorrhaging.

"It's going to be all right," Megan said. With Luke's help, they put a helmet on Tahira's head, explaining it would stop the racket and noise. And she could hear them speak to her through the intercom. The gesture wasn't wasted, Megan discovered. Almost instantly, Tahira relaxed as she heard their voices within the helmet.

The medevac lifted off, moving straight up into the cloudy sky. Luke placed a permanent blood pressure cuff on Tahira's left upper arm for the flight to Bagram.

They hooked her up to several instruments to monitor all her functions. The straps across the gurney were there to prevent Tahira from being jostled if they hit air turbulence on the way to the base.

Megan focused on keeping Tahira engaged. Her eyes were wide with wonder. Khalid was a smooth flyer and he kept the medevac moving at top speed, hopping over several mountain ranges and then dropping into the brown desert plain that led to Kabul. Bagram was twenty-six miles north of the capital.

She forced herself not to talk with Luke other than for medical purposes. The longer they flew, the more Tahira relaxed. Her blood pressure moved down, indicating she was no longer as fearful.

They landed at Bagram's hospital in a flight oval just outside the emergency room of the massive building. Khalid had brought the medevac in for a smooth, gentle landing. Megan spotted a surgery team waiting nearby. She turned and told Tahira about it.

"It is a team?" she asked in wonder, still holding Megan's hand.

"Yes, just for you and your baby. There is a woman doctor who is going to help you, Tahira. Her name is Dr. Laura Hunter. She's a baby doctor. You'll be in very good hands with her."

"And will you be with me?"

Megan heard the sudden fear in Tahira's voice. She understood she was the only person Tahira had to lean on in this new, strange world. Giving her a smile, Megan said, "I'll be with you every step of the way. And I'll be giving your husband radio updates all the time so he doesn't worry." Or blow off Aylin Sahin's head, but Megan didn't say that. She was sure Tahira didn't even realize her husband had taken a hostage. And she wouldn't know.

Once the medevac was down, Khalid cut the engines and the blades slowed. Luke was nearest the door and slid it open. Instantly, the team of five people in desert fatigues rushed forward, a gurney on wheels propelled between them. Megan kept up patter with Tahira as she released the straps across her. She told her what was going to happen next. In a minute, they had her transferred to the gurney. Megan scooted out the door and moved to Tahira's side, placing her hand against the woman's shoulder. As they moved toward the hospital emergency room doors, wheeling the gurney, Megan made her first call to Gholam. He answered immediately.

"I want to talk to my wife."

Megan placed the radio in Tahira's hand. She spoke soothingly to her husband.

By the time they wheeled Tahira into the emergency room, Luke was at Megan's side. He was giving Dr. Laura Hunter all the medical information on Tahira. The woman was already in green scrubs, ready for surgery even though he knew Tahira didn't know what was going to happen in a few minutes. As soon as Tahira had talked to her husband and signed off, they wheeled her into a surgical prep room.

Megan saw Luke move back near the door of the room. His job was over. She gave him a quick smile and he responded in kind before he left. Returning her attention to Tahira, she continued to speak quietly in Pashto to the woman so she wouldn't become frightened and confused by all the activity going on around her. A nurse came up and put another medication in her IV.

"Tahira, this will help you rest," Megan told her.

"You will feel drowsy and soon you will be asleep. When you wake up, I'll be here. I'm not leaving your side."

Tahira started to speak, but her lashes sank downward. The drug took effect. Stepping away, Dr. Hunter gave quiet orders to prep the patient.

Megan felt shaky. She was safe. She was no longer under a rifle bead with Gholam wanting to kill her. Suddenly, as she watched the doctor begin to examine Tahira, she felt faint. Leaning against the wall, eyes closed, Megan allowed all the fear of dying to overwhelm her. Then she pushed it aside since she wanted to be in the surgery with Tahira.

Megan knew her way around the hospital and went down the hall with the team. She didn't see Luke. It was a busy place with doctors, nurses, paramedics and other staff in constant motion. She pushed a door open. Inside were clean scrubs and deep sinks to wash and clean off her arms and hands before donning surgical gloves. Megan knew she wasn't going to help in the surgery, but she would be present to give Dr. Hunter anything she needed to know about Tahira.

As she scrubbed her hands and arms with surgical soap, Megan prayed that nothing would go wrong. Aylin Sahin's life hung in the balance. And so did Tahira's and her baby's lives, as well.

Chapter 17

Luke waited impatiently outside the surgical theater. Tension ate at him. It had been an hour and a half since Megan went in with the surgery team to operate on Tahira. Tiredness washed through him. He had barely slept since her kidnapping.

The doors opened.

Megan gave Luke a weary smile and a thumbs-up. She stood back as the gurney bearing a conscious Tahira rolled by. In Tahira's arms was a newly born baby, crying lustily in her arms. The whole surgical team was all smiles.

"Success," she told Luke, standing near him as she pulled the radio from beneath her scrubs.

"Went well?"

"Like clockwork. Dr. Hunter rocks. They gave Tahira a spinal block so that she could be awake to receive her baby girl." Holding up the radio, she said, "I need to make a call to Gholam. And then I want to have Tahira talk to him directly."

"Good idea." He gestured toward the team down at the end of the polished green hall. "Let's follow them to her room?"

"Duh." Megan gave him a silly smile. "I'm so exhausted, Luke, I can barely think straight, much less walk straight."

He gave her hand a quick squeeze. "I know. You're doing great, though. Captain Shaheen is here at the hospital. He has an idea, but let's get Tahira assigned to a private room first."

Luke had a crafty look gleaming in his gold-and-green eyes. How strong and virile he was, his shoulders squared, the darkness of a beard shadowing his face. Just his unexpected touch made her go soft with yearning. "Oh?"

"Yes," he said, walking with her. "We're all hoping Khalid's plan works."

"Tell me about it?"

"Khalid wants to convince Gholam to fly in to stay with his wife and new baby. He was talking to another OB-GYN doctor earlier and she said it would be a minimum of four days Tahira would be kept here after her surgery. Khalid will do the flying. He feels Gholam will have far more trust in another Afghan."

"Really?"

"Do you think he'll go for it?"

Grimacing, Megan said, "I don't know. He hates Americans so much."

"Khalid's going to remind him it was Americans who saved his wife's and baby's lives."

Megan shrugged. "It's a toss-up." They rounded a corner and then took an elevator with Tahira and her medical team down to the second floor. Megan smiled at Tahira and touched her shoulder. Although she'd just had surgery, she glowed, the black-haired baby girl wrapped in a pink blanket lying in her arms.

"Okay?" Megan asked her in Pashto.

"Oh, yes. I long to speak to Jabbar…to tell him the good news."

Holding up the radio, Megan said, "As soon as we get you to your room and settled I'll make the call. Then you can speak to him yourself." Tahira's eyes widened with joy. She gently kissed her baby's tiny, wrinkled forehead.

Luke spotted Captain Khalid Shaheen in his olive-green Army flight suit near the open door to Tahira's assigned room. The tall, lanky combat pilot smiled broadly and congratulated Tahira as they rolled her into the room.

Megan hesitated at the door with them. "What's the plan, Captain Shaheen?"

"Did Luke get you up to speed?"

"Yes, sir, he did. Should we tell Tahira first? Let her make the plea to Gholam?"

Khalid grinned. "Exactly right."

"I learn fast," Megan said, her mouth curving. "Let's go on in."

The three of them stood quietly in the room as Tahira spoke excitedly to Jabbar. At one point, Tahira held the radio toward Khalid.

"Please, my husband wants to speak to you."

Taking the radio, Khalid nodded.

Megan listened intently to the conversation between the pilot and the Taliban leader. She saw hope burning in Tahira's dark eyes, clinging to every word.

Khalid gave them a thumbs-up. He turned to Megan and whispered, "Gholam's agreed to come here."

"Yes," Megan said softly. "That's good news."

Seeing the weariness in her blue eyes, Luke reached out and touched her cheek. "You're incredible."

His whispered words, the grazing touch of his fingers across her cheek, made her weak with need. There was a burning light in Luke's gaze as he smiled down at her. It was a very male smile. A man wanting his woman. All Megan wanted was to be alone with Luke and love him.

"Okay," Khalid announced, turning off the radio and smiling over at Tahira, "Jabbar has agreed to fly in." He handed the radio to Megan. Looking at his watch, he said, "I'm going to Ops right now. I'll file a flight plan and take off. If everything goes well, I'll be back here in about two hours."

"Wonderful!" Tahira cried. "Thank you so much, Captain Shaheen. I know my husband has great faith and trust in you."

Khalid nodded. "Jabbar is in good hands with me." He looked over at Luke and Megan. "You'll stay with her until I return?"

"Absolutely," Megan said, moving to Tahira's bedside. She gently touched the sleeping baby's soft black hair. "We'll keep Tahira company."

Khalid strode to the door and Luke opened it.

Tahira sighed and looked up at Megan. "I am so happy, Megan. You helped bring this all about. I am very sleepy now."

"I'll take your daughter and put her in the bassinet," Megan said softly, leaning down and scooping up the tiny bundle. "I'll be here all the time, Tahira. I won't leave until Jabbar arrives, so you can relax and go to sleep."

A trembling smile touched Tahira's lips. "Thank you, my good friend. I know my daughter is in loving hands."

Luke watched the new mother quickly fall asleep. He rolled the bassinet to her bedside. Just by the way Megan held the baby, he knew she would be a good mother. The tenderness in Megan's face as she nestled the sleeping baby told him everything. He wanted so badly to be alone with Megan. Luke stilled his impatience. Two more hours.

"It's over," Megan whispered. They stood outside Tahira's room. Khalid had just escorted Gholam to his wife's private room. Two Marine guards were posted outside the door.

Luke wanted to slip his arm around Megan and pull her close, but he couldn't. "They're bringing in another bed so they can stay together." He smiled down at her. "You don't have to babysit anymore."

Rubbing her face, Megan said, "All I want is a hot shower and bed. I'm so tired, Luke."

"Would you like to go somewhere with me where we'll be alone? No prying eyes?"

Slowing her step down the hall, Megan said, "Yes… but where?" Bagram was a big base, but there were no facilities for privacy. Especially between lovers.

Luke placed his hand beneath her elbow. "Follow me," he said enigmatically.

Stymied, Megan trusted Luke with her life. They took the exit stairs down to the first floor. He led her out the rear exit door. The early-evening sun almost blinded her and she held up her hand to shade her eyes.

As they moved down the few concrete steps, there was a car and driver waiting for them.

Halting, Megan eyed him quizzically. "Luke, what's going on?"

He smiled. "Khalid is giving us the guest bedroom at their villa outside Kabul. It's completely safe and guarded. He knows we love each other. They won't be home until tomorrow evening. There's a housekeeper who will show us the room and cook for us."

The words fell gently upon her dizzied senses. If not for Luke's hand on her arm, Megan wasn't sure she could stay upright. Now that the crisis was over, the adrenaline was leaving her system. "That's so kind of them...." Even her words were slurred.

Luke opened the door to the beat-up green Toyota Land Cruiser and urged her in, "Climb in...."

Megan remembered sitting in the backseat, snuggled up in Luke's arms after they drove outside Bagram's gates, heading toward Kabul. The sense of love radiating from him, his arms around her, lulled her to sleep for the first time in two days.

Luke pressed a kiss to Megan's soft red hair. She slept hard for an hour before the driver drove carefully down one of the few paved roads near Kabul. "Hey," he whispered against Megan's ear, "we're here. Time to wake up...."

Megan heard Luke's voice and felt his lips against her hair and cheek. Lifting her head, she sat up, disoriented. She saw the Toyota was parked on a red-tiled plaza. A two-story home rose above them. Blinking and rubbing her eyes, she noticed the ten-foot-high wall around the estate, concertina wire on top of it. Grim-looking Gurkha Indian guards stood attentively nearby with rifles.

"Okay?" Luke asked as he threaded his fingers

through her hair. It was silky and he wanted to continue touching her, but Megan's eyes were drowsy. He understood the depth of her exhaustion.

The driver opened the door.

Luke guided Megan out of the vehicle. A guard nodded and gestured for them to follow him to the front door. As he wrapped his arm around Megan's waist, she leaned against him. Birds were singing. The sky was turning a darker blue as the sun began to set in the west.

The door opened and a housekeeper with a grotesque scar on her face bowed and stepped aside. The sentry left and returned to his duty.

Megan looked around the quiet, beautiful home. It was filled with antiques and colorful Persian rugs covered the white-tiled floors. A small woman with a white apron around her waist gestured for them to follow her down another hallway. They were shown a suite. Megan thanked the housekeeper in Pashto.

Inside the suite, Megan stood in shock. There was a colorful American quilt on the large bed and a nearby American rocker. The decor was decidedly 1930s Americana. Luke shut the door behind them and his hand slid around her slumped shoulders.

"You're in culture shock," he said, looking down into her half-closed eyes. "At this point, Megan, you need some serious sleep."

Frustrated, Megan lifted her hand and grazed his cheek. "But I want to love you, Luke." Her voice fell into a hush, laden with emotions. "After I was kidnapped the only thing I regretted was not telling you that I love you, Luke." She drowned in his green-and-gold eyes, felt her love being returned tenfold. His hands slid from her shoulders upward and framed her face.

"Listen," Luke whispered, leaning down and brushing her lips with his, "you're so tired you're slurring your words." He touched her lips and felt them part beneath his. How long had he wanted to kiss this brave woman?

With a soft moan, Megan threw her arms around his shoulders, pulling him hard against her. Their mouths met, hungry and eager. Luke embraced her, holding her solidly against his male body. Inhaling his scent was an aphrodisiac that awakened all her senses. His mouth was commanding, guiding and she felt starved for him in every way. Megan could feel his heart beating against hers. The moistness of his breath feathered across her cheek as he eased his mouth from hers. Megan opened her eyes. She drowned in his and suddenly noticed regret in them. Why?

"You need a shower and sleep, Megan. I don't want to love you like this. You're still in shock." Luke gave her a very male smile. "I want you, but I want you rested. We aren't going to get many times like this, and I want you to enjoy it as much as I will."

"You're right," she said, resting against him. Luke wasn't as tired as she was. Megan could see the glimmer of humor in his gaze. Leaning down, he kissed her wrinkled brow, her smooth, flushed cheek and, finally, her nose. "You've been through hell. It takes time to come out of it."

"You should know," Megan whispered. Resting her head against Luke's powerful chest, she sighed and closed her eyes. "I just want to hear the beat of your heart, Luke. I want to sleep with you holding me…."

Pressing a kiss to her hair, he said in a husky tone, "I never want to leave your side, Megan. Not ever."

The words seared her wildly beating heart. Her emotions rushed like a torrent through her. His face blurred

before her. Tears leaked out of her eyes and Megan felt
the warmth trickling down her cheeks. "I—I thought
I was going to die, Luke. You don't know how many
times I thought of you. I was so scared. I didn't know
what Gholam would do. I thought for sure he was going
to kill me."

"I know, I know," he rasped, holding her tightly,
rocking her in his arms. "But you're safe now. You're
with me and everything's going to be all right."

His words were like an invisible unguent. A sob
worked its way up and out of Megan's throat. "I'm sorry
I'm crying," she choked, her words muffled against his
uniform. How wonderful his strong arms felt around
her right now!

"Shh, don't apologize," Luke whispered, feeling her
tremble. Rocking her, Luke took Megan's full weight.
As he threaded his fingers through her hair, love welled
up within him. A fierce protectiveness swept through
him. She finally surrendered to the terror she'd had to
endure. Closing his eyes, he simply held Megan and allowed her to expend that terrible poison that had threatened her life.

What would life be without her in it? Luke couldn't
conceive it. Not then and not now. The woman in his
arms was so strong and resilient, able to handle even the
possibility of death staring her in the face. She'd been
an ardent warrior on Tahira's behalf, despite danger
to herself. Megan had stood up to Gholam, who hated
Americans. Sliding his hands around her shaking shoulders, he soothed her and held her safe. In a war zone,
there was no place to hide. No place to ever feel safe.
Luke understood, like many veterans who had three or
four tours in Iraq and Afghanistan, that it took a terrible

toll on a person's soul. No one was ready for what war took away from them.

Through it all, Megan had been courageous. She'd fought like a tiger for Tahira's and her unborn baby's lives. There were few people who could challenge Gholam and live to tell about it. Sliding his hand down her long spine, he wanted to let her know how much he loved her.

Gently, Luke lifted her damp strands of hair against her cheek. "Better now?" he asked. Seeing her eyes red-rimmed, he gave her a game smile. "It's good to get it out, Megan. Tears are always healing."

Megan lifted her hand and wiped away the last of the tears. "I'm surprised I held them back for this long." Looking up, she saw such intense love burning in his eyes. Swallowing convulsively, Megan whispered, "I love you so much, Luke. You'll never know how much strength it gave me when I was kidnapped by Gholam. I pictured your face, how strong and quiet you are in an emergency, and it would calm me." She leaned up and placed her lips against his, needing him now as never before.

Tasting the salt on her tear-wet lips, Luke groaned, the sound moving through him. Her mouth was soft, tender and hauntingly needy. Few would ever understand how the threat of death changed a person. He knew too well. It made a person appreciate life as never before. It made you live in the moment, fully. His mouth curved against hers, lips parting and allowing him entrance into her. Moving his tongue slowly, provocatively across her wet lower lip, he felt her tremble. Her hands curved against his chest, sliding and feeling him as a man who wanted her. Life and death. It was all mixed together in a cauldron of fire and burning desire to survive.

Reluctantly, Luke forced himself to release her lips. He opened his eyes and fell into Megan's blue gaze. Easing his hands across her shoulders, he whispered against her mouth, "I'm going to start the shower and afterward, you need to sleep. I'll be here with you. I'll hold you in my arms, Megan. I promise."

Chapter 18

Megan awoke slowly, feeling drugged. Her mind refused to work. Luke's warm, heavy arm lay across her waist. When she realized she was pressed against him, head nestled in the crook of his shoulder, Megan felt joy thrum quietly through her. She opened her eyes to the barest hint of dawn outside the massive floor-to-ceiling windows. Luke's moist breath fell softly against her cheek and temple. Like the greedy person she was, Megan absorbed the moment, cherished and inhaled his male scent. Life was precious. And only for a stolen moment.

Driven by need, Megan eased up on one elbow and looked down on his shadowed, sleeping features. He appeared so boyish and no longer worried or anxious, She marveled at how handsome Luke really was. Slipping her fingers across his brow, Megan pushed several dark brown strands of hair aside. She felt him stir. His beard had darkened the hollows of his cheeks. It gave him a vulnerable look that thrilled her senses. As his eyes slowly opened, she smiled softly, leaned down and began to kiss his brow and cheek before coming to rest against his mouth.

It was so easy for Luke to roll onto his back and bring his arm up across Megan's shoulder. Meeting her searching lips, he groaned and brought her fully against him. Her hair swirled against his face, the scent of nutmeg intoxicating his awakening senses. Her lips were searching and hungry. Heat roared through him, dissolving his drowsiness and making him fully aware how much he wanted to love Megan.

In moments, Megan lay against the length of Luke's body. Only her thin green nightgown provided a barrier between them. He wore only a pair of pajama bottoms. Where their hips met and melded, she felt his desire for her. Drowning in his kiss, his mouth worshipping hers, they gradually parted. Their breathing was ragged. As she stared down into his eyes, Megan saw a glitter of gold. Luke had such a strong face. She had come to know him on the battlefield, watched his calm and focus. And now, as his hands ranged downward from her shoulders, memorizing her ribs and waist and coming to rest across her hips, Megan felt her heart burst wide open.

"I don't remember when I fell in love with you, but I did." She kissed his brow, nose and mouth. Just to slide her lips against his, to taste Luke, enflamed her.

"I don't want this moment to end," he rasped against her wet lips. Looking up into her shining eyes filled with desire, he slid his fingers through her silky red hair. The desire in her eyes, in her face, sent a tidal wave of pleasure through him. "I loved you from the moment

I saw you." Luke's mouth curved upward. "You are so kind, thoughtful and caring toward everyone, Megan." As he touched her flushed cheek, his voice deepened. "We aren't going to have many times like this together for a year...."

"A year seems so long."

"We belong together, Megan. That's more than anyone else has out here."

Bowing her head, she pressed her cheek into his large palm. Anguish flowed through her. "I didn't want to fall in love with you, Luke." The words came out filled with pain.

"I know...me, neither." He saw the suffering in her blue eyes and heard the tremble in her voice. Her body pressed against his was all he'd ever want. "But I'm not sorry. Are you?"

Shaking her head, Megan absorbed his strength and warmth. Tears came to her eyes and for a moment, his face blurred before her. "I—I worry every time you go out on a mission, Luke. That...you'll be killed."

Capturing her face, he brought her down, their lips barely touching. "Don't worry. I have you to return to. Megan, you're everything to me." He kissed her hard and long, as if to convince her of what he already knew. Luke pulled a drawer open and unwrapped a condom. After rolling it on, he turned and laid down next to her.

Heat exploded between them and Megan moaned as his mouth and body devoured her. The gown was pulled away, and she felt the rawness of his hips melting into hers. In moments, they had divested themselves of their garments and come together once more. Only this time, Luke guided her onto her back, a glint in his eyes as his hand moved slowly around the curve of her

breast. Arching into his exploring hand, she thrust her
hips against his, wanting him now. Forever.

In moments, his lips tugged gently upon her nipple,
tasting one and then the other. His fingers, strong and
memorizing, slid across each of her ribs. His hands
flowed across her flared hips and he began a slow assault upon her thighs, coaxing them apart. Breath coming erratically, lost in this splendor, Megan kissed him
with wild, hungry abandon. She eagerly opened to
him, feeling him move her against him, monitoring
his strength as he guided her.

As they came together, she gasped, arching against
him. Megan felt his pounding heart beating in unison
with her own as they flowed rhythmically into each
other. The scent of him fueled her hunger. His mouth
found hers, his tongue teasing hers.

Megan wanted nothing more than to mate with him.
It was a powerful, predatory, survival need driving her
hips against his. Each thrust proved her love for Luke.
It drove Megan forward into his arms and body. The
moment congealed and she suddenly felt an eruption
of heat flowing out from the core of her body. A soft
cry tore from her lips. Luke caught the cry, his mouth
melding against her parted lips. His large hands drove
her deeper as he enclosed her hips and brought her into
a primal rhythm with him.

Luke felt his entire life melt into Megan's strong,
loving body. Never had he wanted to love a woman
more than her. Never had he wanted a woman as much
as he'd wanted her. Their desperate situation, the fact
that either of them could be killed tomorrow, drove him
recklessly to give her his body, his heart and his soul.

Slowly, so slowly, Megan felt the weight returning to
her body. She lay across Luke, her head resting weakly

against his shoulder, her hand moving across his chest. Never did she want this moment to go away. Closing her eyes, Megan memorized his thundering heart beneath her ear, the flow of his moist breath across her cheek, his calloused hands ranging across her sensitized skin.

A rooster crowed somewhere outside the window. Megan frowned, wanting to stop the sounds of dawn, of an awakening world around them. Pressing her lips to the column of Luke's neck, feeling his power, his utter masculinity, she whispered, "I want the world to go away...."

He smiled. "I hear him, too." Opening his eyes, Luke took in Megan's strong, supple body across his. His strength was returning, filling her once more. Such was his love for her. "The world isn't going away. We know that. What we can do is treasure these moments in between."

Flesh tingling in the wake of his fingers' small trails of fire down across her back, Megan sighed. "By this evening, we'll be back at the base."

"Don't think about it. We're here now."

Megan felt him move deep within her. His masculine power amazed her. She was hungry for him all over again. There was nothing else. He was right, she belatedly realized. All they had was right now.

"I want to marry you when we get home, Megan." Luke saw surprise flare in her blue eyes and then tears made them sparkle. Her lips, well kissed, parted. She smiled and touched his hair.

"I've been waiting for you all my life, Luke." Her voice grew hushed as she drowned in his darkening eyes. "I didn't know it until I met you. And I think I knew from that moment on, we were destined for each other."

Lifting his hand, he outlined her soft eyebrow, flushed cheek and stubborn chin. "At first, I tried to tell myself it was crazy." His mouth moved into a wry smile. "But you're not a woman I could ignore. You held my heart in your hands from the beginning."

Leaning down, Megan cherished his lips beneath hers. "I love you," she whispered against his mouth. "I'll never not love you."

"Are you ready?" Megan stood watching Luke as he picked up his medical pack from the bedroom floor. The morning had gone swiftly. Her body glowed from the continued bouts of loving him. She was already dressed in her utilities, her pack on her shoulder, helmet in her other hand. The Kevlar chafed her rib cage, reminding her of the harshness they would soon return to.

The dark look in his eyes as he hefted his pack across his broad shoulders told her he felt the same way. Neither of them wanted to leave this safe place.

"Ready." Luke moved around the bed, reached out and grazed her cheek. Megan's solemn face lifted. He leaned down and whispered against her mouth, "We've got the heart and strength to get through this."

His kiss was cherishing and warm. Once outside that door, they couldn't touch again. Not like this. War meant dying. War meant loss. She could lose him in a heartbeat. As his mouth lifted from hers, she opened her eyes and drowned in his glittering gaze. It was the look of a warrior, a man who would cheat death over and over again to be with her. Luke was a survivor. He'd already survived two tours. He could survive this one.

As they drove back to Bagram, they sat close. The drive was dangerous in itself, and already, Luke felt his old instincts, his alertness, returning. He wanted to protect Megan. Looking at her profile, he knew she was emotionally gearing up for their return. He also noticed the strength and stubbornness he'd come to know so well. Luke picked up her hand and rested it on his thigh. She tilted her head, their gazes meeting.

"Our love will see us through this," he said.

At Bagram, they stopped at the hospital. Captain Hall had wanted an after-action report. Megan walked up to the nurses' desk on the floor where Tahira stayed. Two armed guards remained outside of Tahira's room. Luke stayed at her side.

"Oh," the nurse said, smiling, "Tahira is doing fine! Her baby is eating and she's got plenty of milk."

"What about her husband, Jabbar Gholam?" Luke asked.

The nurse shrugged. "You know, I think a miracle has happened."

"What do you mean?" he demanded.

"Gholam has been talking to a Marine colonel who came for a visit. Now, I don't know what they talked about, but the colonel was all smiles when he came out of the room."

Megan gave Luke a confused look.

"Maybe Gholam is going to give up being a Taliban leader," Luke told them.

"That would be nice," the nurse said.

"Can we go see them?" Megan asked.

"No, I'm sorry. Only staff is allowed."

Luke studied the guards on duty at the door in the hall. "Do you know when they're going to release Tahira?"

Moving through the computer screens at the desk, the nurse said, "In two more days."

Megan shrugged her pack on her left shoulder. "We

need to get to Ops. There's a flight taking us back pretty soon."

Luke nodded and thanked the nurse and they exited the hospital. A driver in a Humvee drove them over to the busy Operations building sitting at the side of the many runways at Bagram. The main air base for all of Afghanistan was bustling with activity.

As they left the Humvee and walked through the doors, men and women crowded around them. At the Ops flight desk, Luke dropped his pack on the deck and gave the scheduling sergeant their names and orders.

"You're hitching a ride to Lar Sholtan with Captain Khalid Shaheen." The sergeant pointed out a large glass window to the left of him. "Over there. That CH-47. Go on out. He's waiting for you."

Megan followed Luke as they went through the sentry gate. "Good that we can fly back with Captain Shaheen. That's nice."

"It is."

The rear of the CH-47 was open and several loadmasters were putting huge pallets of supplies under cargo netting into the helo's belly. Spotting the tall Afghan officer in his flight suit, Luke lifted his hand.

"There's Captain Sahin!" Megan said, pointing toward the cockpit.

"I wonder if the Turk is any worse for wear," Luke said, walking at her side.

Megan grinned. "Maybe we should ask a different question. Did Gholam get beat up by her?"

Chuckling, Luke nodded and said nothing. Jets took off on another runway into the late-afternoon sky. Their thundering engines shook the air around them.

Megan smiled as Khalid walked up and met them.

"Hi, Captain Shaheen. Nice you can fly us back. Thank you."

Khalid smiled and placed his hands on his narrow hips. His eyes danced with mirth. "I hope you had a pleasant break at our villa."

Luke grinned. "Yes, sir, we did. Thank you."

"It's there for you anytime you can get away," Khalid said.

Megan wanted to hug the Apache pilot, but stopped herself. "Thank you…it means the world to us."

Khalid's smile disappeared. "I know it does. My wife, Emma, and I are constantly flying, constantly in danger. We look at our villa as the only safe place where we can be alone and together. We understand your dilemma better than most."

Megan nodded. She saw the last pallet being moved into the huge two-engined workhorse of a helo. "How is Captain Sahin?"

"She's fine. Pissed off, but that's to be expected. Gholam couldn't stand her overbearing presence and locked her up in the goat barn to escape her." Khalid chuckled. "Most people don't understand the Turks ruled the world for a while. Aylin's got that same fire, courage and hardheaded competitiveness of her ancestors." Khalid glanced up at the cockpit of the CH-47. "Gholam's lucky she didn't rip his head off. He didn't know she's a black belt in karate and a qualified sniper."

Luke became serious. "Sir, what do you know about Gholam?" He told Khalid about the information the nurse at the desk had given them earlier.

"Oh, that." Khalid grinned happily. "Gholam has turned. He's given his word that he'll no longer work with the Taliban. Colonel Putnam from Kabul has gotten his word on it. And now his village will be allowed charity and all kinds of help." Hooking his thumb over his shoulder, Khalid said, "As a matter of fact, this cargo is heading for his village. As soon as we drop you off at Lar Sholtan, we're delivering food, medicine, clothing and blankets to his village."

"That's great," Megan said, relief in her tone.

Khalid patted her shoulder. "Thanks to you. Without your influence, without being over there, this wouldn't have happened. You know that? Did Colonel Putnam get in touch with you?"

Megan shook her head. "No. He didn't." Confused, she glanced at Luke, who had a slight, relieved smile on his face. "I didn't do anything, Captain Shaheen."

"Yes, you did." Khalid gave her an intent look. "General Maya Stevenson has already heard from Colonel Putnam. He's raving about your influence as a woman in the village. By being kind and helping Tahira, you turned Gholam from enemy into friend. By your example as an American woman, he saw your care and genuine concern for his wife. It turned him. Now he no longer sees Americans as the great Satan. Well done."

Megan was shocked. "I was constantly butting heads with him over his wife's treatment. I didn't see him believing anything I said."

"Megan, you have a gentle way of being authoritative and confident," Luke said. "Gholam might have wanted to disbelieve you, but there was something about *you* that made him trust you."

Laughing and embarrassed by all the praise, Megan told them, "If anyone turned Gholam, it was Tahira, not me. He might be a big, bad warrior, but when she spoke, he melted into a lovesick puppy dog."

Khalid traded a knowing look with Luke. "I think we are all putty in the hands of our women, don't you?"

Megan saw Luke's smile widen.

"No question."

"Come on, it's time to fly," Khalid told them, turning and walking toward the rear ramp.

Hurrying to catch up, Megan laughed.

"What's so funny?" Luke asked.

"You guys."

"What? That we have the women we love? And we'd turn this world inside out to keep them safe? Love them? Adore them?"

As she stepped up on the metal ramp, Megan was thoroughly amused. Luke seemed happy and at ease. She knew they'd get through this year because they had each other. "I like being put up on a pedestal. It feels good." She saw the gleam in his eyes, the love shining through to her. Only to her.

They walked up the ramp and slid between the strapped-down pallets in the center of the helo and chose two nylon seats. Luke took her medical pack and set it next to his. The whine of one engine and then the other filled the long, hollow interior of the bird. They put on their helmets.

Megan pulled the mike close to her lips as the ramp ground upward and locked into place with a slamming thud. The two loadmasters sat on either side of the helo at the rear.

It felt good having Luke next to her. His body, his warmth, steadied her. The helo began to tremble. She saw Captain Sahin, the Turkish woman, would be flying the bird. Just looking at her profile, Megan was reminded of an avenging eagle. Her mouth was pursed, her eyes narrowed and focused. Her gloved hands flew over the controls with confidence.

As the helo broke connection with the earth, it shook

and shuddered. Megan remembered her family tradition, why she was here. Her love of being a field medic and stopping suffering was all that mattered to her. And then there was Luke. Looking to her left, Megan studied him in the semidarkness of the cargo hold. All he wanted to do was help those who suffered so much in this war.

Closing her eyes, Megan allowed the shivering of the helo to work through her. As they gained altitude and left Bagram, the rear ramp would be opened, a .50-caliber machine gun placed in the center of the deck. One of the loadmasters would then sit down, legs on either side of it, and watch for potential Taliban attack from below. The skies were never safe over Afghanistan.

Her heart moved and blossomed with a fierce love for Luke. War had brought them together, but war would not separate them. They would plan their wedding over the rest of the time left on their tours. It would be a positive against so much hardship they would endure. For now, their love would remain a secret. And every now and then, Megan knew Luke would find small but cherished ways to let her know just how much he loved her.

* * * * *

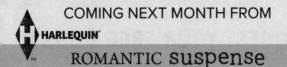

COMING NEXT MONTH FROM

HARLEQUIN®

ROMANTIC suspense

Available February 19, 2013

#1743 WHAT SHE SAW
Conard County: The Next Generation
by Rachel Lee

When Haley Martin poses as Buck Devlin's girlfriend to help solve a murder, she never imagines that he's putting her life, her dreams and her heart at risk.

#1744 A BILLIONAIRE'S REDEMPTION
Vengeance in Texas • by Cindy Dees

Willa Merris may be off-limits, but Gabe Dawson is a billionaire and can break all the rules to keep her safe... if she'll let him.

#1745 OPERATION REUNION
Cutter's Code • by Justine Davis

Will family loyalty ruin Kayla Tucker's chance at a true, lifetime love, and will past secrets destroy everything she holds dear?

#1746 COWBOY'S TEXAS RESCUE
Black Ops Rescues • by Beth Cornelison

Black ops pilot Jake Connelly battles an escaped convict and a Texas-size blizzard to rescue Chelsea Harris, but will he also lose his heart to the intrepid small-town girl?

HRSCNM0213

REQUEST YOUR FREE BOOKS!
2 FREE NOVELS PLUS 2 FREE GIFTS!

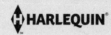

ROMANTIC suspense

Sparked by danger, fueled by passion

YES! Please send me 2 FREE Harlequin® Romantic Suspense novels and my 2 FREE gifts (gifts are worth about $10). After receiving them, if I don't wish to receive any more books, I can return the shipping statement marked "cancel." If I don't cancel, I will receive 4 brand-new novels every month and be billed just $4.49 per book in the U.S. or $5.24 per book in Canada. That's a savings of at least 14% off the cover price! It's quite a bargain! Shipping and handling is just 50¢ per book in the U.S. and 75¢ per book in Canada.* I understand that accepting the 2 free books and gifts places me under no obligation to buy anything. I can always return a shipment and cancel at any time. Even if I never buy another book, the two free books and gifts are mine to keep forever.

240/340 HDN FVS7

Name	(PLEASE PRINT)	
Address		Apt. #
City	State/Prov.	Zip/Postal Code

Signature (if under 18, a parent or guardian must sign)

Mail to the **Harlequin® Reader Service:**
IN U.S.A.: P.O. Box 1867, Buffalo, NY 14240-1867
IN CANADA: P.O. Box 609, Fort Erie, Ontario L2A 5X3

Want to try two free books from another line?
Call 1-800-873-8635 or visit www.ReaderService.com.

* Terms and prices subject to change without notice. Prices do not include applicable taxes. Sales tax applicable in N.Y. Canadian residents will be charged applicable taxes. Offer not valid in Quebec. This offer is limited to one order per household. Not valid for current subscribers to Harlequin Romantic Suspense books. All orders subject to credit approval. Credit or debit balances in a customer's account(s) may be offset by any other outstanding balance owed by or to the customer. Please allow 4 to 6 weeks for delivery. Offer available while quantities last.

Your Privacy—The Harlequin® Reader Service is committed to protecting your privacy. Our Privacy Policy is available online at www.ReaderService.com or upon request from the Harlequin Reader Service.

We make a portion of our mailing list available to reputable third parties that offer products we believe may interest you. If you prefer that we not exchange your name with third parties, or if you wish to clarify or modify your communication preferences, please visit us at www.ReaderService.com/consumerschoice or write to us at Harlequin Reader Service Preference Service, P.O. Box 9062, Buffalo, NY 14269. Include your complete name and address.

HRS13

SPECIAL EXCERPT FROM
HARLEQUIN® ROMANTIC SUSPENSE

RS

Harlequin Romantic Suspense presents the
third book in the thrilling Black Ops Rescues
miniseries from best-loved author Beth Cornelison

Black Ops pilot Jake Connelly battles an escaped convict
and a Texas-size blizzard to rescue Chelsea Harris, but will he
lose his heart to the intrepid small-town girl?

Read on for an excerpt from

COWBOY'S TEXAS RESCUE

Available March 2013 from
Harlequin Romantic Suspense

A rattle came from the trunk lock, and she tensed. *Oh, please, God, let it be someone to rescue me and not that maniac killer!*

The lid rose, and daylight poured into the pitch-dark of the trunk. She shuddered as a stiff, icy wind swept into the well of the trunk, blasting her bare skin.

"Ah, hell," a deep voice muttered.

Her pulse scampered, and she squinted to make out the face of the man standing over her.

The gun in his hand registered first, then his size—tall, broad shouldered, and his fleece-lined ranch coat made him appear impressively muscle-bound. Plenty big enough to overpower her if he was working with the convict.

A black cowboy hat and backlighting from the sky obscured his face in shadow, adding to her apprehension.

"Are you hurt?" he asked, stashing the gun out of sight and undoing the buttons of his coat.

"N-no." When he reached for her, she shrank back warily.

Where was the convict? She cast an anxious glance around them, down the side of the car, searching.

She jolted when her rescuer grasped her elbow.

"Hey, I'm not gonna hurt you." The cowboy leaned farther into the trunk. "Let me help you out of there, and you can have my coat."

His coat… She almost whimpered in gratitude, anticipating the warmth. When she caught her first good glimpse of his square jaw and stubble-dusted cheeks, her stomach swooped. *Oh, Texas!* He was a freaking *Adonis.* Greek-god gorgeous with golden-blond hair, cowboy boots and ranch-honed muscles. He lifted her out of the trunk, and when he set her down and her knees buckled with muscle cramps, cold and fatigue, she knew she couldn't dismiss old-fashioned swooning for at least some of her legs' weakness. He draped the coat around her shoulders, and the sexy combined scents of pine, leather and man surrounded her. She had to be dreaming.…

Will Chelsea find more than safety in her sexy rescuer's arms? Or will the convict come back to finish them both off? Find out what happens next in COWBOY'S TEXAS RESCUE

Available March 2013 from Harlequin Romantic Suspense wherever books are sold.

HRSEXP0213

HARLEQUIN®

ROMANTIC suspense

Willa Merris may be off-limits,
but Gabe Dawson is a billionaire and can break
all the rules to keep her safe...if she'll let him.

Look for the third book in the
Vengeance in Texas miniseries.

A BILLIONAIRE'S REDEMPTION
by Cindy Dees

Available March 2013 from Harlequin Romantic
Suspense wherever books are sold.

A PROFILER'S CASE FOR SEDUCTION
by Carla Cassidy

(Book #4) available April 2013

HARLEQUIN®

ROMANTIC suspense

Coming next month from
New York Times bestselling author

Rachel Lee

When Haley Martin poses as Buck Devlin's
girlfriend to help solve a murder,
she never imagines that he's putting her life,
her dreams and her heart at risk.

Look for the next electrifying book in the
Conard County: The Next Generation
miniseries!

WHAT SHE SAW

Available March 2013 from
Harlequin Romantic Suspense wherever books are sold.

Heart-racing romance, high-stakes suspense!